S0-BXE-177

Previously published Worldwide Suspense titles by MICHAEL NIEMANN

LEGITIMATE BUSINESS
ILLICIT TRADE
ILLEGAL HOLDINGS
NO RIGHT WAY
PERCENTAGES OF GUILT

THE LAST STRAW

MICHAEL NIEMANN

WORLDWIDE

TORONTO • NEW YORK • LONDON
AMSTERDAM • PARIS • SYDNEY • HAMBURG
STOCKHOLM • ATHENS • TOKYO • MILAN
MADRID • WARSAW • BUDAPEST • AUCKLAND

To the victims of inhuman policies who have perished along borders worldwide.

WORLDWIDE™

Recycling programs for this product may not exist in your area.

ISBN-13: 978-1-335-45267-2

The Last Straw

First published in 2021 by Coffeetown Press, an imprint of Epicenter Press, Inc. This edition published in 2023.

For questions and comments about the quality of this book, please contact us at CustomerService@Harlequin.com.

Harlequin Enterprises ULC
22 Adelaide St. West, 41st Floor
Toronto, Ontario M5H 4E3, Canada
www.ReaderService.com

Printed in U.S.A.

THE LAST STRAW

ACKNOWLEDGMENTS

I am grateful for the support and the critical eye of my "Monday Mayhem" writers group: Jenn Ashton, Carole Beers, Sharon Dean and Clive Rosengren. Alison McMahan inspired the theme and gave crucial feedback after reading the first draft. Jennifer McCord's candid remarks on the first draft were equally important. John Love's comments were invaluable. Together, they made this a better novel.

ONE

VALENTIN VERMEULEN WAS BORED. He was sitting at his desk in the Office of Internal Oversight Services, United Nations headquarters, New York City. He got up to refill his coffee cup more often than was good for him. It was the fifteenth of October in 2018, a Monday afternoon and nothing to look forward to except quitting time. The hands on the wall clock seemed to be stuck just shy of four o'clock. He checked his phone to see if his partner, Tessa Bishonga, had texted him. She hadn't. He browsed news websites. Nothing interesting had happened since lunch break.

Vermeulen was an investigator at OIOS, a position he'd held for fifteen years. His primary task was to uncover fraud throughout the UN operations and name those who committed it. Much of his work involved traveling to out-of-the-way places where the UN operated. All that travel over the years had taken its toll. Now rapidly approaching fifty, his face—always a bit rough—had grown more haggard, creased like Kraft paper that had been crumpled and resisted any efforts at smoothing. His blond hair had started fading into a color he refused to call gray. Although still six feet tall if he stood erect with his back against a wall, there was rarely a wall to press his back against. As a result, his head was usually bent forward a bit. But his pale blue eyes had lost nothing of their sharpness, and he kept in decent shape.

Despite occasional setbacks and run-ins with his superiors, he liked his work. Yes, the travel was tedious most of the time. He didn't like being away from Tessa for weeks at a time. Still, on-site investigations were a hundred times better than his current task, checking up on how various UN entities had implemented the critical recommendations OIOS had sent them.

Investigations, whether they exposed fraud or not, usually unearthed inefficiencies, sloppy procedures and other shortcomings. Those were cataloged and, at the end of an investigation, a list of recommendations was submitted to the agency or operation in question. The most important ones were labelled *critical* in the hope that those in charge would implement them sooner rather than later.

The follow-ups were both tedious and mind-boggling. Tedious, because it was, well, paperwork, something he deeply hated doing. And mind-boggling because the excuses dreamt up by agencies to explain why they'd failed to implement even the simplest controls were so inane, it drove him up the wall. How hard could it be to put in place a rule that no one could dispense gas to vehicles that didn't have the UN logo on them? How difficult could it be to double-check the references potential contractors provided?

Changing bureaucratic behavior was like changing the course of a supertanker. The forward momentum was so dominant that changes in procedures took a long time to filter down to those who had to adopt new ways of doing their jobs. Vermeulen also knew that it was easy to come up with new rules in the air-conditioned offices at One, United Nations Plaza. He didn't have to follow them in some faraway place where conflict, poverty and sheer lack of institutional capacity put to shame the concerns of bureaucrats like him.

When his cell phone rang, he hoped it would be Tessa, because he really needed her to whisper sweet things into his ears. Seeing her name on the display improved his mood instantly.

"Am I glad you called," he said.

"Why? What's going on?" Her voice sounded warm as always, albeit a bit surprised.

"I'm bored out of my mind."

"That's all? You sounded like you were in trouble again."

"I'd prefer trouble over this."

"Wow. It's that bad, huh? Good thing I called. I have a proposition for you."

"Does it involve your lips on mine?"

He heard her giggle.

"You're sweet, but, no, it doesn't involve heavy petting. My fellow editors and I have decided to work on a special issue on the militarization of borders. My part of it will deal with the US/Mexico border. So I'm going to Arizona. D'you want to come along? It sounds like you could use a break."

"When are we leaving?"

"Wednesday."

"So soon? Where would we be staying?"

"Hotels, motels, why?"

"So there could be breakfast in bed and your lips on mine?"

"Only if you come along."

"It's a deal. I do have to get my boss's okay first.

But that shouldn't be a problem I have so many days of leave accrued, they've been begging me to take them so they don't have to pay me for them."

He went to Jenna Sibinski, the administrative assistant who held most of OIOS together, to tell her he was going to take a week off.

"Better fill out the leave request form. You know that Suarez does everything by the book."

Vermeulen made a face and went back to his desk. He filled out the form and sent it off. He tried to get back to work, but the anticipation of a trip with Tessa made concentrating difficult. He took out his phone and dialed his daughter Gaby's number. She managed the Africa section of a major logistics firm from her office in Düsseldorf, Germany. Given the time difference, it was late there, but she often stayed up late.

It took a while before she answered.

"What trouble are you in now, Dad?" She must've been asleep.

"Sorry sweetheart, I didn't mean to wake you."

"It's midnight. What did you expect?"

"I guess I didn't calculate the difference correctly. Anyway, I'm not in trouble. Just wanted to let you know that I'm taking a few days off to accompany Tessa to Arizona."

"You taking time off? Wonders never cease."

"Come on, I take time off," he said.

"Only when you've been in trouble and your boss thinks it's better for you to cool your heels away from the spotlight."

He had a reply ready, but kept his mouth shut. Gaby knew him and she wasn't that far off.

"What's Tessa doing in Arizona?" Gaby said.

"She and her colleagues are working on a project about borders. She's covering the American angle."

"That's a lot to cover. I've seen the pictures. Terrible. People here are wondering what's wrong with the administration."

"Many people here are wondering the same. So, just letting you know. Go back to sleep we'll talk later."

THAT EVENING, his vacation days applied for and granted, Vermeulen was home and cooking in the kitchen. Since Tessa and he had moved in together, his eating habits had changed a lot. Gone were the days of refrigerators filled with old soy sauce packages, a half jar of pickles and moldy yoghurt. She had let him know in no uncertain terms that take-out was for emergencies and pizza only.

Vermeulen had adapted faster than he expected and even had developed a reliable repertoire of dishes he could make quickly. Roasted sweet potatoes and Brussels sprouts with chicken sausage was one of them.

"Any problems getting your days off?" she said while pouring two glasses of wine.

"Nope. They've been begging me to take them for a while now. I hope the ticket prices weren't outrageous. Don't they want you to book them four weeks ahead of time?"

"Yes, they do. But I know this place that offers great deals on last-minute tickets. In the end, the airlines want their planes full. It wasn't as bad as you think."

The sweet potatoes were ready. He pulled off their skins—burning one fingertip in the process—and mashed them in a bowl with some salt and pepper. He put the bowl back into the oven and started chopping cilantro and basil for the sauce. After mixing the herbs with olive oil, a smashed garlic clove and lime juice, he said, "We can eat anytime."

Halfway through the meal, Tessa said, "Do you know anyone in Tucson? I've never been to Arizona. I have a few contacts and introductions through my networks, but nobody I know personally."

"I'm in the same boat, except Alma Rodriguez—you remember her, right?—she moved there from New Jersey a few years ago."

"Was she the immigration activist who saved your bacon that time you were in the clutches of ICE?"

"Yes, that's her."

About seven years ago, he was about to crack a human trafficking ring only to be arrested and held for deportation by a corrupt Immigration and Customs Enforcement officer. Out of gratitude for the selfless action of Alma and her associates, he decided to join them on their weekly protests against the deportations for a while. As far as he remembered, Alma had married but also gotten divorced again. "I'd love to reconnect with her. See what she's been up to. Her little girl has got to be five or six by now."

Tessa was all fired up about her new project. Since they had moved in together, her life as a freelance journalist, always on assignment in other parts of the world, had come to an end. News outlets were less and less willing to front the expenses and supporting herself and a crew while working on spec was untenable even in the short term.

During Vermeulen's case in Mozambique a few years earlier, she'd come into possession of a trove of documents detailing the illegal manner in which outside actors were acquiring land for prohibited purposes. She recognized that this was too big for her to handle and organized an ad hoc consortium with two editors in South Africa and Switzerland.

That collaboration proved so fertile that the three decided to start a web-based publication that focused on so-called long-reads, articles that went beyond the usual snippets and provided in-depth analysis. Enough people were willing to pay for those insights that Tessa's share of the income was satisfactory.

"Militarization of borders, huh?" Vermeulen said. "Isn't that as old as borders themselves?"

"Yeah, that's the normal assumption. But in the years since World War II, there have been changes in the opposite direction. Think European Union, think NAFTA and various other trade schemes. So borders have become way more permeable. All the people on the move these days, refugees, displaced people, tourists, business people, they all depend on the easing of border controls."

"I'm not sure you can throw refugees and tourists into the same pot."

"Well, they are traveling for diametrically opposed reasons, but they are still moving across borders."

"And you see a global trend in that?"

"Sure. We may think of what's happening at the Mexican border as an abomination committed by this administration, but it's happening elsewhere too. Instead of a land border, the EU is using the Mediterranean to keep refugees out. They patrol with warships instead of Border Patrol SUVs."

"But they let in the Syrian refugees in 2015."

"That was a one-time exception. And even then, the newer members in Eastern Europe refused to accept them. Germany and Sweden may have gotten good press back then, but they aren't taking anymore either."

"Still, a border wall? That has got to take the cake."

"Not at all. Spain has two enclaves in Morocco, Ceuta and Melilla, and there you see the same walls and fences. If Europe bordered directly on a third world country, it would have a border wall too. So, the general gist of the project is to focus on that militarization of borders and what it bodes for the future of the free movement of people."

"And your subscribers pay for that?"

"Sure. It's in equal part intelligence gathering—though not surreptitiously or illegally—and prognostication. Our subscribers include government officials and people all over the business world. In their jobs they only see what's directly in front of them. We allow them to zoom out and see a global picture."

He peeled an orange, picked off the pith and gave her half. She smiled. "I really love it when you peel an orange for me."

TWO

October 15th,
Ciudad Obregón, Sonora, Mexico

SOME TWENTY-TWO-HUNDRED MILES southwest of New York City, Camille Delano sipped her ice cold Grey Goose and sighed with delight. The vodka coursed down her throat and warmed her belly. It wasn't her preferred brand, but getting a Kazakhstani vodka in Ciudad Obregón was too much to ask. She'd asked Armando, the bartender at *Bar 434,* to keep a bottle and a glass in the freezer for her. She didn't want her drink diluted by ice cubes. Also, despite living in Mexico for seven years now, she'd never quite gotten over that US-American suspicion of Mexican tap water.

Since she was a regular and a good tipper, Armando was more than happy to accommodate Señora Beltrán. That's the name she gave him when he noticed her the third time. Vivian Beltrán was the name in the US passport she used when she entered Mexico in 2011. Although it was a Spanish last name, she didn't pretend to be a Latina. Her Spanish was good enough to conduct business but not sufficient to pass as a native speaker.

She was a facilitator. She connected people who needed something with other people who could supply it. As a rule, the deals she facilitated were illegal. She wasn't opposed to providing services that were legal, but her commissions for the illegal services were far higher, so that was a no-brainer. She'd been in this business for quite a while now, and she was good at it. She never met the parties in person. The negotiations all took place over the phone.

These days, she mostly worked as the liaison between kidnappers and those who were supposed to pay the ransom. She specialized in high-value individuals. Being almost bilingual was her most important asset. If the individual abducted came from the US, having an English speaker relay the conditions and price of release made a big difference and cut down on misunderstandings. If they were rich Mexicans, the American voice made the whole enterprise sound more international and hence more serious. The family or corporation were more likely to pay if they were approached in a competent manner.

She had an understanding with the local branch of the Sinaloa cartel, which often benefitted from her intercessions. The local cartel boss particularly appreciated her ability to set up untraceable international relay calls, a skill she first honed back in Newark. Doing so kept identities hidden even from the snoops of the US Drug Enforcement Agency. It wasn't difficult to do, but it required using landlines and the cartels employed young men for whom a landline was a strange artifact of a distant past.

Back in the US, she'd been called the Broker. After she was cheated out of her rightful inheritance of her father's illegal operations, she'd set up her own concern. She'd quickly found that facilitating illegal deals was far more profitable than extortion, smuggling or loan sharking, her father's bread and butter activities. There was less exposure, fewer chances to run afoul of the authorities, and no need to keep paying a permanent crew.

Everything was going well until that day in 2011 when she ran into Valentin Vermeulen. She was running a profitable trafficking gig. Once he became involved, things went seriously sideways. She was prepared then as she was now. Her emergency bag was always packed and she'd kept alternate passports and cash in various denominations in a secret spot away from her residence.

She got away, but lost her network and the contacts that went with it. She'd tried hard to let go of the hatred she felt for Vermeulen. It wasn't easy. Reconstructing her livelihood had been hard. The fact that she was living in western Mexico was a constant reminder that he had turned her life upside down. Over the past seven years, the anger had fluctuated like a chronic pain, ebbing, then flaring up again.

The reason she was drinking her vodka this early in the afternoon was due to such a flare-up. The very case that had caused her downfall at the hands of Vermeulen was back on her plate. The trafficking gang in Moldova wanted to sluice a past victim back into the US. Since the man had already been caught once by ICE, a visa was out of the question. The only feasible way was to smuggle him across the US border from Mexico. Management, as the US intermediary called itself, got a hold of her and she facilitated a deal with the Sinaloa cartel to smuggle the man into the US.

The money she earned in this deal didn't make up for the renewed anger at Vermeulen that washed over her like a spring tide.

She caught her reflection in the mirrors behind the bar; shoulder length blond hair, styled in feathered layers to complement her roundish face, gray eyes, and thin lips—not a bad-looking woman, forty-five or not. The way Armando looked at her told her that she still had it. She'd be a success anywhere in the world. Instead, she was holed up in this Mexican backwater. It was all Vermeulen's fault.

"Another vodka, Señora Beltrán?" he said.

She considered the suggestion. One vodka was her usual dose. But the hot ire inside demanded extra numbing. Nobody was waiting for her. At home she'd only be brooding.

"Why not?" She said, nodding.

The bartender pulled the bottle from the freezer and poured another vodka into a chilled glass, just the way she liked it. At first, she thought his solicitousness was nothing more than the desire to keep her tips coming. All the barkeeps she had known did that. Later, she thought he showed more interest than was strictly required. He could have been off doing stuff on his phone, but he hung about, talked with her and corrected her Spanish. In return she helped him with his English, which was probably far better than he let on. That's why she never answered her cell in his presence.

She used to change her bars regularly. In her line of work steady habits were inadvisable. When she stumbled upon *Bar 434*—small, but well designed—she thought it would do for a little while. That was six months ago. After the bartender accommodated her request to keep a bottle of Vodka in the freezer, she introduced herself and asked for his name. As it turned out, Armando had the same last name as her fake passport.

From time to time, she considered changing to a different bar. It'd be prudent. But having someone to talk to about the goings on in Ciudad Obregón was useful, and it didn't hurt to catch him glancing at her occasionally. She smiled and downed her drink. No use avoiding the inevitable.

"Well, time to go home. Good bye, Señor Beltrán."

"Good bye, Señora Beltrán."

The heat radiated off Avenida Guerrero and would continue to do so into the night. It wasn't as hot as the summer months, and the humidity was lower in October. She preferred the winter months when the weather was balmy and dry. The massive thunderstorms of the summer turned the whole town into a sauna. The city itself had been a haven for her. In her first year here, while busy rebuilding her life, she'd explored the neighborhoods close to her apartment. The boulevards with their tree-lined medians reminded her of Europe. During one of these explorations, she'd discovered a small museum that commemorated the role president Álvaro Obregón had played in the 1910 revolution. She'd guessed that the city was named after an important man, but she found the dual role of Obregón—a revolutionary at first and later an adept politician—quite interesting. Often someone good at the first failed at the second.

She walked four blocks east, two blocks north, crossed the street, went west for a block, before going three blocks north to reach her apartment. She varied this pattern every day. Along the way she employed the usual tricks to spot anyone following her—a quick turn, lingering in front of a store display window, ducking into an entrance. It wasn't a foolproof system. Anyone seriously looking for her would find her quickly. There were only so many *gringas* living in the city. She had contemplated dying her hair, but decided against it. She wasn't the only blonde on the streets, and she liked her hair the way it was.

She unlocked the door to her apartment. There were three more in the building, one to her left and two atop, anonymous enough, but not so anonymous that she had to worry about random newcomers becoming her neighbors. She knew the people who lived there enough to greet them and they reciprocated by being friendly without asking questions.

Out of habit, she checked her mailbox. Except for flyers from local shops there was rarely anything personal in it. That's why finding a letter among the Taqueria Fontana coupons was unusual. She examined it. No sender, but her address was correct.

The number of people who knew her mailing address was near zero. She'd never given it to anyone. There was no need. She didn't have friends over for dinner and the intimate encounters with men always took place at one of the local hotels. Occasionally, one of them would become inquisitive. To which she always replied, "I don't do boyfriends or sleepovers."

The letter could only be from one sender. Inside her place, she put down her bag on the little table by the door, slipped her right index finger under the flap and ripped the envelope open. She winced when the paper cut into her skin. *Damn.*

Sucking on the finger, she managed to pull the note out with her left hand. Just as expected, it contained only one line.

Call Management!

THREE

Monday October 15th,
Southern Arizona

Two-hundred-seventy miles north of Ciudad Obregón, a group of seven students and their professor were combing the Arizona desert for artifacts left behind by border crossers. The sun had reached its zenith and the students were sweating. Although not as bad as the mid-summer heat, the temperatures had crept up to ninety-five.

The students were part of the Undocumented Migrants Project, a summer program run by the anthropology department of the University of Arizona. Their professor, Alain Ponce, had told them to collect, tag and bag each of the discarded items they'd found piled up in a shallow dip. Backpacks, gallon-size water containers, clothing and all the other human-made artifacts migrants had left in the hollow. It was tedious work, and having to wear nitrile gloves made the work more miserable.

Still, nobody complained openly. They had signed up because they believed the work was important. Analyzing contemporary human behavior right here in the US had attracted them. It seemed more relevant than trying to understand human practices in some exotic locale or of some long-forgotten civilization. The extra credit didn't hurt either.

"Funny that they should all decide to drop their stuff right here," a blond student said. He wore long pants, a long-sleeved shirt—both made from some high-tech fabric—and a broad brimmed hat. The others were covered as well, but their clothes didn't have the fresh creases from the outdoor store anymore. The long sleeves and pants were obligatory. Without protection, a couple of hours in this sun would burn their skin.

"It's not funny at all," a red-haired student replied. She'd slathered every bare bit of her skin with SPF 50+ sunscreen. "First, this place is lower, so you can stop and rest here and not be seen by the Border Patrol. Second, they are exhausted and just want to lighten the load. Third, as Alain said, at this point they know they've made it across the border and they change clothes and try to not look like someone who's just hiked across the desert."

Professor Ponce stood near the edge of the field of discards writing in a notebook. Of medium height, he had a round face and black hair under his straw hat.

The blond student muttered something about know-it-alls, but he didn't do it quietly enough, so the red-haired student retorted, "If you hadn't skipped so much of the orientation, you wouldn't say inane things."

"I was just making conversation. It's so fucking dull, picking up and labeling crappy backpacks from a Mexican Walmart. There's nothing special about them. I could just go to the Walmart in Tucson and get the same packs."

The red-haired woman stood up and wiped her forehead. "It's not the damn backpacks. It's that they are artifacts of human migration. That's what we study."

"Yup, that's anthropology for ya," a third student said. He was older than the first two. His outfit showed the wear and tear of multiple summers in rough terrain. "Pick, tag and bag. It'd be no different if these were Aztec vessels. Although you'd have to be a hell of a lot more careful with those."

A scream cut across the hollow. It came from a blonde student the others called Barbie because she had an uncanny resemblance to the doll, including the pointy boobs. She stood, frozen, her finger pointing at a pile of things next to her.

Ponce ran over to her. The others followed suit, the blond guy being the last one to see why Barbie had screamed and why the others stood there agape.

A skeletonized human arm was sticking out from the debris.

They stood silent. Yes, people died crossing the desert. Ponce had told them, so they knew that in an abstract way. He'd also told them that the number of deaths was far higher than the official statistics the Border Patrol published. None of that seemed to have prepared them for the actual evidence of death. Ponce figured it unlikely that any of them had ever seen a dead body or a skeleton.

"Step back everybody," Ponce said. "Nobody touch anything."

"What if there's a whole body under the stuff?" the older student said.

"I don't care, Nick. A dead body means it's the Sheriff's jurisdiction. They tolerate my work, so I make sure I don't interfere in theirs. I don't need any hassle from them."

He saw the blond kid take out his phone to take a picture. "Listen this isn't some spectacle, or something for your Instagram feed. No photos, please, show some respect for the dead."

The kid made a face. Ponce fixed him with a stare. "There are thousands and thousands of people south of here waiting for a word from loved ones who made this journey. They worry and fear the worst. Just imagine the trauma such a photo would cause. No pictures."

The blond kid put his phone away.

He walked to the top of a hill, took out his phone and made his call.

Nick crouched on his haunches and examined the arm from a couple of feet away.

"Whoever the arm belongs to couldn't have died long ago, there's still sinew holding the bones together. What do you think, Megan? You're the physical anthropologist."

Megan, the redhead, crouched next to Nick. "It's hard to tell. Vultures clearly had a go at it, that's for sure. I don't see any ants or beetles. I'd say a week. There might be more of the body under this debris."

"I doubt it," Nick said. "If there were, the vultures would have cleared those backpacks out of the way."

He knelt and stuck his head close to where the arm emerged from the pile of clothes, backpacks and blankets. "I may be wrong, there seems to be more."

"So it can't have been here more than a few days," Megan said. "The vultures haven't had time yet to dig through all the stuff yet."

Barbie stared at them as if they were a couple of

ghouls. "How can you talk like that? It belonged to a human being, who was alive a few days ago."

"I'm sorry. You're right," Megan said. "It's an occupational hazard. I look at it like a puzzle and forget the human. Thanks for reminding me."

"Whoever it is, they're dead," Nick said. "We do want to know how they died. That's part of our job. We know that bodies disappear fast in the desert, even the bones. This pile of discards is very fresh. Migrants have been here just a day or so ago."

Ponce had finished his call, saw Nick kneeling by the arm and yelled, "Nick get away from there. I just talked to the sheriff and the deputy told me to keep away from the body. They'll be here in a couple of hours."

THEY WAITED FOR three hours. Barbie had spread a cloth over the arm because, she said, it seemed the decent thing to do. The work had stopped and the students had congregated near the edge of the hollow, sitting in a circle a respectful distance from what might be a whole body. Nobody wanted to talk. Ponce knew that collective silence easily led to moroseness that would undermine the fragile esprit de corps he'd built over the last week.

"I'm sorry you had to encounter this," he said.

His students didn't answer. They didn't look at each other. Each seemed to be in their own world. The blond kid with the creased clothes looked especially lost.

"Why are they choosing this dangerous area?" he said after a while. "Don't they know?"

Megan sighed and said, "Jeez, Chad. You really didn't pay attention at all, did you?"

Chad didn't rise to the bait. "I've never seen a dead

body. In class it was all theory. Here it's scary real. Why are they risking their lives? I'm just trying to understand."

Ponce recognized a teachable moment when it presented itself. It had been part of the prep for the summer program, but he knew that constant repetition was crucial to make sure the students remembered anything.

"It goes back to nineteen-ninety-two when those students in El Paso filed that lawsuit. You remember, the one about the border patrol harassing them in their own high school. They won and the border patrol couldn't randomly stop people on the US side anymore. So they came up with operation 'Blockade.'"

Chad nodded. He seemed glad that someone was talking to him. The others were also listening. Anything to take their minds off the bones under the cloth.

"Around that time NAFTA was ratified, opening up the borders to free trade," Meghan said. "Because of the increase in US goods flowing to Mexico, its government devalued the peso to make US goods more expensive and maintain some balance."

Ponce nodded, grateful that his students pitched in. "With their money worth less, many more Mexicans tried to come to the US to earn dollars. That led to more border crossings."

Nick nodded. "That's when the Border Patrol really tried to stop crossings in big cities along the border. They didn't stop the flow, though. The border crossers were simply pushed into the desert."

"You covered that in class," Barbie said. "But what happened before nineteen-ninety-two? I saw that movie *Touch of Evil* in my film class, and everybody—Americans and Mexicans—was going back and forth across the border. That was, like, in the sixties, right? What happened after? That's what I don't understand."

"A great film, but that was in the fifties," Ponce said. "A lot has happened since then."

The students were all ears now. It was like a bizarre campfire evening and Ponce was telling stories. He was in the middle of recounting the debt crisis of the 1980s, telling them how the high interest rates in the US and an earlier devaluation of the peso had cut Mexican incomes by almost forty percent, when the Cochise County Sheriff's SUV rolled up.

A deputy climbed from the vehicle and walked stiff-legged to the group. He was tall, at least six feet, and lanky.

"Who's in charge of this here group?" he said.

Ponce rose.

"That would be me. Alain Ponce, Associate Professor of Anthropology at Arizona University."

"You don't say," the deputy said. "That was my major before I switched to criminal justice. What y'all doing out here?"

"We're cataloging the things migrants leave behind. It's part of a multi-year program at my university. I have all the necessary authorizations, Deputy—" he peered at the name tag "—Perez."

"I bet you do. So where'd you find the body?"

"Over there." Ponce pointed at the cloth. "We don't actually know if it's a body, we only saw an arm."

Perez stepped into the hollow, checked the area around the cloth, then lifted it. He crouched and took in the spot without doing anything. He turned back to the students.

"None of you touched anything? Moved anything?"

"No, we just put the cloth over it," Ponce said.

Perez went back to his SUV and returned with a camera. He took a few pictures of the arm.

"You got gloves?" he said to Ponce.

"Sure."

"Okay. You want to help me see what's under there?"

Ponce shrugged, then nodded. He went to the van and took a fresh pair from the box.

They started lifting a couple of backpacks. Nick and Megan had inched closer, their professional interest must've pushed away their queasiness. It looked like there was indeed a whole skeleton under the discarded stuff.

"We were both wrong," Megan said. "Vultures have picked it clean."

"Yeah," Nick said. "But why was the skeleton covered with stuff? Vultures didn't do that."

"You got that right," Perez said.

"Maybe another group arrived here later and covered it," Ponce said. "Migrants often cover a body with stones to keep the animals away."

"Well, it's here and I got to deal with it," Perez said. He radioed it in and requested that the funeral home in Bisbee send a hearse.

Ponce turned around and nodded to Nick and Megan. "Come and make yourselves useful."

They began to uncover the rest of the bones. When Megan revealed the head, she shrieked and jumped up.

Deputy Perez saw what she was pointing to—a round hole in the forehead—and said, "This wasn't a death from exposure, it was murder."

The students stood wide-eyed. Ponce knew why.

Death from exposure was too common. Murder was an entirely different ballpark.

Perez stopped everything and took more pictures from multiple angles. He radioed his office again and requested another deputy to search what had become a crime scene.

While they waited, Perez interviewed Ponce, Barbie, Megan, Nick and the other students. After that, they waited.

An hour later, another SUV slid to a stop. A portly deputy climbed from the cab.

"Hey, Perez, nice mess you've got here," he said.

"Don't I know it?" Perez said and turned to the rest. "This is Deputy Hamilton. Hamilton, these are the students working here. Ponce over there is their prof. They found the bones."

"So if they hadn't stuck their noses into this, we wouldn't have to deal with a stiff?" Hamilton said and shook his head.

"Well, it looks like a crime was committed."

Hamilton snorted and pointed at the debris. "Look at this mess. Every damn backpack is evidence of a crime. Anyway, the hearse should be here shortly. Where are the bones?"

Perez took Hamilton to the site. They set about uncovering the rest of the skeleton.

Ponce looked over their shoulders. The narrow pelvic opening of the skeleton indicated that it was of a man.

They were almost done when the radio squawked and let them know that the hearse was parked as close to the site as possible. Ten minutes later the driver of the hearse arrived carrying a rolled-up stretcher. He was short and wheezing, like a man who spent too much time behind a steering wheel. The deputies moved the bones onto the canvas and Hamilton helped the funeral assistant carry the remains to the hearse.

"What's going to happen to the remains?" Ponce asked Perez.

"Our county doesn't have an ME, but we have a contract with Pima County, so they're bringing it to Tucson for the postmortem."

Hamilton came back before too long and the two deputies searched the site for additional evidence. They bagged everything within a foot of the skeleton: bags, clothing, shoes and a little notebook. An hour later they took off.

The students and Ponce stood, uncertain what to do next.

"Let's pack up what we have and go back to Tucson," Ponce said.

FOUR

Monday, October 15th,
Ciudad Obregón, Sonora, Mexico

THAT EVENING, Camille Delano hailed a ride to the Walmart in the *Zona Norte Comercial*. She hadn't used the public phones there in a while. Not that there was anything wrong with them. It was a question of security. If she used the same phones regularly and if anyone ever asked about it, somebody might well remember the *gringa* using this phone all the time. Better to nip that in the bud and use each pay phone only after a decent hiatus.

She bought a new phone card for two-hundred pesos at the service desk and found the pay phones near the restrooms. She pushed the card into the slot. The display told her she'd have more than enough credit for the call she was about to make. Accessing the relay network that would conceal her phone number and location required punching a series of numbers. She memorized them a long time ago. Standing by a public phone, fumbling with your purse, staring at a piece of paper was a surefire way to attract attention.

The usual clicks and buzzes happened in the regular intervals. Eventually she heard a ring. It was answered immediately.

"Management."

"I received a message to call," Delano said.

"One moment."

More clicks and a high-pitched beep followed before a male voice said, "We have a situation."

"Related to the deal I facilitated earlier?"

"Yes."

"I'm listening."

"The man has not arrived in the US. The Moldovans are upset."

"Maybe he did a runner."

"No, the group of migrants with which the man traveled was intercepted by our operatives and the man wasn't with the group. They interrogated each migrant separately, but the story was the same. The group was ambushed by members of a rival cartel, four killed, and our man was taken away. The latest news is that a skeleton was found in the Arizona desert close to where the migrants said the ambush had occurred."

"I don't see how that involves me?"

"The Moldovans want to be reimbursed."

"By whom? The cartel they hired? You've got to be joking."

"They don't care who pays, but they want their investment back."

"I'm sure they do, but they aren't going to get it."

"That's not how they see it."

"How much are we talking about?"

"A million dollars."

Delano shook her head. "They are in Moldova. They have zero leverage over the cartels here."

"They intimated that Chechen hit squads travel internationally."

"To go after a cartel? They don't know what they are talking about."

"You'll get double your fee."

"Double my fee won't do me any good if I'm dangling by a rope from an overpass. I've built a working relationship with the Sinaloa cartel. From what you're saying the man was killed by a rival cartel. I only have contacts among the Sinaloa people."

"Use them. Contact us when you have an update."

The receiver went silent. She hung up the phone and pulled out her card and went outside into the evening heat.

This was a bad proposition. She didn't need the double fee. She was successful, made more than enough money.

When a kidnapping went wrong, she wasn't involved in the aftermath. She'd go on to the next one. This was different. Dealing with cartels was dangerous. She played a small part and did it well, so they left her alone. Confronting them, even as a messenger, was suicidal for a lone operator like her. At the same time, she was under no illusion that the Chechens would be looking for her if she ignored the order of Management.

A bloody nightmare.

She went back into the Walmart, headed for the payphone and dialed her contact at the cartel. When the man answered, she identified herself and asked for a meeting with the local boss.

"*No es posible.*"

She wanted to tell the contact that this request was above his pay grade, but couldn't think of the Spanish words. "*Es una emergencia. Deja un mensaje en este número*." She recited the number she used for messages and hung up.

Back outside, she half wanted to go back to *Bar 434*, but she decided against it. She would have to find a new bar, hell, an entirely new city before this was over. The Moldovan's demand for a refund would not sit well with the cartels. Shooting the messenger would be the cartel's natural reaction.

She hailed a ride. As she waited, she thought that maybe it was time to retire. It seemed like such an impossible idea. She had enough resources to go anywhere in the world. And do what? Sit on a beach, drink vodkas and fend off young guys like Armando, looking to be her boy toy? The thought alone was revolting. Trouble was, she had no dream of managing a small bookstore in some out of the way place, or a restaurant, or any legitimate business. All her adult life, she'd been on the wrong side of the law. She could be a consultant, but any matter she could consult on would be illegal.

A depressing thought, really, to think that the sum total of your abilities only qualify you for activities that are bound to put you in danger. It was depressing enough to make an ice-cold vodka seem very tempting.

She asked the driver to take her to the apartment instead. The next weeks were going to be tricky. To get out of this alive required a plan. More vodka wouldn't be conducive to that.

FIVE

Tuesday, October 16th,
Tucson, Arizona

THE SKELETON ENDED up on the examination table of Doctor Nicole Post of the Pima County Medical Examiner's office. It was the second postmortem on Tuesday morning. Since it was a skeleton, she'd pulled in her colleague Olga Kaminsky, the ME's forensic anthropologist. Over the past decade, the two had become local experts at dealing with the skeletal remains of undocumented border crossers. Of course those weren't the only cases they investigated, but UBCs constituted an increasing share of their work.

They couldn't have been a more unlikely team. Post, like her name suggested, was tall and sturdy, with a no-nonsense short haircut and a face that radioed a *git 'er done* attitude. Kaminsky seemed almost fragile with her wavy blonde hair and soft face that belied the fact that she'd participated in the exhumation of some of the most gruesome mass graves in the Western Hemisphere. Between the two of them, they'd handled well over a thousand UBC cases during the past decade.

"What've we got here?" Kaminsky said.

"Came in from Cochise County. A bunch of anthro students working in the desert found it."

"Oh yeah, Alain Ponce's group. I bet those kids got a big scare. Anything else we should know?"

"The deputy emailed, saying that it looked like other migrants found and covered the bones. They picked up stuff they found around the skeleton."

They put on their masks, goggles and gloves and started their examination of UBC 132.

"He was a tall fellow, wasn't he," Post said. She measured the length of the skeleton, almost six feet, and wrote it down. "Taller than any of the other UBCs we've had this year."

Kaminsky nodded. "Whatever that means. Did you see the fractures on the right arm?" Both the ulna and radius had been broken near the middle and then set poorly. The bones didn't quite line up. "He must've had a deformed arm. A strange place to break one's arm. It almost looks deliberate."

"You mean someone broke his arm?" Post said.

"Maybe. We haven't seen such breaks here before."

"Are you saying torture?"

"I don't know. Maybe he couldn't afford a doctor. Or the doctor did a lousy job."

Post started with the feet. Feet tell you a lot about a person's life. Many of the UBCs she saw were walkers. They walked most of their lives, usually carrying things. That meant a visible amount of wear on ankle and knee joints.

"He's definitely not one of our regulars. His leg joints are in pretty good shape, but his left fibula and tibia are thinner than his right, you see that?"

Kaminsky, who'd started at the head, looked up. "Yeah, I can see that from here. No fractures, though."

"Must've been muscle or nerve damage, but he clearly limped and had done so for a while."

Post concentrated on the pelvis area next. "I'd say he was early to mid-forties, the wear on the pubic symphysis is consistent with that age and it matches the general bone density, too."

"Sounds about right," Kaminsky said. "But he sure had crappy teeth for a man that age. He's had every kind of cavity you can imagine. Probably ate sugar by the spoonful."

"But he still has all his teeth?"

"Yeah. He has a lot of dental work, way more than the usual UBC. So he had access to a dentist, but not a good one. They didn't use silver amalgam for the fillings. Looks like some kind of alloy that probably wasn't the healthiest thing to have in your mouth. I want to say Eastern Europe."

"Eastern Europe? Are you sure?"

"These alloys haven't been used in North America or Western Europe in decades. In graduate school we looked at dental work from different parts of the world and this looks just like the samples I saw from places in Eastern Europe."

"Okay. That's different."

They didn't have to spend much time on the hole in the skull. Post knew her calibers by heart. It was caused by a 9 mm bullet. No doubt.

"Let's sum this up," Post said. "We have a skeleton, possibly of Eastern European origin, likely killed by a 9 mm bullet and found along the border among the detritus left behind by undocumented border crossers. That about sum it up?"

Kaminsky nodded.

"Well, ain't that a weird case."

"You said it."

"How long do you think he's been out there?"

"That's tricky," Kaminsky said. "Some tests have shown that a body can disappear completely in as little as nine days. These bones are mostly clean, but ligaments are still present. Vultures have been at it, but didn't get a chance to finish their job."

"Like someone interrupted them?"

"Yes, it might have been the UBCs who covered the body. If that's who did it."

"That must've been pretty recent. I mean vultures wouldn't be deterred by a few backpacks."

"Yeah, but once the flesh is gone, the scent isn't all that powerful anymore. Like I said, it's hard to tell. I'd say less than three months but more than a week."

"Shoot. Not very precise. But if that's what it is, I'll put it in the report. What about the stuff the deputies bagged?" Post said.

"I'll have a look at it. But don't hold your breath, we don't even know if it's connected to this guy. If he was dumped there—and it looks like that, doesn't it?—none of the things they bagged would mean anything."

Post shrugged and left to type up her report.

Kaminsky lingered and studied the head of the skeleton one more time. "Who are you? What's your story?"

KAMINSKY WENT TO the evidence room to check on the bags the Cochise County deputy had dropped off with the skeleton. It didn't look very promising. She sighed, snapped on a pair of gloves, and opened the first one.

A daypack: she unzipped it and looked at the label inside. *Made in China.* That was to be expected. The pack contained a thin T-shirt and a pair of women's panties. Both items were well washed and the tags were almost illegible. She could make out *Hecho en México* on the T-shirt.

"Unless you were a cross-dresser, this wasn't your pack," she said.

The second daypack was also made in China and it was empty. She searched the side pockets and found a bus ticket from Tapachula to Mexico City. Most likely a Central American migrant. The man from Eastern Europe would've gone straight to Mexico City. No reason to go to Guatemala and then take a bus north.

She sorted out all the plastic bags that contained backpacks and put them to the side. The skeleton didn't strike her like a backpack guy. Sure, he might have gotten one for the desert trek, but chances weren't all that good she'd find something useful inside. Most clothing for sale anywhere in the world was made in China, India, or some other cheap labor country. How would she know if she had his backpack and his clothes? The labels would be no different from all the others. More personal items were her best bet: notebooks, address books, books, watches. She sorted through the evidence bags and put the most likely candidates in one pile.

The first bag she opened contained a man's wallet. It looked well used but not falling apart. She unfolded it and looked through the compartments. All the money was gone, which made sense. There was no ID card or any other paper that could give a hint as to its owner.

The rest of the smaller things ended up being equally useless. She found a driver's license, but it was Mexican and for a man who was much shorter than the skeleton. There was a loyalty card for Soriana supermarkets. But there was no clue as to the identity of the skeleton.

She rummaged through the remaining evidence bags and noticed a small booklet, like a pocket diary. She took it out of the bag and tried to open it. The pages were stuck together. It must've gotten wet. She went to the computer and connected to the University of Arizona Meteorology website and checked the rainfall over the past month. There had been a couple of storms in the region, so moisture could have damaged the notebook.

The Pima County ME office didn't have the special equipment to deal with caked-together diaries. She thought of soaking the booklet in water. It was one way to get the pages unstuck. The downside was that whatever writing was inside could become even more illegible. She called Scott Geran, a colleague at the University of Arizona School of Anthropology, telling him of her problem.

"Come on over tomorrow around one," he said. "We'll see what we can extract from your artifact."

SIX

Wednesday, October 17th,
Tucson, Arizona

AFTER LUNCH KAMINSKY entered the anthropology building at the western edge of the campus. It was a familiar spot. She attended lectures there and had a number of acquaintances on the faculty. She taught the occasional graduate course in forensic anthropology, but had rejected the offer to teach undergraduates.

Scott Geran, one of the professors she worked with occasionally, waited for her. He ran a couple of labs and had access to technology she could only wish for at the ME's office. His pallid complexion and rotund body made clear that he was the lab kind of anthropologist, not the rugged outdoorsy kind. Geran looked at the diary, nodded and said, "Not very old, just wet and then dried. Is it part of a case?"

"I don't know yet. We found a skeleton and this was in the vicinity. For all I know it belonged to someone else. It was at one of the spots where migrants dump their stuff."

"Doesn't sound very promising. But let's see what we can do."

He froze the diary in what looked like a regular freezer.

"You keep your lunch in there?" Kaminsky said.

"No way. We store stuff you wouldn't want near your lunch even in a frozen state."

After a half hour, he took the frozen diary and laid it into a vacuum chamber. As the pump extracted the air from the glass, Kaminsky could see the diary expand in thickness.

"This would have been a lot more difficult with a really old book," Geran said. He let air back into the chamber and took out the diary. "The pages are really brittle now, so careful. I suggest you use gloves and tweezers."

He took her to a table where she sat down and tweezed apart the pages. Whoever had owned this hadn't been a consistent diarist. There was writing on several of the pages, but it was too faded to be deciphered. It was a Latin alphabet, but that was all she could make out. Maybe there was more writing and it just had faded completely, although the age of the booklet didn't suggest that. The freeze/vacuum process had made the cover and binding so brittle that she had to separate the pages from the diary. She placed four pages each into a plastic cover. After twenty minutes of careful examination she ended up with twenty pages encased in five sleeves. She knew as little as when she'd started.

Geran popped his head into the room and asked about her progress.

"Not any, so far. I need an infrared or ultraviolet viewer."

"I figured as much, let me take you to the microscopy lab."

One story up, they entered a narrow room with several high-tech apparatuses only one of which looked like a microscope. Next to them stood a computer and a large monitor.

"Which page do you want to start with?" Geran said after turning on the computer.

She handed him the first sleeve. He slipped it under the lens of one of the apparatuses. All she could see were marginal traces of writing. The ink was really washed out.

"Let's try the infrared filter first," he said. He clicked a couple of check boxes on the screen. The result was even worse than regular light. The pages were white, as if there were no writing on them at all.

"Oops, that's not really what I expected," Kaminsky said. "Does that mean these pages are not readable?"

"No worries. It just means that whatever ink is left is transparent to infrared. Let's try another filter."

He clicked different boxes on the screen.

"This is a blue-green filter."

The paper on the screen became all black but the writing appeared clear and white.

"Wow. That's amazing."

The first page contained just two words, *Mihaly Luca.*

"That looks like a name," Geran said.

"Yup, and it doesn't sound Mexican or Central American."

"The last name does, sort of."

"Okay, but not the first name. That could be a version of Michael. Hang on."

She pulled out her phone and typed the first name into her search engine. A couple of taps later she said, "Just as I thought, it's an Eastern European variation of Michael, common in Hungary. That also fits with my analysis of the skeleton's teeth. I thought the dental work looked Eastern European. I think we can assume that the diary and the skeleton go together. I mean what are the chances of two Hungarians coming across the border."

Geran shrugged. "Not high? Let's look at the other pages." He moved the pages under the lens and they looked at each page. There was writing in a language neither understood.

"It doesn't look Hungarian," Kaminsky said.

"You know Hungarian?"

"No, but I grew up in Chicago not far from the Hungarian neighborhood and the words on the store signs looked different."

They stared at the script for a while.

"It's got something Italian to it," he said.

"It's definitely not Italian."

"I'm not saying it is, but there are words that look Italian."

"It could be a Romance language."

The remaining pages in the sleeve contained equally unintelligible words. The next sleeves didn't produce any useful information either. She'd have to find someone to decipher the words. When they reached the last of the sleeves, she'd pretty much given up on finding anything useful on the diary pages. The first page changed her mind.

It was the address book part of the diary. The entries didn't follow any obvious order. They weren't alphabetical, either by last or first name. Sometimes, there were only initials or no name at all. Oddly, the pages didn't contain anything that looked like a street address. There were only numbers, which could be phone numbers, but they varied in length. Most of the numbers started with a six, some with "235," which looked like a US area code.

Kaminsky used her phone again to pull up the Wikipedia page on telephone numbers in Hungary. The numbers didn't fit the pattern. She checked the surrounding countries. Bulgaria, Romania and Ukraine looked different too. She tried Moldova last and that's where she stopped. For one, all mobile phone numbers started with the six. Landlines had two or three-digit area codes and the ones starting with "235" could be numbers in a town called Orhei. Landline numbers could be five or six digits long, which explained the varying lengths. Moldova was the best bet yet. She checked and found that the official language of Moldova was Romanian.

She made notes to that effect and was about to thank Geran for his help, when he said, "Check this out."

He had moved the last page under the camera. There was only a number on that page and that number looked suspiciously like an American number, three digits, three digits, four digits. The first set read "212," the area code for Manhattan.

"Maybe he has a relative there?" Geran said.

"Then he could've gotten a visitor visa, no?"

"You're right. Probably just a friend."

"It's a good point, though. Why did he choose this dangerous route if he had other options?"

Geran shrugged. "Maybe he wanted to stay longer then ninety days."

"Yeah, but then he could've just overstayed his visa. Nobody checks on those. How many undocumented Irish do you think are in Boston? As far as I know, the largest number of undocumented aliens in the US are folks who overstayed their visas. It's odd. I'll send my report to the sheriff in Cochise County and they can do with it what they want."

She thanked Geran, took printouts of all the pages with her, and went back to the ME office, where she typed up the report. Once she was done, she called Deputy Perez.

"A very unusual skeleton," she said after he answered. "The man's name is Mihaly Luca and he's from Moldova in Eastern Europe. He's definitely not your usual UBC. You already know that he was killed by a shot to his head. The only item that I can directly link to him is a diary. I took it to the university to have it analyzed. It's all in the report. There's one odd thing. There's a US phone number in the diary. Manhattan area code."

SEVEN

Wednesday, October 17th,
Tucson, Arizona

THEIR PLANE LANDED in Tucson that afternoon. Neither Vermeulen nor Tessa had checked any luggage and headed straight to the rental car counters just outside the terminal. Vermeulen waited while Tessa completed the paperwork for their car. Outside the air-conditioned structure rental cars stood lined up in the bright afternoon sun. They got into theirs—it was quite hot from standing in the bright afternoon sun—and headed to their motel.

Driving through Tucson, he saw how different this place was. Whereas New York City was vertical, Tucson was spread out like wet bread dough. A few high-rises downtown didn't make up for the fact that the city had simply expanded horizontally. Space was no issue here. There was always more desert to be annexed.

Tucson looked very much like a desert city, an endless repetition of low-slung buildings in some shade of beige. Maybe the sun eventually bleached away all paint anyway, so why bother painting any other color. Although he didn't like pink as a house color, here, the occasional pink structure was almost a relief. The city's parks department had made a valiant effort to break up the monochrome appearance by planting lots of trees along the residential streets. But even these looked tired after a hot summer.

Their motel, just off Speedway Boulevard looked like motels everywhere. Tessa preferred locally-owned ones rather than the chains. This one wasn't far from the University, where she planned on interviewing a contact. Even though the outside was nondescript, their second-floor room was quite the opposite. The wall behind their bed was painted a deep red and there was a large abstract mural on the white wall that enclosed the bathroom.

"Wow," he said. "Not your plain vanilla decor."

"I like it. Something different. Who needs white walls?"

Vermeulen plopped himself on the bed. "Oh good. Not too much of a bounce. Feels like a firm mattress. I think I'll survive the week."

Tessa rolled her eyes. "You're on vacation, of course you'll survive the week. And I know you've slept on far worse beds."

"Sure, but they were also a lot cheaper. What's the plan? It's too early for dinner."

"I gotta make some calls and confirm appointments. You can call Alma Rodriguez. Maybe we can meet for dinner later. But please do it outside, though, 'cause I'm gonna be making my calls in here."

He took out his phone and started for the door. Before he reached it, his phone rang. *Unknown number.*

Vermeulen tapped the green icon and said, "Hello?"

"Good day. This is Deputy Antonio Perez with the sheriff's department of Cochise County. Who am I speaking with?"

"What?" Vermeulen looked at his phone and the

strange number. On a scale from likely to implausible, it was way past the implausible end. "The sheriff's department where?"

"Cochise County, Arizona. Who are you?"

He'd received a lot of odd calls in his life, all of them related to his work. Back in Antwerp, where he'd been a prosecutor until 2002, he'd gotten calls from snitches and crooks. Later, at the United Nations, the calls came in languages he didn't understand and from numbers that he'd never remember. But this was a first, a random call from someone wanting to know his name.

"I'm not in the habit of giving my name to random callers."

He ended the call.

"Who was that?" Tessa said, standing next to the desk chair.

"Some guy who claimed to a deputy sheriff and asked who I was. A scammer."

"A deputy where?"

"Does it matter?"

"There are no sheriffs in New York City. Why would they call a Manhattan area code?"

"Because the scammers live abroad and don't know better. Anyway, the guy said he was from Cochise County. I have no idea where that is."

Tessa stopped, let go of her roll-aboard and checked her phone. After tapping a couple of times, she said, "Cochise County is the next county over from Tucson. Are you sure you understood that correctly?"

"Yes. The man said his name was Perez and he was a deputy from Cochise County."

Tessa tapped more on her phone. A minute later she held the phone up to Vermeulen. He read the screen. It was the personnel page of the Cochise County sheriff's department. A couple of names down from the top, he saw the name Antonio Perez.

"How'd you know that it wasn't a scam?" he said.

"It seemed a little too specific. If I were a scammer, I wouldn't give the name of a county in rural Arizona. I would just stay general and say, 'I'm calling from the police.' I mean, here we are in Arizona and the first call you get is from Arizona."

"Should I call back?"

"Of course, what's the worst that could happen? But outside, please."

He went to the balcony, closed the door behind him. After finding the website of the Cochise County Sheriff's department he tapped on the main number. A receptionist answered and he asked to speak with Deputy Perez. The same voice answered.

"Okay, Deputy Perez," Vermeulen said. "You are who you say you are. I just needed to make sure that this wasn't a crank call. My name is Valentin Vermeulen. How did you get my number?"

"Have you ever been to Arizona?"

The question made Vermeulen perk up. The deputy wasn't giving any information but started with questions. He was investigating something. "No, I haven't. So where did you get my number?"

"Have you ever been to Mexico?"

"What is this, Twenty Questions? No, I've never been to Mexico. I would really appreciate your telling me how you got my number and why you are calling me."

"We found your phone number in a notebook."

"Okay, we're making progress. Whose notebook?

You didn't by chance transpose a number? Or misread it? Or omit the country code?" Vermeulen said.

There was a pause at the other end, long enough for Vermeulen to think that this settled it and that the call had been in error.

"Sorry," Perez said eventually. "There's a one at the beginning and the numbers are correct."

Vermeulen's gut tightened. The one was both the long-distance code in the US and the international country code for the US. He thought of people around the world who might have his number. An impossible task. There were too many missions to keep track of.

"Does the name Mihaly Luca mean anything to you?"

That name did sound vaguely familiar, but Vermeulen couldn't place it. His phone number wasn't a secret. His business card included both his office and his mobile number. He'd distributed his cards liberally in many parts of the world, but the recipients were always people he met doing his job as investigator for OIOS. Those included government officials, UN officials, local and international contractors, and folks working for charitable organizations. "I'm not sure. In my line of work I meet a lot of people."

"What do you do?"

"Listen, this is starting to feel like an interrogation. I'm under no obligation to tell you anything. I'm happy to help, but you should at least tell me what this is about."

There was another pause at Perez's end. This one didn't take as long. When Perez spoke again, he did so in a much more reserved tone, as if he was annoyed by Vermeulen's reaction. "The notebook was found near the skeleton of a dead migrant in the desert. We're sure that it belonged to that migrant."

A skeleton in the desert? With his phone number? That made no sense at all.

"I'm sorry," Vermeulen said. "But I can't think of any reason why my number should be in a dead migrant's notebook. I can't think of anyone in my circle of acquaintances who might attempt to enter the US via the Mexican border. Sorry, I can't help you."

"This Mihaly Luca, was murdered. So this is a murder investigation. There must be a reason your number was in his notebook."

He was about to tell Perez that his number was circulated widely when the part of his brain that had been mulling over the name spit out a result. The recognition struck him as if he'd touched a bare wire. Of course, Mihaly Luca. The sad looking man in the York County prison in Pennsylvania. He'd been caught by immigration and awaited deportation. Vermeulen questioned him during the investigation of fraudulent UN letters that had been used to obtain visas for the US. It was a bad case of human trafficking.

"Are you still there?" Perez said.

"Uh, yes, I am."

"So does the name mean anything to you?"

"It does. I'm remembering this case now. It happened seven years ago. I interviewed Mister Luca in Pennsylvania. He was about to be deported."

"Are you law enforcement? Immigration?"

"No, I work for the United Nations. This was a case of human trafficking and I got pulled in because some the victims had been given fake UN letters so they could get visas to the US. I only saw Luca once."

"So how did he get your phone number?"

"I'm not sure. He asked me to write to his family that he was okay. I wrote the letter and I may have included my phone number in case they had urgent questions."

"We definitely need to talk with you," Perez said. "Your area code tells me you are in Manhattan, is that correct."

"It is."

"I'll pass it on to the County Attorney, Carson Mac-Millan. He'll call you."

Vermeulen hesitated. The last thing he wanted was getting drawn into a murder investigation. "About what?"

"To testify before the grand jury."

"Why? I don't know anything about Luca. I saw him once seven years ago. That's all."

"Are you in Manhattan now?"

"Uh, no," Vermeulen hesitated. He didn't want to lie to the deputy, but a grand jury appearance? Not what he came for. The better part of his conscience prevailed. "I'm in Tucson."

Vermeulen could hear the surprise in the deputy's voice.

"Tucson? You've got to be kidding. That's less than two hours away. He'll definitely call you."

EIGHT

Wednesday, October 17th,
Tucson, Arizona

VERMEULEN OPENED THE door to their room to let Tessa know what had just happened. Tessa waved him off, the phone at her ear. He went back outside and called Alma Rodriguez instead.

"Hi Alma," he said after she answered. "It's Valentin Vermeulen."

"Valentin? What a surprise. How are you? It's been a while."

"I'm fine. How about you? Sorry, I'm not very good when it comes to staying in touch with my friends. The exciting news is that I'm in Tucson."

"You are? How nice. What brings you here?"

"My partner Tessa is contributing to a project on the militarization of borders worldwide and she's doing the US angle. I'm just tagging along. What are you up to?"

"I'm still working for the *Arizona Rescue Committee*."

"Good to hear. You've always been such a committed activist. I'm glad you're continuing that work. It can't be easy these days."

"It isn't. Things are worse than what you read in the news."

Vermeulen heard an exhaustion in her voice that sounded much deeper than long working hours.

"It's that bad?"

"It is. Just before you called, I got my monthly email from the Pima County Medical examiner. Last month, they found the remains of over a hundred dead migrants in the desert. I'm looking at the details right now. And that's just this stretch of the border. The worst part? The real number could easily be double that."

It took Vermeulen a moment to let that sink in. Those numbers never made it into the news. "That has to be so hard for you and your colleagues."

"It should be for everybody."

Vermeulen swallowed. She was right.

"I've been working on immigration issues for a long time," she said. "Two-thousand-eighteen has been the worst year, and it doesn't look like it's getting any better."

"Nothing like deportations you were working on in New Jersey?"

"Deportations?" He could hear her snort. "That used to be our biggest issue. Right now it's about saving lives. The asylum process is being systematically dismantled and we're seeing the results right here."

The anger in her voice startled Vermeulen. He remembered Rodriguez as an outgoing and positive activist. "How's your daughter Catalina? She's got to be, what, five now?"

"Not yet, only four." Rodriguez's voice brightened. "Or four-and-a-half, as she is eager to point out. She's the center of my life and keeps me sane. She started preschool this fall and is doing well there."

"The reason why I'm calling is to see if we can invite you and Catalina for dinner tonight. It'd be nice to catch up and meet Catalina."

There was a moment's hesitation before she responded with a tentative sounding yes.

"It's okay if it doesn't work. I know it's short notice," he said. "We're here for a week. I'm sure we'll have time to get together."

"No, that sounds great. I'd love to. Where do you want to meet?"

"I don't know my way around town, so if you have a favorite place, let's go there."

He sensed the tension easing in her voice.

"Oh, that's easy," she said. "I'll introduce you to the best *taqueria* in Tucson."

She gave him the address and they agreed to meet there at seven.

"I better let you go," he said. "I'm sure you have your hands full."

"Yup, there's a group of refugees who just surrendered to the Border Patrol in Douglas and asked for asylum. I've got to rustle up one of our pro-bono lawyers to represent them. We'll see you tonight."

RODRIGUEZ TURNED BACK to the spreadsheet on her computer. Hearing from Vermeulen awoke some bittersweet memories. The steady flow of deportations during the Obama years was her primary concern then. Compared to those years, what she was facing today seemed so much worse. The deaths she now documented here in Arizona weighed on her conscience like nothing before. Each row in the spreadsheet represented a life lost, squeezed from the body not by the relentless climate, but an administration that did its level best to foreclose any and all avenues of entry.

Some days all she could do was close her eyes and let a wave of darkness wash over her. She dreaded that volatile combination of deep sadness and red anger. Her hands pressed against her face, she willed her mind into calmness. Once the wave had run its course, she opened her eyes again. She slid her fingers through her long dark hair and took a deep breath before looking at the screen again.

The number of bodies with identification was rather large. There must have been another Border Patrol sweep in the sector. That's when they found bodies still in their clothing and with some form of ID. Most of the identified victims were asylum-seekers from Honduras and El Salvador. Unlike migrants from Mexico, the refugees kept their IDs so they could apply for asylum. If they ever made it to the front of the line.

Her boss, Gloria Fuentes, came into the room. In her fifties, she had graying hair and a round face with almond eyes. She was short and her body matched her face. She took one look at Rodriguez and said, "A new spreadsheet?"

Rodriguez nodded.

"Will it ever stop?" Fuentes said.

"It has to."

Both had worked for the *Arizona Rescue Committee* for several years now. In addition to documenting deaths, they also operated a missing migrant hot line, informed relatives of any deaths, organized legal representation and left water and food in the desert to help border crossers.

"What about that group of refugees surrendered to

the Border Patrol in Douglas," she said. "Can you rustle up a lawyer who could get down there?"

"I think we already have someone in Douglas." Rodriguez flipped a few pages on her desk. "Yup, William Morgan the Third is down there. I'll call him to let him know about the new arrivals."

The entire staff made a point of calling the pro bono lawyer by his full name, William Morgan the Third. When he first showed up, sent by a big law firm in Phoenix as their token contribution to pro bono work, he'd introduced himself that way. At first, they thought he was making a joke, and it took a minute before they realized that he was serious. He came from a Boston patrician family and graduated Harvard Law. They had yet to find out what made him take a job in Phoenix.

Rodriguez took her cell phone and dialed his number. He answered with a gruff, "What now?"

"Hey, William Morgan the Third, are you still in Douglas?"

"Just about to leave, and, please, stop that thing about my name."

"There's a new group of asylum seekers in Douglas. Can you check and start the legal stuff if needed?"

"Oh man, I was hoping to get back to Phoenix at a reasonable hour."

"Just change your definition of reasonable and you'll be fine."

"That's easy for you to say."

"We're all working longer hours."

"But you got air conditioning and I don't. My shirt is so starched with sweat, it'll stand up on its own."

Rodriguez relented. "Sorry, but you're already down there and sending someone else will take more time."

"I know. I'll take care of it. What are you doing for dinner?"

"I actually have an invitation."

"Oh." Morgan hesitated. "A new boyfriend?"

"No, an old friend and his partner from the East Coast."

"Too bad. I was planning on taking you out. Maybe another day."

They had this strange game going, where he asked her out for dinner and she'd decline politely. He couldn't be more than twenty-six and looked even younger. There was no chance in hell she was going to get involved with a Boston lawyer eight years her junior. At the same time, his invitations had some innocent quality to them. It didn't feel like he was hitting on her.

And it was tempting. He was handsome and she'd been single since her divorce four years ago. Taking care of her daughter Catalina was all she did besides work and it'd be nice to eat dinner with someone and not talk about children or work.

"Why'd you wanna do that?" she said.

"Uh, I don't know. I guess I want to get to know the people I work with. All we do is talk on the phone."

He sounded innocent, as always, but still. "A nice thought, not tonight though. But you make a good point. Maybe we should have an office party where we invite all the lawyers so we can get to know each other."

Phew. That was a good deflection. Nice, friendly, but also clear.

William Morgan the Third got the message and said, "Yeah, that's a great idea."

She ended the call and turned back to the spreadsheet. The next part of the task was the hardest, compare the names on the body list with the names in the missing persons database. Each time there was a clear match it fell to her to notify the relatives. Her nightmare outcome was to send a death notice to a family whose relative wasn't dead after all. So she took great care to make sure that all the data points matched—not just names and dates of birth, but also dates of departure, dates of last contact and so forth. She'd rather not notify a family than send out a false notification. So far, she'd succeeded.

By the time she had to leave to pick up her daughter, she had matched twenty missing persons with the bodies found. That was a lot more than normal.

She was going to be awake all night thinking about writing those twenty letters in the morning. At least there was dinner with Vermeulen; a small reprieve.

NINE

Wednesday, October 17th,
Tucson, Arizona

TESSA STEPPED OUT on the balcony. "Done for now, what did you want to tell me?"

Vermeulen gave her a summary of the call from the deputy. Her reaction was the same as his. "What? A seven-year-old case?" she said. "And the man turns up dead in Arizona?"

"I know, I can't believe it either."

"There has got to be a story behind all this."

"I'm sure there is, but I'm not really interested in being part of it."

"You may not have a choice. If it's a murder investigation, you'll be questioned."

"Didn't you promise me a vacation?"

"Not quite. I promised you a break from your boredom. Looks like you just got that."

Vermeulen sighed. "Not the break I was looking for."

"Oh, come on. You'll talk to the deputy. What's the worst that could possibly happen?"

"If the past is anything to go by, a lot."

"I know it sounds callous, but maybe Luca's case can be the thread that holds my story together. The changes in asylum policy are terrible and have caused enormous trauma and suffering. Yet the magnitude of what's happening here is almost numbing for readers. Specific cases help highlight how cruel it really is."

Vermeulen shook his head, more to himself than his partner. This was going to be trouble.

AT SIX-THIRTY THAT EVENING—showered and somewhat rested—the two headed to the best *taqueria* in Tucson to meet with Alma Rodriguez. It was a bit of a trek south on Sixth Avenue, but it was impossible to miss the yellow building. The entire restaurant consisted of two white-washed rooms, one with a tiled counter to order food, and the other with four tables and chairs. A *Tecate* neon sign buzzed in the window.

Rodriguez and her daughter sat at one of the tables. A young couple sat at another.

When she saw Vermeulen enter, her face lit up.

She got up and they hugged with the tenderness of old friends.

"Valentin," she said. "It's so good to see you. How long has it been?"

"Too long, for sure."

"This is my daughter, Catalina." She turned to Catalina and said, "This is my friend Valentin. We helped each other back in New Jersey. You weren't even born then."

"You helped me," Vermeulen said. "Not the other way around. It's nice to meet you, Catalina. How old are you?"

The girl had her black hair tied into a pony tail. She wore blue shorts and a yellow top with red flowers emblazoned on the front. She half hid behind her mother and shyly said, "Four."

He crouched down and said, "That's cool. You like tacos?"

Catalina nodded.

He got up again. "This is Tessa Bishonga. I don't think you ever met."

The two women greeted each other.

"Hey, Catalina. Which tacos do you like?" Tessa said, staring at the large board hanging on the wall behind the counter. The number of choices was overwhelming.

"I like fish tacos," Catalina said.

"Okay, that's what I'll have too."

They ordered their respective choices and sat down at the table.

"So tell me why you are here," Rodriguez said.

Tessa explained her project in broad strokes, the global angle, and the increase in migrants everywhere.

Rodriguez nodded. "This sounds like a worthwhile project. We in the trenches of this struggle often forget that this isn't just one administration in the US, but a world-wide phenomenon. I'd be happy to help, if you need any information."

"That would be great," Tessa said.

"And you're tagging along, being a good partner?" Rodriguez said.

"Yup, that was the plan, but since we landed something unexpected happened."

Vermeulen gave her a quick rundown of his conversation with the deputy. "It sounded like he was just fishing for information. They have a difficult case on their hands and I'm the only lead they have. Not really what I was planning on."

"It's one of his old cases coming to life again," Tessa

said. "The case where you met. When it was all over, only some of the perpetrators were caught."

"Mama, what's a perpetrator?"

"Sorry," Tessa said. "I forgot there's a little one at the table."

"A perpetrator is someone who does something bad," Rodriguez said to Catalina, before turning to the other two. "Let's talk about something else. What are you two doing these days?"

Tessa talked about her reporting and curating the subscription website. Vermeulen talked in very general terms about work at the United Nations.

"We moved," Tessa said. "It's a bigger apartment on West 119th Street. I think Valentin misses his little bachelor pad but it was too small for two people. Where do you two live?"

"Mama, what's a bachelor pad?"

Leave it to the four-year-old to make the adults smile.

"It's a small apartment where only one person lives," Rodriguez said. "To answer your question, we have a two-bedroom apartment a little north of here."

"I have my own room," Catalina chimed in. "I can draw and play with my dolls. My bed is purple."

"How nice," Vermeulen said. "What do you like to draw?"

A server brought their meals, and Vermeulen's question went unanswered while they focused on their food for a while.

"What about you?" Vermeulen said, wiping his mouth with a napkin.

Between bites, Rodriguez caught them up on her journey from Newark to Tucson. "I realized I just wasn't cut out for a career in human resource management.

Working in a corporate office, hiring and, worse, firing people, that just didn't feel right. My personal life also fell apart. The divorce was hard on both of us," she said, nodding to Catalina.

The girl had deconstructed her tacos. The shredded cabbage and condiments were piled on one side, the corn tortilla on the other, and the pieces of fish in the middle. Apparently, she had developed a system, eating her way from one pile to the next. It was a messy affair, but she was wholly absorbed in it.

"Tucson is a long ways from New Jersey," Tessa said.

"Yeah, I know, but the more I learned about what was happening at the border, the more I knew I needed to be there. Texas just scared me…"

"Why is Texas scary?" Catalina said.

"Oh *mi amor*, it's so big, we'd get lost in it."

The answer must've satisfied the girl because she started tearing the tortilla into small pieces. Rodriguez seemed to notice the mess around her daughter's plate for the first time. She grabbed a napkin, wiped Catalina's hands and said, "Are you gonna eat this or are you just playing with it?"

Her tone was sharp and Catalina scrunched up her face, getting ready to cry.

"Catalina, would you like some dessert?" Vermeulen said.

Catalina's face lit up, "Yes, pleease, flan."

"How about the rest of you?"

The two women nodded.

"Maybe you and Catalina can go and order flan," Tessa said.

"Alright, let's go," Vermeulen said to Catalina and they went to the counter. When they came back with four servings of flan, Vermeulen heard Tessa ask how difficult it was to visit people in detention. Seeing they were in a serious conversation, he sat down and asked Catalina why she liked flan so much. But he listened more to the adults' conversation than to the girl's explanation.

Rodriguez said, "It's hard to tell. Attorneys always get in. The resettlement people usually get in. We get in sometimes, depending on who's in charge. Family gets in, mostly. Journalists and strangers? Hard to tell. Sometimes it just depends on the mood of the day and the visiting hours."

"Where would I try?"

"Hmm, you could try the Border Patrol lockup here in Tucson, or the one in Douglas. The ICE facilities in Phoenix and Eloy are private prisons. There you'd have to check visiting hours."

"Would you have time to accompany us for a visit?" Tessa said.

Rodriguez frowned. "I can't. I rarely have time to leave my desk."

Catalina ate her dessert by licking only a thin layer from her spoon, then repeating it, making noises like a puppy drinking. She said, "Yummmm. I love flan."

"Catalina, stop that," Rodriguez said.

Her daughter made a face but ate her dessert quieter.

Rodriguez turned to Vermeulen. "I've been thinking about the call you got from the Cochise County deputy. Were those the remains found by the anthropology students?"

Vermeulen shrugged. "No idea."

Tessa raised her eyebrows. "What were anthropology students doing out there in the desert?"

"This group is working with Alain Ponce, a prof at the university. They are documenting migration by focusing on the items left behind by migrants."

"What do they do with it all?"

"Tag it and bag it."

Tessa straightened. "Do you have the number of the professor?"

"Sure."

Rodriguez found the contact on her phone and showed it to Tessa who tapped it into hers.

"You might also talk with Olga Kaminsky, she's the forensic anthropologist who analyzed the remains. She's in Tucson. Here's her number."

"Thanks," Tessa said.

In the meantime Vermeulen and Catalina finished their flan at the same time.

"It's a tie," Vermeulen said. "I like flan as much as you do."

Catalina frowned as if that was not possible.

"Let's go, sweetheart. It's getting late." Rodriguez grabbed her purse and got up.

"No Mama, I want more flan?"

"Don't be rude."

Catalina pouted but got up.

They said their good-byes.

"I'll be in touch," Tessa said.

After Rodriguez and Catalina left, Vermeulen looked at his watch. "It's still early and I could use a beer."

"Let's call this Kaminsky and see if she wants to join us."

TEN

Wednesday, October 17th,
Tucson, Arizona

Olga Kaminsky couldn't get the skeleton from Moldova out of her mind. It was the broken arm that kept her mind busy. Like many who work with the dead, she had developed a technique for keeping the skeletons she analyzed at arm's length. That was especially true for the ones found in mass graves that showed signs of terrible abuse, like the ones in Guatemala. No forensic anthropologist could do their job otherwise.

Most of the time, she simply focused on the bones and avoided visualizing them as fully fleshed human bodies. She knew all the evil human beings did to each other. Sticking to the bones engaged her scientific mind and left the human part with all its messiness, fear, pain and trauma behind.

That habit of avoiding the human part of her emotions kept her sane, but it also meant she had few close friends. And that was putting it generously. Her colleague Nicole Post, maybe because they shared work with the dead, was her best friend. But Nicole was married and had two kids, so there was a limit to how much they could hang out. There were a few anthro colleagues from the university, but that was it. In the middle of the week, there were no after work gatherings. She was alone, again.

A train whistle blew as she opened the door to *The Buffet*. It was one of the oldest bars in Tucson just a few blocks from the university. If you looked up the word 'dive bar' on Wikipedia, the entry should feature a picture of *The Buffet*. The cramped space featured a large horseshoe shaped bar with stools, a pool table that took up most of the space on the left side of the bar, a shuffleboard along the right wall and just one tiny table in a corner.

She slid onto a bar stool. Her eyes took in the graffiti, the drawings, the lists of anything listable, names, and crude pictures of anything under the sun that covered the wall. On top of that were stickers, posters, and mirrors advertising liquor brands. They made the space feel even smaller than it was.

The TVs were tuned to some 24-hour sports channel. She never paid attention to them since they were muted. The music from the jukebox was usually enough to keep her company.

Evie, the bartender, saw her come in and set about making a martini. Kaminsky was a regular.

"Any interesting bones on the table these days?" Evie said.

Kaminsky didn't want to talk shop and said instead, "Is it true that when the walls are all full the owner will paint everything over?"

"Yeah, that's the story. Although this place hasn't been painted for as long as I've been here, and that's quite a while. So maybe it's just a story."

She put the martini on the counter.

"Know what?" Kaminsky said. "I think I'll sit at the table."

"Jeez, is it something I said?"

"Nothing you say could make me do anything. I'm just a bit preoccupied today."

Evie nodded and went about wiping the counter.

Kaminsky settled at the table. She took a sip from her martini and shivered a little. As always, the air-conditioner was set to arctic and, like the dim light, the frigid temperature took a moment to get used to.

Her gaze wandered to the coasters decorated with all kinds of drawings that Evie had pinned to the shelf full of liquor bottles. There was no rhyme or reason to the selections. Some were accomplished, others just had scrawls. It was all part of *The Buffet.*

Those broken arm bones that had been set badly didn't leave her alone. Although there was no telling what people might do to break their bones, accidental fractures tended to occur in the same areas of the arms. The laws of physics applied to bones as much as to any other aspect of human life. Most arm bone fractures came from falls, the very human reaction of putting one's hands out to break the fall. Therefore the bones tend to break near the wrist, or, depending on how far the arm is stretched out, in the upper third of the ulna. That's due to the distribution of the force of the sudden impact.

She took another swallow and sucked on the first olive.

The fractures in the skeleton were neither of those. They almost looked like a textbook nightstick fracture. Almost, because those occur in the ulna only. A cop swings the nightstick, the protester raises the arms in defense, and the nightstick hits the inside of the forearm and breaks the ulna, but it wouldn't reach the radius on the other side of the arm.

To break both ulna and radius at the lower third required a deliberate action, like tying the arm down and smashing it with a hammer or a baseball bat. Nicole had been right to ask about torture.

Kaminsky didn't know the first thing about Moldova. She knew that some of the former Soviet states had degenerated into repressive kleptocracies, where the government wasn't all that different from the mafias. Was Moldova one of those?

If it had been a case of torture either by the government or a mafia, the man would have been eligible for asylum. No better way to demonstrate a credible fear than to show your broken arm. In that case, he could have easily made it to any of the western European countries who still upheld the right to asylum.

She finished her martini.

So why did Mihaly Luca come to Mexico and brave the desert to come to the United States?

She dialed Nicole's number. Quite surprisingly, her colleague answered immediately. "What's up, Olga?"

"Wow, aren't you like making dinner or something?"

"It's my night off. Kids and dad are off to the taco truck, they'll be back in a little while. So better make it quick, 'cause you don't want to get between me and my taco *Al Pastor*."

"Our skeleton from Moldova. Was he right or left handed?"

"From the different thicknesses of the bones I concluded left handed. Why?"

"Just curious about the broken forearm, is all. Enjoy your dinner."

"Where are you? Want to join us? I'll just text them to bring a few more."

"That's so nice of you, but, no thanks. I got plans. See you in the morning."

She ended the call before Nicole could laugh out loud. Kaminsky never had plans, and Nicole knew that. It's just that being around kids made her feel even more awkward.

The people who smashed Mihaly Luca's arm didn't break his dominant arm. The torture wounds she'd seen weren't so selective. Torturers hurt people where it mattered most. These people didn't do that. It made the whole thing seem more of a warning, like saying, we could really fuck you up, but we're not doing that quite yet, because we're giving you one more chance. One more chance to do what? And why did that involve coming to the US via the southern border? Well, those were thoughts for another day.

Her phone rang. She answered.

"Hi, this is Tessa Bishonga," the caller said. "I got your number from Alma Rodriguez at Arizona Rescue. I'm a journalist, working on an article on the militarization of borders, and heard from her about the skeleton you examined. Can I buy you a drink and ask you about that?"

Kaminsky hesitated. Since Alma had given out her number, this Tessa Bishonga was probably okay. Did she want company? It was the middle of the week—why not? It would be better than drinking her martini alone.

"Sure. I'm actually at my favorite bar already. Come to *The Buffet*. Just search for the directions. I'll wait for you."

VERMEULEN NOTICED THE slight woman sitting at the sole table right away. She seemed out of place, her delicate features and stature out of sync with the rough surroundings of a dive joint. The bar dominated the room and the walls were thick with graffiti. This was a place where people came to drink, play pool and leave the outside world behind. He liked it. It reminded him of a strange little restaurant he'd stumbled across in Antwerp a couple of years back.

The woman, in turn, examined the newcomers. She raised her hand and waved. Apparently, Vermeulen and Tessa looked equally out of place, although the bar's clientele spanned many ages and hues of skin color.

"Olga?" Tessa said, trying to speak over the music that seemed rather loud.

"The very same, nice to meet you, Tessa. And this must be Valentin."

"I am, nice to meet you too," Vermeulen said. "Can I get you another Martini while we're up?"

"No, I think I'll have a seltzer with lime."

"I'll have a beer, an amber," Vermeulen said to Evie. Tessa decided to go with a martini. The bartender drafted the beer, stirred the martini, and served the drinks.

"Why are you interested in the skeleton?" Kaminsky said after Vermeulen brought over the drinks.

"I knew the man," he said. "I met him seven years ago."

"Oh," Kaminsky said. "Was that your number in his notebook? The two-one-two area code?"

"Yes, it was. You can imagine how shocked I was when I got a call from a deputy right when we got off the plane in Tucson."

"What are the chances?" Kaminsky said.

"You got that right. When I met him back then, he was in deportation proceedings because he came to the US with a visa that was obtained with fraudulent credentials."

"I see," Kaminsky said. "That explains why he came via Mexico and the desert. He wouldn't be eligible for another visa. I was wondering about that."

"Luca was the victim of a trafficking ring then," Tessa said. "We assume that he was trafficked again."

"And something went wrong," Kaminsky said. "Hence the bullet hole?"

"Looks like it, doesn't it? Trafficking someone from Moldova to the US can't be easy. Given the complex route, I'm wondering how the gang in Moldova communicated with the cartel in Mexico and who got in between."

"Sorry, I can't help you there," Kaminsky said. "All I know is what I learned from the analysis of the bones and that notebook."

"You didn't see anything else in the notebook that struck you as interesting?"

"Besides your phone number? Nope. A bunch of phone numbers, a bit of writing. I don't speak Romanian, so I saw nothing I could make sense of."

"And they didn't recover anything else at the scene?"

"Nah. A backpack, some clothing, but it didn't belong to Luca. You should speak to Alain Ponce. His students bagged a pile of things at that location. Maybe there's something. You should know that his right forearm had a strange fracture. Did he have that seven years ago? He would've held his arm at an odd angle."

"I don't remember. It was a no-contact visit in a prison."

"Anyway, that fracture was almost certainly the result of torture. Someone broke it on purpose."

"Why torture?"

"He was left-handed. Whoever did that broke his non-dominant arm. That tells me they wanted to send him a warning."

Vermeulen and Tessa looked at each other, but didn't say anything.

"I got Ponce's contact info," Tessa said. "We'll contact him tomorrow."

"So, I'm curious why you are chasing a seven-year-old case."

"I'm not," Vermeulen said. "But Tessa is interested in the militarization of borders and Luca's fate could help shine the light on that."

"If you're smart, you're going to leave this alone," Kaminsky said. "Nobody gets across the desert without going to the cartels. And they are ruthless. They kill journalists who write about their crimes. You don't want them to get an inkling that you're interested in them. The moment they find out, you're a target, and don't think the border will protect you."

Tessa shrugged. "I've reported from war zones. How bad can it be?"

"I don't know about war zones, but presumably those combatants target each other. Here you're a target the moment you show an interest. I mean it. Leave it alone. They'll make an example of you just because they can."

ELEVEN

Thursday, October 18th,
Tucson, Arizona

ALMA RODRIGUEZ FINISHED writing the last letter informing relatives of the death of a loved one. She spread that gut wrenching task over several days, thinking it would keep the trauma manageable. Today it didn't feel that way.

The last letter—to a family in the Atlántida province of Honduras—hit home, and not only because the family lived in a town named Arizona. She knew about the struggle of the indigenous community there against a dam. She knew that for the past ten years, indigenous environmentalists were the top targets for assassinations, followed by journalists who wrote about it. Was the young man one of these, who fled rather than be executed? Or did he flee the gangs because he didn't want to join?

So many lives in peril and no safe haven anywhere.

Fortunately, the ME office sent those spreadsheets only once a month.. Rodriguez was grateful for the reports even if she hated seeing them. Part of her wanted to know, to document the magnitude of what was happening. She was convinced that, at some point in the future, there would be a reckoning when she and others had to show without the shadow of a doubt what her country had done to those most wretched.

A sound from her computer alerted her to a new email. She opened the message. It came from Tessa Bishonga. She wanted to know more about the skeleton from Moldova. Had Rodriguez come across other border crossers from Moldova or Eastern Europe? Had she come across border crossers who said something about a murder, or a gun shot, or about someone speaking a strange language?

Rodriguez leaned back in her chair. That was strange. Off the top of her head, she didn't recall any talk about a murder or Eastern Europeans, but then she didn't really talk to folks on the frontlines. She looked at the coordinates where the skeleton was found and figured that maybe some of the folks who'd made it to Douglas last Monday might have heard or seen something.

She picked up her phone and called William Morgan the Third.

"I got a couple of questions," she said after he answered.

"Shoot."

She could hear music and people noise in the background.

"Where are you?" she said.

"Oh, my girlfriend thought I needed some R&R after my mission to the border. So we're getting some luscious ice cream."

"You have a girlfriend?" She realized she sounded more startled than curious and quickly added, "I mean, you've never mentioned her."

"Well, I didn't want to brag, you know. But she's perfect. Like she stepped out of…"

"TMI. Listen, about the migrants you met in Douglas last Tuesday. Did any of them mention something bad, like a murder or a gun shot?"

"Uh, no. But I didn't ask either. Why?"

"Well, I just got a message from a journalist. She's looking into the case of the skeleton from Eastern Europe. The coordinates of the skeleton were not far from where your group crossed the border. She wanted to know if any of them had mentioned anything."

William Morgan the Third was quiet for a moment. Rodriguez heard a ding.

"You know," he said. "The people in that group were Central Americans. They seemed very subdued, but who wouldn't be after sitting in a tight Border Patrol holding pen for much of the day? One of them said something about a great sadness—sorry, my Spanish isn't perfect—but I just assumed he meant his situation. Maybe something did happen to their group."

"Where are they now?"

"Back in the holding pen, awaiting their transport to an ICE detention facility."

"Thanks, I'll make a note of that. I don't think anything will come of it anyway."

"And keep in mind, they might be shipped to a different facility without notice. So if you think you might want to talk to them, you better hurry down there. For all I know, they may already be gone. Their lawyer is usually the last to know."

"You have their names?"

"Yup. I made sure their asylum claims were properly filed. I never trust that the Border Patrol does that right. I'll email them to you."

They were quiet again. Rodriguez was glad they were comfortable with silences. There was another ding.

The music still played in the background, but it didn't sound like an ice cream parlor, more like canned music.

"You're not really at an ice cream parlor, are you?"

"Nope, I'm headed up to my office in Phoenix. It's a very slow elevator."

"Do you really have a girlfriend?"

"I'm a junior partner here. Do you know the hours I work? The pro-bono work is my only escape. The firm is glad I fill their quota, but my regular work piles up anyway and waits for me. I haven't got time for a girlfriend."

Rodriguez had a smile on her face. "Liar."

"Well at least I got you jealous," he said. "When are we going out for dinner?"

"*¡En tus sueños!*"

"Well, a guy can dream. What about that staff party you promised me on Monday."

She'd totally forgotten about that. "I'll talk with Gloria and let you know."

"Don't forget again. *Hasta luego.*"

A few minutes later, his email arrived, and she saw the cover pages of eight I-589 forms: eight names, eight lives in limbo for who knows how long. The 180 day period between application and final determination specified by law was wishful thinking given the backlog and the lack of immigration judges. Add to that the new rules from the Trump administration, eliminating all discretion for immigration judges, and these new claimants could be waiting for many months and even years before a final decision.

A migrant from Europe was rare, but not unusual. There were border crossers from all over the world who made their way to the Mexican side of the border. Not too long ago, she had to scramble and find a French speaker to interpret for two refugees from the Democratic Republic of Congo. But they didn't trek across the desert to enter without documents. They went to the border post and asked for asylum.

She didn't know the first thing about Moldova. In her mind, Europe was the photos she'd seen of lavender fields in France, mountain lakes in Switzerland, or the stately buildings of Madrid. Sure, there had to be poor areas, but fleeing for one's life? That seemed inconceivable.

Even if the man was persecuted and hoping for asylum, why did he come all the way here? Wouldn't asylum in France, Switzerland or Spain be easier and closer? She knew that the whole world had turned against refugees, but European countries couldn't be as bad as the US, could they?

Okay, assuming he had a reason to come the US, why did he not do what the refugees from Congo did; to present themselves at the border post, ask for asylum, get the paperwork started and wait for the hearing.

She checked the missing persons reports they'd received in the past week. There was no mention of someone from Moldova missing. She grabbed her phone and dialed the number of Jack Camacho, who coordinated the desert support actions along the border. His group of volunteers made daily hikes into the desert to help any border crossers they might encounter and leave water and beans for sustenance.

He didn't answer and she left a message asking about refugees from Moldova. There was nothing more she could do. The skeleton had taken enough of her time. There were too many living people who needed her attention.

TWELVE

Thursday, October 18,
Tucson, Arizona

WHEN VERMEULEN'S PHONE rang late that morning with yet another unknown number he was no longer surprised. His expectation of having time off had disappeared into thin air.

"This is Vermeulen."

"Hello, Mr. Vermeulen. This is Carson MacMillan, the County Attorney for Cochise County. I'm on speaker phone and with me is Deputy Perez with whom you spoke yesterday."

"How can I help you, Mr. MacMillan?"

"I have to tell you that we're recording this call. I hope that's okay with you."

"Why is that necessary?"

"As the deputy informed you, this is a murder investigation and I'm conducting a preliminary interview."

"As I told the deputy, there isn't really a whole lot I can contribute."

"Depending on your answers, I might call you for testimony before the grand jury."

"I really don't know anything of value to your investigation, but go ahead and record the call."

"Let's start with your name, can you spell that for us?"

Vermeulen did so.

"And what's your address?"

Vermeulen gave that, too.

"What do you do for a living up there?"

"I'm an investigator for the Office of Internal Oversight Services at the United Nations."

That stopped MacMillan for a moment. "An investigator, you say? Are you law enforcement?"

"No. I investigate potential fraud inside the United Nations operations around the world."

"Sounds like police work to me."

"It's more like forensic accounting? Making sure the money is spent for what it's been allocated. If I find fraud, the matter is turned over to local authorities or handled by the disciplinary mechanisms at the UN."

"Thanks for that clarification."

Vermeulen thought MacMillan sounded bemused.

"So," MacMillan said. "As Deputy Perez has already indicated, we found your phone number in a notebook that in all likelihood belongs to a murdered migrant. We've now confirmed that this migrant comes from Eastern Europe, Moldova to be specific. Does that ring a bell for you?"

"Yes, it does."

"And according to Deputy Perez, you know the man in question, Mihaly Luca?"

"Yes, I'm sorry to hear that he was murdered. Do you know anything about the circumstances?"

"Can you tell us how Mr. Luca ended up having your phone number in his notebook?"

Since Vermeulen truly didn't know the answer to that question, he didn't have to work hard at being the flummoxed witness.

"The last time I saw Mr. Luca was about seven years

ago. He was detained by Immigration and Customs Enforcement at York prison in Pennsylvania. I spoke to him in the context of an investigation of visa fraud using forged letters from the United Nations."

"Why'd you give him your phone number?"

"I didn't give him my phone number. After I questioned him about the traffickers who were behind the visa fraud, he asked me to contact his family in Moldova. I wrote a letter to them and I must have included my phone number there."

Deputy Perez chimed in, "Did you say traffickers?"

Vermeulen heard barely suppressed excitement in Perez's voice. That was worrisome; better to proceed with caution.

"Yes, I did."

"Care to explain?"

"It was a complex case. I got involved only because the traffickers used forged letters from United Nations offices to obtain visas to the US."

"How did Mr. Luca end up in ICE custody?"

"I don't know. I assume that when Customs and Border Protection agents questioned him on arrival at JFK, his cover story didn't hold up. By the time I got involved, Mr. Luca was already in detention pending removal."

"Did he say anything to you?"

"Not much, he was clearly very frightened and didn't divulge anything that would point at who he was involved with."

MacMillan looked at the deputy, then back at the camera. "Could Mr. Luca have come back to see you?"

The cat was finally out of the bag. Those two were eager to tie him to Luca's skeleton, and, by extension, to the traffickers. That could not happen. It was time to push back.

"Absolutely not. I wrote one letter to his family seven years ago. Nobody ever replied to that letter. Neither Mr. Luca nor his family have tried to contact me in any way, phone, mail or internet. There's no reason whatsoever to assume that. If Luca wanted to contact me, he could have called me."

"Why do you think he came back via the desert in Arizona?"

"I have no idea. It sounds to me like you're on a fishing expedition. I understand that you have to follow every lead in a murder investigation, but I've told you all I know."

"Can you hang on for a moment?" MacMillan said.

The sound cut out, leaving Vermeulen to wonder what they were doing. There couldn't be that many murders in the county. The Wikipedia page for Cochise County listed a population around 130,000. These were small town authorities doing a murder investigation. What could possibly go wrong?

A lot; and Vermeulen wanted no part in it.

The sound came back on.

"Can you tell us more about this trafficking situation you were involved in."

Vermeulen's chest tightened again. It was the second time they homed in on the traffickers.This wasn't about Luca, it was about the traffickers. And Vermeulen was the only link they had.

"I wasn't involved in any trafficking situation, I was investigating how the people got the forged UN letters to obtain US Visas for their hapless victims."

"Those people happened to be traffickers," Perez said.

"Yes, they were, but that was for other authorities to

investigate. My job focused solely on finding out how they got those letters."

"So, did you meet any of those traffickers?" MacMillan said.

Vermeulen grew hot under the collar. His attempts to deflect MacMillan line of questioning hadn't worked. "Yes, uh, I met two individuals who were implicated in the scheme."

"Who were they?"

"One ran a criminal enterprise in New Jersey and the other was a UN employee in Vienna?"

"Austria?"

"Yes, Vienna, Austria."

"So this was an international operation?"

"Yes, it was."

"What happened to the traffickers you met?"

"The UN employee was arrested and tried. The crime boss in New Jersey disappeared before the authorities could arrest her."

"Okay, thanks Mr. Vermeulen. I'll turn this over to the Cochise County grand jury. They'll decide how to proceed with this case and whether to issue any indictments. You will be called upon to testify."

Vermeulen shook his head. This was the outcome he'd wanted to avoid. "I'd like you to answer a couple of questions?"

"Sure," MacMillan said.

"Am I a suspect in the murder of Mr. Luca?"

"No, not at this moment."

"Am I a witness to the murder of Mr. Luca?"

"You know, Mr. Vermeulen," MacMillan said. "I believe you've been straight with us. At the same time, I can't help feeling that there's more to the story."

"I'm sorry, Mr. MacMillan, but from one lawyer to another, feelings don't count."

"You're a lawyer?"

Vermeulen could have kicked himself. That was an unnecessary mistake. Now he'd engaged MacMillan on his own terms. He sighed. "Yes, I was, back in Belgium. I'm not registered as one in the US. That doesn't change my point. I know nothing about why Mr. Luca came to the US this time around. I know nothing about who might have trafficked him. Whatever you are investigating, I can't add anything else."

"Belgium, huh? Thought I detected an accent. Where are you staying in Tucson?"

Vermeulen gave him the address.

"You'll be hearing from us. Bye now."

After they ended the call, Vermeulen exhaled. But the tension didn't leave his body; so much for the vacation Tessa had promised. The memories of his investigation seven years ago were as vivid as if it had occurred last week. The visit with Luca in York prison, the fear in Luca's eyes, his desperation over the safety of his family, it all came back. And now he was dead. Vermeulen couldn't fathom why Luca would want to come back to the US. It had to have been something very serious.

He called Tessa, who had gone to meet with a local journalist, and told her the gist of the conversation.

"They really want you to testify?" she said.

"Most likely. They'll give the case to their grand jury, and if I heard the County Attorney right, he'll lean on them to call me as a material witness. I think they're desperate. I'm the only lead they have and they must think that if I talk long enough they'd find a clue that allows them to solve the crime."

"But Luca can't be the only death they've encountered."

"I'm sure it isn't, but this is a murder case."

"There have got to be more violent deaths than this one," she said.

"I think so, but who knows how many victims are actually found. It's a vast desert out there."

"Did they give you any hint as to why they thought your testimony would help?"

"They perked up when I mentioned Luca's connection to the trafficking case back then."

"They think Luca was killed by traffickers?"

"That's probably a safe assumption."

"Interesting." Tessa paused a moment. "I know that the Mexican cartels have expanded their operations from drugs to human trafficking. But this case implies that they have connections all the way to Europe. That's new."

"The traffickers on this side of the Atlantic killed Luca. That doesn't sound like some new achievement in cooperation."

"I didn't say cooperation, I said connection. We also know Mexican cartels hold migrants for ransom."

"But Luca's family was dirt poor," Vermeulen said. "That's why he signed up to come here the first time around."

"Maybe the cartel bypassed Luca's family and went straight for the traffickers in Moldova."

"Oh."

"Right."

"But that would mean they've been in contact beforehand. How else would a cartel know to target him?"

Tessa sounded very animated. "Mexican cartels have had European connections for a while. They got people in Spain and have ties with the Sicilian mafia in Palermo. They could be expanding."

Vermeulen thought about that. "Okay," he said after a moment. "That still doesn't explain the death of Luca."

"Ever since *El Chapo* was extradited to the US in 2017, there's been vicious fighting between several cartels. His Sinaloa cartel is under pressure. It could be someone else muscling in on the action. They grab Luca and demand ransom from the Moldovans. The folks in Moldova refuse because they think they had a deal. Luca is killed."

"Oh man, what kind of world are we living in?"

Tessa didn't say anything.

"Sorry," Vermeulen said. "I know the answer. It's just that the utter depravity of the world is sometimes too much to handle. And going after the poorest? Whatever happened to Robin Hood."

"Sorry, sweetheart, that's just a legend."

"So where does that leave me?"

"I don't know. I can see the Moldovans not taking this lying down. Luca was an investment of theirs. Whoever killed him messed that up."

"So now we'll have a transatlantic cartel war?"

"Maybe. I'm pretty sure nobody has investigated those connections. That's scarily fascinating, criminal globalization. It's gonna be one of the segments of this project."

"What about me?" Vermeulen said.

"You go and testify. I'll do my research. At the end we can take a couple of days to relax. I hear Sedona is a lovely spot to unwind."

THIRTEEN

Friday, October 19,
Bisbee, Arizona

VERMEULEN GOT INTO their rental car to drive from Tucson to Bisbee for his testimony before the Cochise County grand jury. The subpoena had arrived the evening before, delivered by a local deputy.

The drive took almost two hours and passed through a desert landscape, which the relentless sun had faded to the color of oatmeal. Yellow grasses and pale green shrubs provided some relief. After leaving the interstate, the road he followed climbed to higher elevations and the landscape became more verdant. Each time it descended, beige became the dominant hue again. He drove through Tombstone, which didn't ring any bells in his mind until he saw the sign directing him to the O.K. Corral. He wasn't in the mood for western lore and stayed on the highway instead of cruising the Old West part of town and learning more about the shootout.

Bisbee sat on higher ground and was much greener. Located in a steep valley, the town's roads were narrow and curvy. Weaving his way past restaurants, hotels and shops, he found the superior court building at the top of a hill. It was an impressive five-story art deco structure. The entry doors matched the 1930s style, with tall brass-framed windows inlaid with stylized Greek figures leaning on massive swords. The town must've been very rich at one point. The huge piles of mine tailings all around the town told the story of Bisbee's past wealth. Somehow, it had managed to morph from a mining town into a quaint tourist town.

The County Attorney's office next door was rather plain in comparison. Vermeulen entered and gave his name to the receptionist. MacMillan came out and guided him to his office. The man had a pale skeletal appearance, but his demeanor was jovial and easygoing.

Once seated, he went through the procedure of the grand jury and the testimony. On the surface, it was just a repeat of what he'd said during the phone conversation. Vermeulen knew it had been recorded, which should've been enough for the grand jury. There was something else going on. Vermeulen could only guess that it had to do with traffickers. The unpredictability of the next hour or so made his mouth dry. There had better be a glass of water for the witness.

After they got done, Vermeulen had a little time to grab an early lunch. He wasn't very hungry and had a bowl of soup. He was tempted to get some coffee and a treat, but decided he didn't need any more stimulation.

He entered the wood-paneled room where the Cochise County grand jury met. The jurors had been on a break as well and the clerk gaveled the proceedings to order once Vermeulen sat in the witness seat. There was a glass of water for him.

"We're back with the grand jury," MacMillan said. "The next case involves the murder of a man in the border zone near Douglas. We know the man was murdered because the skeleton had a bullet hole in the skull. Evidence recovered near the skeleton, combined with the forensic analysis indicates that the man's name is Mihaly Luca and that he is from Moldova in Eastern Europe."

MacMillan paused and looked at the jurors.

"Is there anyone on the jury who knows Mr. Luca? Please raise your hand." He waited a moment. "I see no hands."

The court reporter recorded it and MacMillan continued, explaining the contents of the notebook and finding Vermeulen's phone number.

"Mr. Vermeulen is a witness, there are no other witnesses. Is there anyone here who knows Mr. Vermeulen?" MacMillan waited again. "I see no hands."

MacMillan looked at the court reporter, then at the grand jury.

"The indictment is for murder in the first degree. In the weeks before August 12, a person or persons unknown committed first degree murder, by intending or knowing that conduct would cause death, caused death with premeditation in violation of A.R.S. 13-1105.A.1 and 13-1101."

He stopped, looked at the clerk and said, "Have all these statutes been read, or should I read them to you?"

The clerk said that they'd been read.

MacMillan nodded and said, "The State calls Mr. Valentin Vermeulen."

After Vermeulen was sworn in, MacMillan asked about Vermeulen's job, his career at the United Nations, his work beforehand at the prosecutor's office in Antwerp. After twenty minutes, he finally came to the heart of the matter.

"Do you know the deceased, Mihaly Luca?"

"Yes, I do."

"How did you come to know Mr. Luca?"

Vermeulen repeated the story of his investigation seven years earlier, how he met Luca at York prison, how Luca had been lured to the US with the promise of ten thousand dollars and how he'd been caught at JFK by Customs and Border Protection agents. He took pains to stay as close to what he'd said before as possible.

"Did you know at the time what the promised ten thousand dollars were for?" MacMillan said.

"No, I did not. Mr. Luca was too scared to tell me. He feared for his family in Moldova."

"Did you find out later?"

"Yes."

"Please tell the jury."

"The money was intended as payment for body parts."

"Who promised the payment?"

"A ring of human traffickers."

"Was this a local organization?"

"No, there were several organizations in different parts of the world who collaborated in this crime."

"Did you meet any of these traffickers?"

"Yes, two of them. One was a United Nations employee in Vienna, Austria. The other was the leader of a criminal syndicate in New Jersey."

"Can you explain to the grand jury how this trafficking ring worked?"

Vermeulen recounted what he remembered of the operation. So far this was going well. He relaxed a bit.

"What happened to the traffickers?" MacMillan said.

"The UN employee in Vienna was arrested. The

leader of the crime syndicate in New Jersey disappeared. I don't know where she is."

"Do you have any reason to assume that these traffickers are behind Mr. Luca's new attempt to enter the US?" MacMillan said.

This wasn't part of the testimony they had discussed. Vermeulen sat up.

"None whatsoever."

"How can you be sure?"

"Mr. MacMillan, you asked me if I had a reason to assume something. I don't. That's all I can say."

"But it could be the same traffickers."

"I don't know who caused Mr. Luca to come here and I'm not going to speculate."

"I understand. But indulge me."

"Mr. MacMillan, we are both lawyers, you understand as well as I do that my speculating on what might have happened isn't going to do one thing to move this case forward. It may even lead to a dead end. If you are trying to solve this murder, you'll have to start with the evidence you have. If that's not enough, you'll have to find more."

"Okay, let's try this another way? Would it be plausible to assume that Mr. Luca was trafficked again?"

"Yes."

"Why?"

"He was poor and, as far as I know, had neither a personal reason nor the means to come to the US."

"Would it be plausible to assume that the same people who trafficked him seven years ago are doing it again?"

Vermeulen didn't answer. This line of questioning was intended to pin him down, to make statements that could later be used against him. MacMillan was smarter than he'd given him credit for. His ire rose. Coming here had been a bad idea.

"Mr. MacMillan, as I've said before, that would be speculation, and I'd rather not do that. I don't know why Mr. Luca came back or who brought him here. The people involved in the earlier case are either in jail or have disappeared. That's all I can say."

"But not all involved were jailed, were they?"

"I don't know how many people were involved, therefore I can't answer this question either."

MacMillan paced back and forth behind his dais and held his tented hands against his lips as if he were thinking very hard. He turned abruptly and said, "You came here as a cooperative witness, did you not?"

"Of course."

"Then why are you not cooperating?"

"Mr. MacMillan, I answer your questions to the extent that I have the information you ask for. When I don't have that, it would serve no purpose for me to speculate. All that would do is put words into the record that aren't based on facts. I'm pretty sure the grand jury is supposed to evaluate the facts, not personal musings."

"How many traffickers do you know?" MacMillan pounced.

The question jolted Vermeulen like an electric shock. What was that all about? Was this a new tack, an effort to incriminate Vermeulen? Or was he just grasping at straws? He took his time to think. He'd already listed two, so he had to give MacMillan those.

"Two, the UN diplomat and the woman in New Jersey."

"Their names?"

"Mr. Kurtz and a Ms. Delano. I don't have a first name for Kurtz. Delano's first name was Camille."

"And you're sure you don't know any other traffickers?"

"In my work I've met a lot of people all over the world. Some of them may well have been traffickers. I just don't know. I gave you the names of the two people I know for a fact were traffickers."

MacMillan turned to the grand jury and said, "Do any of you have questions for Mr. Vermeulen?"

Vermeulen had focused on MacMillan during his testimony and now turned his attention to the group of fifteen. The men were all white, but there was a Latina among the women. As far as Vermeulen could tell, they ranged in ages from late twenties to sixties.

An older man said, "Mr. Vermeulen, do you think that Mr. Luca came again to sell body parts?"

Vermeulen shrugged.

"I don't know. People migrate for many reasons."

"But they trafficked him for that reason once before. Why not try again?"

"It's been seven years since the last time. The criminal network may not even exist anymore."

"Thank you."

"Any other questions?" MacMillan said.

A woman raised her hand. MacMillan nodded.

"Mr. Vermeulen, when you investigated that trafficking ring earlier, did you find out how many others were working with the two people you named?"

Vermeulen looked at the woman then to MacMillan. That was a question MacMillan should have asked. The county attorney realized that too. He was shuffling through his papers.

"It is my understanding that Ms. Delano had hired two men to do her dirty work," Vermeulen said. "I never met them or knew their names."

"How about in Vienna?"

"There was Mr. Kurtz's boss. His oversight of Mr. Kurtz may have been poor, but there was no evidence that he was involved."

"What was his name?"

"I'm not sure I remember. He was Russian. Oh, wait, his name was Oserov."

"What was Mr. Oserov's position then?" MacMillan said.

"He was Director-General of the United Nations Office in Vienna."

"And does he still hold that position?"

"Not as far as I know."

"Did Mr. Kurtz have any helpers?" The woman said.

"I assume so. I only ever saw one man with him."

"What was his name?"

"If I remember correctly, his name was Popescu."

"Were there any altercations?" MacMillan said.

Vermeulen hesitated. None of this had anything to do with Luca's skeleton. The annoyance that had lingered just below the surface reappeared. A small-town attorney seemed to be fishing for information to make a name for himself.

"I don't see what that has to do with this case."

"I'm simply trying to ascertain how dangerous these traffickers are."

"As I said, there's no reason to assume they are the same."

"So were there altercations?"

"Yes, there were. These men were dangerous."

"Why didn't you reveal that information before?"

"I didn't think it was germane to the case you have before you."

"Please leave that determination to me. Any other questions for Mr. Vermeulen?"

Nobody raised their hands.

"Mr. Vermeulen," MacMillan said. "I can't shake the feeling that you know more than you are telling us."

"I can't help you there. I've told you all I know."

MacMillan ended the proceedings and the grand jury members got up to stretch their legs. Apparently, there was another case waiting.

Vermeulen left the room and couldn't figure out why MacMillan had it in for him. It wasn't a development he'd expected.

FOURTEEN

Friday, October 19th,
Ciudad Obregón, Sonora, Mexico

LATER THAT MORNING, Delano went to check her messages as she had every day that week. This time she went to the maternity hospital to check. There was one. A male voice told her to be at a restaurant called La Focaccia at four in the afternoon. The date stamp on the message told her that the message had been left that morning. She checked her watch. Four and a half hours to kill.

She decided to spend the time at the library of the *Instituto Tecnológico de Sonora.* It was a busy public space, a good place to lose a tail. They were following her, she was certain of that. At night, she'd watched the street outside her apartment, hoping to catch watchers. They were good, she never saw the same car twice, or someone loitering in a doorway. The library made it easier to spot someone following her. They couldn't just rustle up a student at a moment's notice. Besides, she liked the architecture, the dark red circular entrance that protruded from the sand colored walls of the building.

In the foreign language section on the second floor, she picked a random English language novel from the shelf and settled at a table that gave her a good view of the doors. The novel was marginally interesting, which suited her purpose. The reading area wasn't too busy, a few students with their laptops, busy writing assignments. None of them used any books. There was not a lot of foot traffic either.

Her fee had been deposited in her offshore account. Management had always been punctual when it came to finances. It was a good chunk of money, but, unlike in the past, dealing with them now felt off. Her stomach was always the first to send out warning signals and it did so now. This wasn't the right job for this time.

She got up, replaced the novel and ambled through the stacks, pretending to search for another book. The aisles were empty. Nobody lingered suspiciously. She took another book and settled back at her table. There were only two students left in the area. One was a young woman with long brown hair, typing up a storm. The other was a man, mid to late twenties with a fashionable day-old stubble. He was also staring at a laptop but not typing much.

Was he the watcher? A little older than your average student, a little distracted, he fit the bill. It was time to put it to a test. She took her book and walked the length of the corridor to the other side of the library. Along the way she left the book on a table and settled in the current periodicals section. Nobody had followed her. So far so good. She scanned the headlines of *El Diario de Sonora*.

Car accidents, police busts, some big celebration in Hermosillo, nothing of interest. She found a day-old copy of the *New York Times*. Fewer car accidents, but not all that different from the local news. A rustling noise made her look up. The young woman, a messenger bag slung over her shoulder stood a couple of shelves farther back, checking out an academic journal.

Okay, not the guy then and a reminder that her assumptions about the *macho* culture were dangerous blinders. She pulled out her phone and hailed a car service to the intersection of Calle Antonio Caso and Calle Albert Einstein. The two streets bordered a large parking lot, plenty of options to get away.

TWO RIDES LATER, Delano was sure she'd shaken any tails as she strolled along Avenida Nainari, a lovely boulevard with a nice median of trees. This was definitely the upscale part of town. The houses looked solid and well kept. There were commercial blocks interspersed. La Focaccia occupied the western part of one such block, right next to a bike shop and an organic grocery store. The store had some customer traffic as did the bike shop. The restaurant seemed less busy.

She circled the location of the restaurant once at a distance of a city block. There was a steady flow of traffic. The neighborhood didn't have any specific vibe to it, but it looked familiar. She'd been here before. An intersection later, she knew why. The museum commemorating Álvaro Obregón was only two blocks away from the restaurant.

Despite the atmosphere of normalcy, Delano's body was tingling with tension. She'd brought her Glock 29, shoved into the outside pocket of her purse. Whatever accuracy the small size of the pistol sacrificed was made up for by the punch of the 10 mm bullets. Worst case scenario, she'd have to shoot her way out of the restaurant, not that it had to come to that.

At three o'clock she entered La Focaccia. Since it was

between lunch and dinner, there were no patrons inside. One table outside was occupied by four teenagers, who could've been skipping school. The interior was vaguely rustic, bricks for the bottom half of the wall and green-painted stucco to the ceiling. Large chalk boards listed drinks and specials. Tables and chairs were standard restaurant issue, and the obligatory red and white checkered tablecloths covered each table. A staircase led up to the second floor. She didn't go up.

There were no patrons inside. She looked for exits. The pizza oven and the kitchen area were separated from the restaurant by a knee wall and a swinging half door. There was a door at the back of that space. The only other door was the entrance leading to Avenida Nainari.

Not the worst place to meet, especially since she was the only one here. She chose a table that gave her a full view of the entrance and easy access to the kitchen area. A youngish waiter in black pants and black shirt hurried to her and asked her what she wanted.

"*Agua mineral*," she said.

He placed her accent right away and asked if she wanted ice cubes.

She shook her head.

"*¿Quieres una carta*?"

"*No*." She wasn't here to eat.

He went to a large refrigerator near the back door, took out the bottle of water and poured it into a glass for her. She settled in, her purse on her lap and her right hand in its pocket holding the Glock.

At three-thirty, two men entered the pizzeria. They were about the same height, had dark hair, and mustaches. One was beefy and the other one lanky. Other than that, there was nothing remarkable about them; muscle for a boss or sub-boss. They scanned the restaurant, their eyes resting for a moment on Delano. The beefy one had already turned and stepped outside when his partner did a double take and examined Delano more carefully. He frowned.

Delano smiled and pulled the Glock from the purse. Her party had arrived. The lanky guy's right hand moved toward the small of his back.

"I wouldn't do that," Delano said and pointed the Glock at him. "Hands where I can see them."

Despite her accent he got the message and raised his hands. Since the door was still open, the other guy could come back any moment.

"Come here," she said.

The guy slowly stepped closer.

"Tell your boss I'm here for a friendly conversation. As you can see, the place is empty. You two wait outside and I'll talk to him alone. Okay? Go."

He was outside in a flash.

A moment later the door opened again and a middle-aged man wearing tan slacks, a white shirt and a linen jacket entered. About her age, he had a fleshy face that spoke of alcohol, late nights, and brutality. His longish hair was held in place by pomade. He looked like the kind of gangster she'd seen hanging out in strip clubs in New Jersey. He probably did the same here. Half a cigar smoldered between two fingers of his left hand. She smelled it across the room. It wasn't Cuban. He gave her the kind of once-over that set her teeth on edge.

"Señora Beltrán?" he said. His voice had a nasal quality that didn't quite fit with his face.

"Yes. Don Martinez?"

"I am Don Martinez. What do you want from me?"

"Thank you for meeting with me. Kind of you to come personally." Her default approach to tricky situations was courteousness, it put your opponent at ease, or, as the case may be, off balance. She spoke Spanish instead of English for the same reason.

Martinez acknowledged the sentiment with a half-smile and a short nod. "It's the first time we meet, no?"

"It is."

"And yet, we do business together. We should've met before." The look on his face left no doubt as to the kind of meeting he imagined.

"I make it a point to work in the background."

"I see. And why come into the open now?"

"I need information."

He smiled like someone who'd just seen an opening. "We all do sometimes. What kind of information?"

"Not too long ago, I facilitated a transaction to transport a man from Moldova in Eastern Europe to the US via Mexica. His sponsors had paid the necessary monies for this service."

Don Martinez nodded.

"I was informed that the man was murdered. His sponsors are quite upset as they had invested considerable money into this deal. They want their money back."

"And what is your connection to this case?"

"As before, I'm merely the facilitator, the go-between, the person who makes the interactions between two parties possible."

"So you have nothing to gain from the outcome?"

"I collect a fee for my services, but that's all."

"And what makes you think I can help."

"You put me in touch with your organization's people up North. You must occupy an important position. Am I wrong?"

Flattery was her second tool in tricky situations. It always worked with men. A smile played around the corners of Martinez's mouth.

"You are correct."

"Good. Could you find out what happened? That shouldn't be a problem for a man of your status."

"I will need to speak to some people. Can I reach you by the same number?"

"Yes."

She waited until Martinez got up before putting her hand holding the Glock on the table.

"One more thing, Don Martinez. I've been straight with you and I expect the same in return. The fact that you haven't met me even though we've done business should tell you that I can take care of myself. So, keep your men on a leash. They won't survive an unfriendly encounter."

Martinez looked at the pistol and shrugged. It would be like him to underestimate her.

She wouldn't make the same mistake.

FIFTEEN

Friday, October 19th,
Tucson, Arizona

VERMEULEN PULLED INTO the parking lot of their motel in Tucson. His back needed a stretch after the two-hour drive from Bisbee back to Tucson. He'd chosen the way back via Sierra Vista to see something new. The desert was pretty much the same, but the road block he encountered before getting to the freeway was something new. All traffic was sluiced through a Border Patrol checkpoint, each car scanned by more hi-tech scanners than he'd ever seen before. With all that buildup, the encounter with the agent was almost anticlimactic. He'd buzzed down the window and all the agent said was, "Have a nice day." Of course, had his skin been of a darker hue, there would have been questions, and more. That, or the scanners had already ascertained all the agent needed to know about him. Maybe they'd already connected the license plate on the car to the rental company and had gotten his name and immigration status. It was his first encounter with the surveillance going on at the border. How did the locals feel about that?

It was hotter in Tucson than in Bisbee, but all the same, he was glad to be away from MacMillan. Maybe the County Attorney was just posturing in front of the jury, but there was something off about the way the man questioned him. The worst part was that MacMillan ordered him to remain available to answer further questions.

Still in the car, he called Tessa to find out where she was. She was in a cab on her way to the motel. She told him to get ready to drive to Phoenix as soon as she got back.

"Do we have to? I've already driven four hours today. I was thinking more of a long shower, some rest and then a nice dinner."

"We're not on vacation," Tessa said. "At least I'm not. I just got a lead to talk to an attorney who might know more about Luca."

Before he could answer, a taxi rolled to a stop behind him. Tessa scrambled out of the back, paid the driver and came to his window. "Let's go."

"How about we go up and freshen up a bit?" he said.

"I got wet wipes in my purse, that's all you're gonna need. You look bushed, let me drive."

He got out plopped himself into the passenger seat and sighed.

"I saw Alma this morning," she said. "Interviewed her for my article. I had wanted to speak to her boss Gloria, but she had to leave just as I arrived. Did you know that some Border Patrol agents sabotage the water and food left by volunteers for the border crossers?"

"What? Why?"

"I guess sheer cruelty. That's where Gloria was headed, a meeting with the Border Patrol boss in Tucson."

Tessa was navigating along Speedway Boulevard and took the freeway to Phoenix.

"Any other insights that help you with your article?" Vermeulen said.

"She said that the Mexican cartels are now controlling the trafficking, but they also kidnap border-crossers and hold them for ransom, especially if they have relatives in the US. If they don't they make them work and prostitute the women."

"Oh man, this is terrible. On the US side, the authorities lie in wait and on the Mexican side it's the criminals."

Tessa had merged on to the freeway and set the cruise control to seventy-five.

"Did you ask her about Luca?" Vermeulen said.

"I did, but she didn't have anything to add. There are a lot of ways he could've ended up dead in the desert. He obviously was trafficked by a cartel. There's no doubt about that. That he ended up shot dead is unusual. Even if another cartel had kidnapped him, wouldn't they have tried to ransom him for cash?"

"Unless there was nobody to contact. Or maybe the rival cartel tried to make a point."

"Maybe. I have a hook for my article. The militarization of the border has created an almost symbiotic system. The US authorities and the cartels depend on each other. The US clampdown on the border drives the migrants into the hands of the cartels. The brutality of the cartels gives the USA ammunition for ratcheting up the rhetoric. No longer are the border crossers refugees or poor people looking for jobs, they are rapists and criminals."

"Hmm, never thought of it that way. But I think you got something there. Why we are driving to Phoenix?"

"We're meeting with one of the pro-bono lawyers

who is representing a group of migrants who were detained near where Luca's skeleton was found. Alma thinks that maybe they saw something. I want to know what they said to him and see if we can talk to them."

"The lawyer got a name?"

"Yes, William Morgan the Third."

"Wow, really, the Third?"

"Yup, it's an inside joke. Apparently, that's how he introduced himself when he first came to represent migrants."

THE LAW OFFICES of Fillmore, West & East in Phoenix occupied five floors in one of the high rises on First Avenue. Tessa announced their visit at the reception on the third floor and, after showing their IDs to the receptionist, they were allowed to take another elevator two floors up to where William Morgan the Third occupied an office not much larger than that of Alma Rodriguez. Maybe it was larger, but the piles of law books, folders, and legal briefs made the space look as cramped as a hoarder's apartment.

Morgan had hung his jacket over the back of his Herman Miller chair, rolled up his sleeves, and loosened his tie. He was writing on a legal pad and looked up as they entered. He had that Northeast Prep School look that Rodriguez had implied. Blond hair parted on the left side, a well-proportioned squarish face, neither full nor lean. Vermeulen could imagine him on some small college rugby team, wiry and athletic.

"William Morgan the Third?" Tessa said.

He looked a little puzzled. "Yes. Uh, sorry, who are you again?"

"I'm Tessa Bishonga, a journalist. Alma Rodriguez

told me to contact you. I'm working on a piece on the militarization of borders. I'm looking into the skeleton that was found southeast of Bisbee in the desert. This is Valentin Vermeulen, he's an investigator for the United Nations."

The last bit made Morgan sit up. "The United Nations? Is this something international? Sorry, I don't do international law."

Vermeulen raised his hands. "No worries, I'm not here in a professional capacity."

"Alma said you represented a number of border-crossers who may have been where the skeleton was found," Tessa said. "We're trying to speak to anyone who might have seen the man before he was killed."

Morgan pushed a strand of stray hair from his forehead. "Yeah, that was Monday, wasn't it? I remember her mentioning a skeleton."

"She said you heard someone talk about 'a great sadness.'"

"I'm not really sure if it had anything to do with the skeleton. This one man said something to that effect, but you have to remember that by the time I meet people, they're utterly traumatized—the cumulative effect of being forced to leave home, traveling dangerous routes, dealing with the cartels, traversing the desert and then being arrested. They've been through hell, and I thought what the man said was more a general comment on how life was for him."

"Yeah, I can see that," Vermeulen said. "On the other hand, he could have witnessed a murder."

Morgan shrugged. "Maybe."

"Is there any chance we could talk to him and the others?" Tessa said.

Morgan leaned back into his chair and scratched his temple.

"Hmm. Attorneys and family can visit detainees, but journalists? I'm not sure."

"I could pretend to be your paralegal," Tessa said.

Morgan looked at her, eyebrows raised, and shook his head.

"Why not?" she said.

Morgan struggled to find the right words. Finally, he said, "Listen, I started here less than a year ago. I'm at the bottom of the pecking order of this firm. I don't want to stay there. So pretending that two strangers work for me when they don't makes me uncomfortable. It could jeopardize my position here, and also with the authorities."

"I understand," Tessa said. "No big deal. Can you at least give us the names of the people who were in that group Rodriguez mentioned?"

Morgan rubbed his forehead. "I don't know. I'm concerned with the wellbeing of my clients. They've been through so much. They are more than raw material for whatever story you want to write."

Vermeulen saw a flash in Tessa eyes and worried that Morgan didn't know what was going to hit him in about a second. But Tessa simply nodded and said, "I appreciate your concern for your clients. I really do. And I don't blame you for distrusting me or my motives. After all, you don't know me, and we don't have the time to get to know each other well enough for me to dispel your doubts. So I ask you to trust me. To trust that I, as a woman of color, as an African woman, would never disregard the wellbeing of my fellow human beings and certainly not that of the most vulnerable among us."

Vermeulen exhaled quietly. He shouldn't have worried. Tessa always knew how to read situations and say the right words. Morgan had raised his eyebrows again and stood up.

"Okay, then," he said. "Let me see where they are. I don't know if they've been moved since I last spoke with them. Their attorney is always the last to know. And, yes, they're doing that on purpose."

Morgan pulled a sheet of paper from one of the stacks that covered his desk. He tapped his laptop touchpad, typed something, his left index finger following a line on the paper, and tapped again. Apparently, the query had yielded the info he wanted because he wrote down something on the paper. The process took a while, but before too long, he handed the sheet to Tessa.

"This is where all the people I met with that day are now, according to the ICE website. The ones with an asterisk aren't in the ICE system, which means they are either still in Douglas, or they fell between the cracks."

Tessa and Vermeulen looked at the sheet. Of the eighteen names more than half had already been processed and were in custody, some of them in the Tucson Border Patrol facility, others in ICE facilities in Arizona and as far away as Texas or New Mexico.

"They all applied for asylum?" Vermeulen said.

"Yes."

"So they have to wait for their credible-fear hearing in prison?"

"They already had their credible-fear hearing. That happened at the border. Now they are waiting for their trial."

"But they are still in prison."

"Yes, unless someone posts a bond. Many have relatives, but few have the money. Some churches raise enough money to post bonds, but that's just a drop in the bucket. The crazy thing is that the vast majority will show up for their hearing. All this jailing is just costing an arm and a leg, when letting them live in the community would be just as effective."

"This is messed up," Vermeulen said. "I think the Refugee Convention specifically states that asylum-seekers should not be incarcerated."

"It doesn't quite say that, but it does say that we should not impose penalties on asylum-seekers entering the country illegally, which amounts to the same thing."

SIXTEEN

Saturday, October 20th,
Tucson, Arizona

THAT MORNING, Vermeulen and Tessa drove to the Customs and Border Protection detention lockup in Tucson. They figured the weekend, with fewer officers on duty, offered a better chance to get inside. On the drive there, they'd debated the best way of getting inside the facility. Tessa wanted him to use his UN ID to get in. Vermeulen countered that it would do no good, since he had no jurisdiction here. They tried out different scenarios, but couldn't agree on one. When they finally stood at the entrance Vermeulen fell back on the routine he'd employed all over the world—bluster his way inside, using his UN credentials and vastly exaggerating his authority.

"Good morning," he said to the agent at the entrance. "I'm Valentin Vermeulen, investigator with the United Nations Office of Internal Oversight Services." He waived his ID in front of the man. "This is my colleague Tessa Bishonga. We're here to inspect these facilities."

The agent stared at them. "The who with what now?" According to the tag, his name was Keith Boyd.

"The United Nations, Agent Boyd."

"Uh, nobody told me about this."

"My office has sent a memo to the person in charge

here. It's probably in that pile of papers right there." He pointed to a stack of paperwork that looked official, although he had no idea what it contained.

Boyd looked nonplussed. He took the pile of paper and stared at it.

"Would you please let us in," Vermeulen said. "We don't have all day."

"I, uh, don't know anything about a United Nations visit."

"Could I please speak to your superior? You obviously don't know what's going on." Vermeulen's armpits were getting wet. This was the biggest con he'd ever pulled inside the US. "I must say, it doesn't reflect well on you that you haven't familiarized yourself with your daily orders."

Boyd sat up. "Can I see that ID again?"

Vermeulen handed it to him. Since it was real, he didn't have anything to worry about.

"What about hers?"

"She's part of my delegation, she doesn't need an ID."

"But I can't let her in without any form of identification."

Vermeulen turned to Tessa. "Kindly give him your driver's license, Ms. Bishonga."

She reacted with the same stern expression that Vermeulen sported.

The agent wrote down the particulars, returned their IDs and told them to wait for a guide to accompany them.

"The whole purpose of the inspection is that we're not shown only what you want us to see."

"I can't let you walk around inside by yourselves."

"Okay, get us an escort, we still have to visit facilities in Douglas, Casa Grande and Naco."

The man spoke into a walkie-talkie and before long another agent, short and chubby, appeared. His name tag said, Thom Steinert.

"Please come with me," Steinert said.

Inside, he asked them what they wanted to see first.

"The detention areas, of course. We'd also like to speak to a few detainees."

"Okie-dokie." Steinert seemed strangely unconcerned by a visit by UN personnel.

They passed a monitoring office with a bank of screens displaying video feeds from detention areas. Vermeulen stopped.

"We'd like to have a look. That way we don't have to go to each section."

"Okie-dokie."

Steinert opened the door and said, "Visitors" to the two agents monitoring the screens. They looked up and had the glassy eyes that come from staring at screens for too long. The matter of fact way in which Steinert announced Bishonga and Vermeulen gave them instant credibility.

"Do these cover all detention areas?" Tessa said.

"Yes, but not at the same time. The feed changes every thirty seconds or so," one of the guards said.

The screens, poor color and fuzzy, captured Vermeulen's attention. The rooms were crowded. Two of them had so many people lying on the ground and wrapped in mylar sheets, it seemed impossible anyone could move without everyone else having to as well. One room was clearly a bathroom, there were four stalls with knee-high dividers. Still, there were shapes huddled in mylar sheets sitting or lying on the floor. It wasn't clear if they had mats or were lying on the concrete.

"We'd like to speak to..." Vermeulen pulled out the sheet from the lawyer's office. "...Fausto López and Emerson García. Can you find these men, please?"

The two agents monitoring the screens shrugged. Not their job. Steinert took them to a different office. The two agents there looked busy with paperwork.

"These two are looking for Fausto López and Emerson García. Where are we keeping them?" Steinert said. Again, Steinert posed the question as if Vermeulen and Tessa had every right to be there and one of the officers started a search on his computer.

"López has already been sent to ICE, he's at the Florence Correctional Center. García is still here."

"And, where is he?" Steinert said.

The officer gave Steinert the information and the man took Vermeulen and Tessa through a maze of hallways past doors with wire-reinforced glass that gave a close-up glimpse into the horrifically crowded conditions.

"Why are the rooms so crowded?" Vermeulen said.

"Too many people coming across."

"And there are no other facilities nearby?"

"They're also past maximum capacity."

"Are those asylum seekers or migrants?"

"What's the difference?"

"The difference is that asylum-seekers are protected by international law, undocumented migrants are not."

Steinert looked at him as if he'd just outlined a distinction he'd never heard of.

"I just work here."

Vermeulen heard hurried steps behind them and

turned. Two men came running down the corridor. They had insignia on their collars that indicated some rank.

"Who are you and what the hell are you doing here?" the first one said.

"I'm Valentin Vermeulen and I'm an investigator for the Office of Internal Oversight Services of the United Nations. That's the investigative arm of the UN. We are here to inspect this detention facility."

"I'm Jason Markey, Patrol Agent in Charge of this facility, and you have no damn business here."

"I beg to differ. The United States is a signatory to the Convention Relating to the Status of Refugees. That convention spells out the treatment of people seeking asylum. The United Nations is the guardian of international treaties and as such we have every business to be here and ascertain that you are following international law in the treatment of asylum-seekers."

Markey stood there with his mouth open. He turned to the other man. "Do you know anything about this?"

The other agent's name tag read, "Bill Nelson." His collar insignia were different and, given his demeanor, he ranked below Markey. "No, sir. I know nothing about this."

"The legal obligations of the United States are clearly spelled out in the convention and those include inspections," Vermeulen said. His con was getting bigger by the minute. Yes, there were legal obligations, but there were no inspections. Despite the air-conditioning, he felt sweat running down the sides of his body. He looked at Tessa whose face was a stony facade of officialdom.

"The conditions under which you hold detainees here are beyond anything allowable under international standards," Vermeulen said. "There are no beds, nor hygienic facilities. The UN Standard Minimum Rules for the Treatment of Prisoners outline clearly that these conditions are illegal. I'm afraid we'll have to report this."

Tessa's face told him not to push his luck too far. But he couldn't help himself. Seeing the real consequences of the Trump policies made him both angry and despondent, because he knew he couldn't change what he saw.

Markey seemed nonplussed. "What do you expect me to do? I got no resources, no place to put people."

"You could release the asylum seekers pending their trial. I believe that used to be the practice until recently."

Markey shook his head. "I can't. Orders from way above my pay grade. Sorry."

It was the first indication that Markey wasn't one-hundred percent on board with the new policy. Vermeulen had to back off. "If it's no trouble, we'd like to speak with Emerson García. Agent Steinert here was about to bring us to him."

"What's your interest in García?" Markey said.

"His name was forwarded to us by the Human Rights Commission as a person at risk."

The incredulity on Markey's face reached a new dimension. "How'd they even know about him? He can't have been here for more than a week."

"International justice isn't always as slow as people assume it is. So can we speak with Mr. García?"

Markey looked at Nelson, who shrugged and said, "Why not? We don't want to create an international incident, do we?"

Vermeulen's stomach unclenched a fraction. They might still pull off this con.

Markey nodded and told Steinert to take them to meet García. Steinert said, "Follow me" and took them deeper into the facility. Vermeulen resisted the temptation to look back and see what the senior agents were doing.

They passed more rooms. Through the security glass in each door, Vermeulen saw more shapes huddled on the floor wrapped in mylar sheets. It was inconceivable to him what kind of mind would issue policy directives that resulted in such inhumane treatment.

García happened to be in a space that wasn't quite as crowded. Steinert yelled the name and a slight man wrapped in a mylar sheet got up from the floor. He had the haggard look of someone whose life had always been hard. Steinert motioned for him to follow them into an empty room that had a few chairs.

"*Siéntese, por favor*," Tessa said. As usual Vermeulen was impressed by her language abilities.

García took a seat but didn't take the mylar sheet off. "*Es muy frío*," he said.

Although Vermeulen was used to air-conditioning, he had to agree. These rooms seemed very cold. Those mylar blankets didn't look like they made much of a difference, but every detainee they'd seen so far was wrapped in one.

Although Tessa's Spanish wasn't close to fluent, she managed to get the questions across. After some back and forth, Vermeulen understood that the skeleton had already been at the location when García and his group of border crossers arrived at the spot. They weren't so much shocked but saddened by the sight. They used the stuff lying there and some of their own to cover the skeleton. It was the best they could do. There was no time to bury it.

Vermeulen asked a few more questions, which Tessa

translated as best she could, but García had no further information that would help them sort out how the skeleton had gotten there.

When García realized that the interview was coming to an end, he asked that they call his family in El Salvador and a cousin in Los Angeles to tell them that he was okay. He gave them the phone numbers and also asked to tell the cousin his A-number. Vermeulen remembered that this number was crucial to follow anyone who ended up in the US immigration system. Vermeulen wrote the information in his notebook and then met up with Steinert, who'd waited outside the room.

After returning García to the detention room, Steinert looked at the two. "Where to next?"

"I think this will do, Agent Steinert. If you'd accompany us to the exit, we'd be much obliged," Vermeulen said. He looked at Tessa and saw her nodding, as if to say, *Let's get the hell out of here.*

"Okie-dokie," Steinert said and brought them back to the gate.

They waited for Agent Boyd to buzz the door open, but there was no buzz.

"I think the Agent in Charge would like a word with you," Boyd said.

"Well, we're short on time and we have a lot of ground to cover today. We'll be back soon and we can talk then," Vermeulen said.

Boyd didn't seem happy with that reply. "He's on his way."

"It'll just have to wait, we have a meeting with the Chief Patrol Agent of the Tucson sector in twenty minutes. I'm sure your Agent in Charge doesn't want to be responsible for making us late."

"I guess not," Boyd said and pushed the buzzer.

The gate opened and Vermeulen had to keep himself from running outside. They managed a hurried pace in line with the claim to be late, got to their car and drove from the lot without much of a squeal.

"We'll never be able to do this again," Tessa said. "Too bad, because we really didn't learn a lot."

"We did too. We now know that the group of border crossers represented by William Morgan the Third found the skeleton *in situ*. The body must have been brought there earlier."

SEVENTEEN

Saturday, October 20th,
Tucson, Arizona

BACK AT THEIR MOTEL, Vermeulen called Alma Rodriguez to give her the news about Emerson García. He didn't tell Alma Rodriguez how he and Tessa had managed to get inside the Border Patrol detention facility.

"The less you know, the better," he said. "But we talked with one of the detainees who had seen the skeleton. He told us that they found it in the hollow and covered it with the discarded things they found there, because they had no time to bury it."

"Sadly, that's a common story. We get news of bodies and skeletons all the time from migrants. In this climate, it doesn't take long before a body is reduced to its bones. The sun and the animals take care of that quickly. The skeleton could have been there for less than a week."

Vermeulen thought about that and it didn't add up. "Why wasn't the body discovered earlier?"

"The *coyotes* who bring the migrants across vary their paths all the time. They have their own network and information, so a specific spot might not be used for a while if there's too much Border Patrol activity in the area."

"Ah, I see. Are they all being brought over by the cartels?"

"Most of them. The crackdown by the US has forced them into the desert. The cartels know that and they control the passage. They want you to sign up with a *coyote* for a fee. If you don't have the money for the fee, and want to try it on your own, you still have to pay the cartels a border tax. Sometimes they make you carry drugs if you have no money left."

Vermeulen shook his head. Tessa had been right about the two sides feeding off each other. "I have some information for you. Mr. García gave me a couple of phone numbers and his A-number so I could inform his family in El Salvador and his cousin in Los Angeles. I don't speak Spanish, so I'm hoping you could do that."

"No problem, that's a big part of what we do at *Arizona Rescue*. We're a little like a bulletin board. Families leave messages for us to pass on to their relatives that try to make it across and we, in turn, inform families when we have news. The worst part is writing letters to those whose relatives were found dead. Those keep me awake at night."

Vermeulen wanted to hang up, but had one more question. "If I understand the current situation, the majority of border crossers are refugees from Central America looking for asylum. Is that correct?"

"I don't have the exact numbers, but, yes, that's what's going on. The net migration of Mexicans is negative. More are leaving the US than coming in."

"So they ask for asylum, get their credible fear hearing and are then put in detention?"

"Yup. What's the question?"

"That seems so counterproductive and expensive."

"Yeah, but there are two issues at stake here. First, this administration wants to send a signal to stop people from coming here. Getting put in detention is part of that strategy, as is making it as hard as possible to even qualify for asylum. The second part is that all ICE detention facilities are private prisons. So they cash in on that."

"I was afraid of that. How can you stand facing this every day?"

"There are days when I nearly despair. But we are often the only friendly voice the families hear. So I grew a tough skin and carry on."

"Do you at least get the weekend off?"

"Sorta. I'm not at the office, but I'm gonna make those calls now. Every day that goes by without news from their loved ones is hard for the families. It's the least I can do."

Vermeulen took a deep breath.

"Thank you. I can imagine that your being here is a godsend for the families."

"It's how I can be useful."

WILLIAM MORGAN THE THIRD did spend Saturdays at his office. It was his normal routine. His workload never ebbed. Pro bono work piled on top of the regular work made those Saturday hours inevitable.

His phone rang and when he saw Alma's name on the display, his mood improved.

"Are you calling to tell me you want to have dinner with me tonight?" he said.

"No. I just got an email from the church volunteers in Douglas. There are seven new unaccompanied minors at Douglas wanting asylum. Do you have time to go down there or should I call the next one on the list?"

"You didn't answer my question," he said.

"And you didn't answer mine, so we are even. Can you represent them or should I call Phil?"

"Don't call Phil. I'll do it. Gets me out of the office."

He hesitated. "Listen, since my dinner invitations have all flamed out so spectacularly, maybe we can just meet for coffee. Or do you like tea? I bet that's it. You're a tea-drinker, am I right?"

"William Morgan the Third, has it ever occurred to you that it's not a question of coffee or tea, but a question of my not wanting to hang out with you?"

"But why? I'm not mean, not too ugly, and I speak in complete sentences."

"And you think I should settle for that?"

That was harsh. Morgan had to swallow. So far, his interactions with Rodriguez had been friendly and he thought the little banter would liven their conversations. He thought she was cute and although he knew she was older and had a daughter, he was interested in getting to know her better—but this?

Before he could say anything, Rodriguez spoke again. "I'm sorry, William. That was uncalled for. I tried to be funny, but I wasn't. I'll check my language better the next time."

"Okay." But the bad taste remained.

"Listen," Rodriguez said. "You know I really appreciate the work you do for the refugees, big time. I'm also flattered by your invitations. It's just that I don't want to get involved with anyone right now. I got a busy job and a daughter to take care of. That's all I can handle at the moment."

Fair enough, he thought. At least she doesn't hate me.

"I understand," he said aloud. "I promise to be less obnoxious. But I do want to buy you a cup of your favorite hot beverage when I come through. I need to update you on the cases anyway."

"It's a deal. Thanks. And I prefer coffee."

EIGHTEEN

Saturday, October 20th,
Ciudad Obregón, Sonora, Mexico

AT MID-MORNING CAMILLE DELANO took a car service to the other Walmart in Ciudad Obregón. She found the payphone and checked for messages. Sure enough, there was a new one. A voice—not that of Don Martinez—told her to be at La Focaccia at four in the afternoon. Good, Martinez kept his word—for now.

Since their last meeting, she hadn't noticed any obvious surveillance. Either the cartel was really good, or it was an example of Martinez being true to his word; maybe, maybe not. Cartel goons weren't good at spy craft. Their MO was to shoot, not to blend into the background and follow their prey.

Walmart was as good as any place to while away the intervening time. She strolled through the aisles and wondered why, even in Mexico, so much stuff came from China. Occasionally, she would turn around suddenly as if she'd just remembered something. There was never anyone suspicious behind her. She didn't think of herself as a snob, but she couldn't think of anything she'd want to buy at the store. In the end, she picked up some laundry detergent and bought two more phone cards for future phone calls at the cash register.

Near the entrance, she got a cup of coffee at the Café

El Vaquero, which wasn't really a café, just a kiosk, and sat on one of the hard plastic benches. She saw people coming and going, some carts overflowing with merchandise, others with only a few items. There was a steady ebb and flow of humanity, almost mesmerizing, if it hadn't been for the harsh light. She'd always thought herself separate from that mass of humanity. Not in the sense of being special, simply in being apart from it.

That apartness came with a cost, a cost that seemed negligible ten, twenty years ago, but that weighed more heavily on her these days. At first, she'd blamed her exile in Ciudad Obregón, but more and more she thought it'd be the same in any city in the US. New Jersey, the state she knew best, hadn't been different—a decent bar that served ice-cold vodka, facilitating illegal deals, and dealing with lowlifes along the way.

Maybe running a bookstore wouldn't be so bad after all—or take up water coloring. She shook her head. The thought alone was ridiculous.

She checked her watch. Almost time to meet Don Martinez.

THE WAITER AT La Focaccia greeted her like a regular. Her association with Don Martinez must've upped her ranking.

"*Agua mineral, Señora?*" he said.

"*No, un café con leche, por favor.*" Better to get them taken care of now than later.

The man smiled and went about fixing her coffee, which he served a few minutes later with the flourish of a waiter in an old movie.

At three-forty-five, the routine from the day before unfolded. The same two men came inside, checked out the premises, eyed her and went outside again. She'd played her part by holding her Glock under the table. Don Martinez entered, the same cruel fleshy face and loafers, but a different shirt and slacks.

He sat down at her table and signaled the owner, who knew to bring a glass of white wine.

"*Señora* Beltrán, I have the information you want. Tell me why I should give it to you."

Delano smiled. "You either give it to me, or you don't. I can't make you tell me."

Martinez made a dismissive sound as if the thought of her making him do anything was preposterous.

"I told you before, I have no horse in this race," she said. "I've had plenty of deals go sour. It's not my concern. I get paid either way. If you want to play games, be my guest, but please play them without me."

That leering grin was back on his face. "I like a woman with spunk."

"I'm sure you do. I'm not that woman. And my Glock is pointing right at you under the table. I might not make it out of here, but neither will you."

Martinez shifted sideways and raised his hands. "Okay, okay. It was only a joke."

She thought she heard the mumbled "*Puta*" but didn't react.

"The man you spoke of yesterday arrived and was transported as negotiated."

Delano gave a slight nod of acknowledgement. "I expected nothing less, but the man was killed. If your associates did as agreed, why is the man not in the US?"

"I'm in charge of the southern part of the state of Sonora," Martinez said. "Other people run the affairs of the border."

"I understand. My client won't hold you personally responsible. What have you found out?"

"It appears that members of a rival organization kidnapped the man. These kidnappers want money. Usually when the money is paid, the person is released. In this case, maybe the money was not forthcoming, or there was no relative to call. I don't know the particulars."

"So your associates up North didn't kidnap the man?" Delano said.

"Of course not. Why would they?"

"Because they already got paid and the ransom would increase the profits."

"You have a faulty view of my organization. We don't kill clients. It sends the wrong message."

Delano kept a straight face. She knew enough about the Sinaloa cartel. It hadn't become one of the most powerful in Mexico because of its excellent customer relations policies, but because they hung their victims from overpasses for everyone to see.

"Who was the rival organization?" she said.

Martinez stroked his chin. "My associates believe they were members of the *Cartel de Jalisco Nueva Generación*. This organization is assuming, incorrectly, that just because our leader, Joaquín Guzman, is in prison in *Nueva York*, our organization is ripe for the plucking."

That made sense to Delano. She knew that *El Chapo* had been extradited. That would automatically lead to violent challenges to the predominant cartel. She also knew that *El Chapo's* sons had taken over the reins. There would be a lot more bloodshed before either party accepted the new dispensation.

"Who would I speak to at the CJNG?" she said.

Martinez looked at her with raised eyebrows. "I suggest you drop this matter. The CJNG is not a negotiating organization."

"Maybe they haven't gotten the right offer yet?"

"Maybe you get yourself killed or worse. They do things to women."

"As does your organization. Let's not have the pot call the kettle black."

Martinez frowned, the adage being lost on him.

"Never mind," Delano said. "If you have a name, I'd like for you to give it to me. Think of it as customer service. After all, you didn't do a very good job protecting the man."

Martinez shook his head. "He wasn't my responsibility. I told you so."

"He was your organization's responsibility. Your organization let him be kidnapped. It owes my client."

"And how is your client going to collect the debt?" Martinez was smiling now.

"I don't know and it's not my concern, I only facilitate transactions. But a word of advice. There are assassination teams for hire around the world. I hear the Chechens are very effective. Your organization is at war with the CJNG. Imagine such a team playing you against the CJNG and vice versa? In my experience, unnecessary bloodshed can often be avoided with just a few words. Getting the names of the persons responsible and suggesting to the CJNG that they reimburse my client would be a good beginning."

Her suggestion of an assassination team made enough of an impression on Martinez to continue the conversation.

"What sum did your clients have in mind?" he said.

"Well, there's the cost of travel, the lost fee for trafficking the man to the US, but, most importantly, the lost earnings. My clients expect a payment of one million dollars."

"How can one man be so valuable?"

"You'd be surprised. The Sinaloa cartel gets the money from CJNG and transfers it back to the Moldovans. Case closed and everybody walks away alive."

"We're at war with the CJNG. They won't give us the money. You're the intermediary, you take it. If they're willing to pay. I doubt that, but I will pass your request to them and hope that you will tell your client that I cooperated."

"I will."

NINETEEN

Saturday, October 20th,
Douglas & Phoenix, Arizona

WILLIAM MORGAN ARRIVED at the Douglas Border Patrol detention center in the afternoon. He checked in and indicated that he was there to register as the attorney for the asylum claims of seven newly-arrived unaccompanied minors. An agent led him to a large windowless room where two fenced pens had been built. One of the pens held boys, the other one girls. Opaque plastic sheets obstructed the view from the boy pen to the girl pen.

The room was cold. Another *hielera*, an icebox, where the kids were only given a mylar sheet as protection. Even Morgan, who was used to air-conditioned offices, shivered when he spoke to the agent. Sixty-six degrees was just plain inhuman for kids who had few clothes.

"Who are you here to see?" the agent said. He was holding a clipboard with papers.

Morgan gave him the seven names Rodriguez had emailed him. The agent flipped through the pages, shook his head several times. He checked his watch.

"Sorry, you just missed them, they're being transported to a permanent facility while their cases are pending."

"What do you mean, I just missed them? I called before I left Phoenix. How can they be gone?"

"You came from Phoenix? That's where they are headed. A van came with orders to pick them up. We don't have any more space here for kids."

"Where is it now?"

"The van? Probably just pulling out of the parking lot. He said he was taking Route 80 via Bisbee."

"A Border Patrol van?"

"Private contractor."

"What's the van look like?"

"I dunno. Just a van. It's white, with tinted windows."

That would describe the majority of vans on the road. "Any markings?"

"Nope, just white."

Morgan raced from the facility, jumped into his BMW and skidded out the parking lot. When he hit the intersection with Route 80, he could see the white van in the distance. There wasn't any other traffic. He accelerated to catch up. When he reached it, he set the cruise control and followed it. Where were these kids headed?

During the drive, Morgan had called Rodriguez to let her know that the children were being driven to Phoenix by a private contractor.

"I won't be able to meet you for coffee after all," he said.

"Did you say private contractor?"

"Yes, in an unmarked white van."

FOUR AND A half hours later, the van left the freeway west of the Phoenix Sky Harbor airport and drove into a neighborhood of mixed-use buildings. It was dark and keeping behind the van was difficult with all the urban traffic around him.

After ten minutes of turns, the van turned into the well-lit parking lot of a nondescript single story office building. Morgan pulled to the curb a few yards away and watched. Whatever this was, it was not an ICE facility or any other government building related to immigration. He knew where all of those were in Arizona and had been to many of them.

A man got out of the driver's side door, went to the entrance door and pushed a buzzer. The door was white glass and obscured what lay behind it. A woman opened the door. The two talked a moment. A minute later, two more people came outside and the driver opened the sliding door of the van.

Morgan counted ten kids climbing from the van. They were led into the building. The driver went back to the van, locked the doors and followed his colleagues inside.

He called his paralegal, apologized for disturbing his Saturday evening, and asked him to look up the owner and tenant of the building. "Oh, and can you check if it is a licensed childcare facility? Thanks, Phil. I owe you one."

He got out of his car and ambled toward the entrance. There was no company name or other identification at the door, just the buzzer. This was highly irregular. A civilian contractor taking kids and driving them for four hours to an office building? That couldn't be part of the zero-tolerance policy. The government was responsible for these kids. How could it turn them over to some contractor with an unmarked van? He walked along the side of the building. The windows had been turned opaque by milky film applied to the inside. He looked around the next corner. There was the same treatment of the windows, but no door. He went back to the entrance.

What was he to do next? The constant changes of immigration rules and procedures felt like a whiplash. Just when he'd gotten accustomed with a new directive from the administration, there came yet another change. It didn't look like a careful implementation of policies, but a random assortment of new ideas, each barely connected to the previous one. The agencies charged with implementing them ended up scurrying around like mice in a cage, eager to please their bosses in Washington, but without the capacity to actually do what they were asked. The result was immigration policy by improvisation, which violated a ton of existing legal obligations. Throw in the private contractors, eager to make a buck by cutting corners, and the result was a humanitarian disaster combined with a bureaucratic nightmare.

His phone rang. It was the paralegal. He told him that the building was owned by a local property developer and had recently been leased to VNM, Inc.

"Can you find out who VNM, Inc. is?"

"I knew you'd ask," the paralegal said. "It's a defense contractor, who has a contract to transport detained immigrant children for the Department of Health and Human Services. And, no, the state website doesn't list this location as a childcare facility; it's also not listed on the website of the Office of Refugee Resettlement."

That's all he needed to know. "Thanks, Phil. I promise I won't bother you again 'til Monday."

He pushed the buzzer.

"Yes," a female voice said.

"This is William Morgan, I'm an attorney and you have seven of my clients inside. I need to talk with them."

There was a pause. Then, "Just a moment, please." Then, silence.

After two minutes of silence, he pushed the buzzer again.

The same voice came on and said, "Non-government persons are not allowed inside this facility."

"I don't care, you are holding minors who are detained by the US government. They are entitled to legal representation and I'm the legal representative of seven unaccompanied minors you have in there. It's in the constitution. Please let me inside. I need to speak with my clients."

"How do you know your clients are inside?"

"I followed the van from Douglas where they were picked up. So open up or I will call the police and have them charge you with kidnapping."

"We have a contract with the US government to transport minors, so your claim of kidnapping is out of line. Please leave or we will call the police."

"You can save yourself the trouble. I'll call them. You will not interfere with the attorney-client relationship."

He ended the call and dialed 911. The emergency operator sounded a bit miffed that he'd used the number since she didn't think it was a real emergency, but she connected him to the police anyway. They said they'd send a patrol car.

While he waited, he saw a middle aged woman stand in the door of a neighboring house. He walked over. She had long blonde hair and the kind of shadows under her eyes, that spoke of a hard life.

"Do you know how long they've been holding kids next door?"

She looked at him a bit skeptical and said, "Who are you?"

"I'm an attorney and seven of my clients are in there."

"Oh, you represent migrant kids?"

"I do."

"It's been going on for several weeks, I think. Started seeing these white vans dropping off kids. At first, I thought they'd put in childcare, but that seemed weird for an office building. They're all Hispanic kids, so I figured it was something with immigration."

"Who used that building before?"

"There was an insurance agent, and then other tenants. I don't really know."

"Have you seen kids leave?"

"Yes, some, but I'm not always here; my schedule is kinda random. The place I work for only calls me when they need me. But then I have to go or I lose the job. Sucks royally, you know, you can never make any plans."

"What kind of work do you do?"

She shrugged. "Waitress."

"Oh man, that's a pain, never knowing your schedule. Any chance you can find a place with more predictability?"

"I wish, but there're not a lot of options."

He saw a patrol car stop and said, "Oh. The cops are here. Gotta go. Thanks for your help. And good luck. Maybe something better will turn up."

He jogged back to the building.

"You the one who called about kidnapping?" the older of the two officers said, after Morgan approached their squad car. He was a bulky man, but his appearance was dominated by a bushy mustache that seemed to have a life of its own.

"Uh, yes, I am. I'm William Morgan and I'm the attorney for seven unaccompanied minors who are held inside."

"And how do you know this?"

"I drove to Douglas this morning to consult with my clients about their asylum status. When I got there, they had just been shipped out. I followed the van which transported them to this location. I asked to speak to my clients and I was refused admittance. Since this is not a federal or immigration related facility, nor a licensed childcare facility, these minors have effectively been kidnapped."

The officer gave him the once over, his mustache looking like it was going to crawl away from the lip.

"Well, Mr. Morgan, Esquire. I just heard from my superiors on the way over that this is a federal mess and that we have no jurisdiction. That company has a contract with the government and they're doing their job. So this ain't no kidnapping. Whatever beef you have with those fellows, you gotta take it up with the Feds. Nothing I can do about it. You have yourself a nice day."

As the squad car pulled away from the curb, Morgan checked his watch. It was too late to do anything. The best he could do was petition for an emergency *habeas corpus.* But for that he needed permission from his firm. He was too junior to go about filing federal *habeas* petitions on their behalf.

He took photos of the building and of the van still parked in the lot and drove to his office. His body ached from sitting in the car for eight hours, from not having eaten anything substantial, and from the weight of his work. He thought of Rodriguez doing this work without complaining and decided to buck up.

At the office he got through to one of the managing partners of Fillmore, West & East to ask for guidance. His boss told him to go for it, for which he was grateful, but it also meant driving to the federal court house and finding a judge who'd accept a petition at nine on a Saturday evening.

TWENTY

Sunday, October 21st,
Phoenix, Arizona

EARLY THE NEXT MORNING, Morgan stood again at the door to the office building ready to push the buzzer. This time a couple of police officers accompanied him because he had a court order, issued a half hour earlier.

The night before, talking to a judge on the phone, he learned that studying contract law was a poor preparation for dealing with immigration issues and criminal law. Fortunately, the judge was patient enough to inform him that a *writ of habeas corpus* was the wrong legal instrument. The government wasn't denying that it was holding the seven minors in question. The judge instead promised to issue an injunction early the next morning, since federal law clearly protected the right of asylum claimants to legal representation.

Morgan pushed the button, a voice answered. He told them that he had come to see his clients and that he had a federal court injunction. Ignoring it would lead to arrest and criminal charges.

The door was opened fast. Maybe the people running this operation had consulted with their bosses and were told not to put up a fuss. The man at the door invited Morgan inside.

One of the cops next to Morgan said, "We all set then?"

Morgan nodded and the officers left. He followed the man inside.

It was a run-of-the-mill office building, a couple of generations behind the latest trends, but not worn-down or neglected. Morgan walked past unfurnished rooms where kids sat on the carpeted floor and leaned against walls. The man brought him to an office. A woman sat behind a desk with a laptop open. She wore a gray business suit and had ash blonde hair that fell to her shoulders. She didn't look like a childcare worker. Her face radiated efficiency, rather than compassion. They must've brought her in from the closest corporate office.

"Good morning. I'm William Morgan, here to see seven of my clients."

"I'm Maude Flanders. My apologies for yesterday's misunderstanding. VNM is committed to superior service for all its customers. Of course we wouldn't stand in the way of an attorney meeting with his clients. Who would you like to see?"

Morgan didn't buy the corporate drivel for a moment. "Before I get to that, I have a few questions. One, this building is not a licensed childcare facility. It's not on the list of approved facilities of the state of Arizona nor the Office of Refugee Resettlement. Why are you housing children here? Two, are there proper facilities like bathrooms, showers, and a kitchen to take care of the minors under your supervision. Three..."

"This is not a shelter or childcare facility. We aren't housing children here," Flanders said.

Morgan felt his anger rising.

"Then what are the children doing here? Clearly,

they've stayed overnight. What is that if it's not housing children?"

"All I can say is that we're not housing children here. This is a temporary holding space." She maintained her stony face as she said this.

"What? The children have stayed overnight. How is that not housing children?"

Her reaction was the same. No expression and a rehearsed answer, "My company has a contract to transport children for the Department of Health and Human Services. That's all I can tell you. Now, who'd you like to speak to?"

Morgan couldn't let this go. "I'm not done yet. How many children are you holding here?"

"I'm not at liberty to disclose that information. Tell me the names of your clients so you can have your conversation."

His hand was shaking with fury when he handed her the list. She typed the names into her laptop and frowned.

"Four of the minors on the list have already been transported to a juvenile facility up North, but we have three of them still here."

"When you say, 'up North,' what do you mean?"

"North of Arizona. From what I see here, they are on their way to Topeka. Three are still here."

She made a quick call and led him to a different room. A few minutes later, a guard brought three boys into the room. Flanders and the guard left.

According to the notes he'd received from Rodriguez, all three came from El Salvador. It didn't take a degree in psychology to see that the boys were traumatized. Their eyes and their restless legs spoke of the misery of the long journey. Two were sixteen, the younger one, fourteen. The two older ones were a pair of brothers. Since they had the same birthday, Morgan assumed they were twins. They couldn't be more unlike each other. Milton García was a bit on the chubby side but Manuel García was taller and skinny. Both had black hair and the downy beginnings of beards. The younger one, Claudio López was small for his age. He had longish hair. Unlike the others, he made no eye contact. The three clearly had trekked through the desert. Their clothes were dirty, and their sneakers worn.

Morgan settled in one of the chairs and got ready to explain the process of asylum applications. Manuel told him in rapid-fire Spanish that they had been interviewed by a border patrol agent, gotten their A-number and then were put in the van that brought them here.

"Okay," Morgan said, his Spanish not very fluent. "Do you understand the asylum process." All three shrugged. "You will have a trial before an immigration judge."

"When?" Manuel said.

"I don't know. In a month, in three or four months? The judge will say if you can stay in the US. Don't lie to the judge. Just say why you fled El Salvador."

"*Calle 18* and *MS-13*," Milton said. The other two nodded.

It was a depressingly predictable answer. The pressure to join gangs and the violent induction process was the primary reason for boys to leave the country.

"Did you get food?" Morgan said.

The boys nodded. "Cheese sandwiches" Milton said, making a face.

"Anything else?"

They shook their heads.

"Did you shower?"

No, they didn't get to shower.

"Where did you sleep?"

"Here," Manuel said.

So they did sleep in the office building. How that wasn't housing migrant children was beyond Morgan. After a little back and forth, he found out from Milton and Manuel that there were no showers, no towels, nor washrags. They washed in the sinks in the office bathroom and used paper towels from the dispensers. He asked how many others there were. They said maybe twenty or more. How long had the others been there? They didn't know, maybe two days, maybe more. Kids were always coming and going, even in the middle of the night.

Claudio López still said nothing. Manuel told him to speak up, he shook his head. Manuel insisted. Claudio got up and limped around the table and showed Morgan a large gash along the left calf. It was mostly scabbed over but there were still weeping spots. He asked how he got the wound and Claudio only said, "In the desert."

"How?" Morgan said. Getting a gash like that took some doing.

"I fell."

Morgan raised his eyebrows. That must've been quite a fall. The boy needed medical attention.

He opened the door and said to the man waiting outside, "You have a medic or doctor around? This kid's leg needs medical attention."

"We don't have one on staff," the man said.

"What? You mean to tell me that you're holding an

injured fourteen-year-old boy, scared out of his wits, and don't provide needed medical services?"

"That's not in our contract."

Morgan shook his head and went back inside.

"Have you called your families? Relatives in the US?" he said.

Milton and Manuel nodded. Manuel explained that they'd gotten their calls right after their interview in Douglas. They also had called an uncle in Phoenix, who would pick them up in a day or two.

Claudio shook his head. Maybe he'd been overlooked. Maybe he'd been too shy.

Morgan stepped outside again and asked why Claudio hadn't been able to call his family yet.

"That's not our responsibility."

"He is entitled to free calls. I don't care what you think your responsibility is. He needs to call his family now. So, you get a medic here and let him have his call or I will sue the pants off you and your company."

The man turned and left. The bored expression on his face told Morgan that the welfare of the youths was the least of the man's concern. He came back rather quickly, holding a PBX telephone set and a cord. "We'll take him to a walk-in clinic after you're done, and here's the phone for his call." He came inside the room, plugged the phone into the wall jack and left again.

Morgan checked the country code for El Salvador on his phone and gave it to Claudio. The boy hesitated. Morgan realized that he was too shy to call in front of Milton and Manuel.

He turned to them. Did they have any other questions? They shook their heads. He asked for their uncle's phone number. The man had promised that they could stay with him until it was time for the trial before an immigration judge. Morgan wanted to stay in touch with the uncle since he'd represent his nephews. Morgan opened the door and told the guard outside that he was done talking to the two.

Once alone with Morgan, Claudio dialed his mother's number in El Salvador. It rang for a long time before someone answered.

Claudio said, "*¿Mamá?*"

Next thing, the boy was talking with so much animation, Morgan thought he'd been switched for a livelier version of himself.

The call lasted about ten minutes. Claudio hung up, his eyes full of tears.

"You want to call someone in the US? You have a relative here?"

"A cousin."

"Go ahead and call your cousin. The sooner you call, the sooner you'll get out."

Claudio pulled the paper with the number from his shoe and dialed. Morgan could hear ringing and the mechanical voice of a voicemail system. It sounded English.

Claudio looked up, confused.

"Leave a message" Morgan said, and Claudio did, but the message he left was short.

Claudio was teary again. He wiped his eyes with his sleeves, but they didn't wipe away the deep sadness. The boy seemed more traumatized than the other two.

"What happened to you?" Morgan said.

He was tearing up again. Morgan, clumsy and awkward, reached out and gave him a hug. He felt the boy's heaving and his tears seeping into his shirt. Morgan held him until Claudio pulled away to wipe the snot from his nose with his sleeve.

"You can tell me."

Claudio sighed and blurted out, "The cartel killed four men in my truck."

"They killed four men? Where? When?"

Claudio didn't know where.

"They almost killed me too."

"What happened?"

"They wanted us all to undress and give them our money."

Now Morgan understood. What a nightmare. He held the boy again. After a while he asked if there were other children on the truck. Claudio shook his head.

"Anything else?"

Claudio thought for a while.

"There was a *gringo.*"

A white man? That was a new one. "With the cartel?"

Claudio shook his head. "In the truck."

"A migrant?"

"Yes."

A white migrant in the truck? "American?"

"Don't know. He didn't speak Spanish."

"Did he speak English?"

Claudio shook his head.

Morgan tried to make sense of the information. A white man was with the migrants in the truck. A white man who didn't speak Spanish or English.

"What happened to the *gringo?*" Morgan said.

"The men took him."

That didn't make much sense, a cartel taking a white man prisoner. But nothing he'd encountered over the last year surprised him anymore. He looked at Claudio.

Poor kid; it was bad enough having to escape from the gangs in your homeland, and here he witnessed even more traumatic events on his way north.

He told Claudio that he'd try to find the cousin, and that he'd be there for the boy's appearance before the immigration judge. It was a shaky promise at best.

A shiver ran down Morgan's spine as he collected the paperwork. How could anyone stay human in the face of all that? His own anger simmered just below the boiling point. It was an occupational hazard for anyone dealing with inhuman policies. What would it take to bubble over? And what would happen then?

He took a deep breath and exhaled slowly. As selfish as it sounded, giving the boy a hug had helped him as much as the boy. Stay kind; it was the only way to do this work without burning out. He knew that, but finding that place every day was a different question.

TWENTY-ONE

Sunday, October 21st,
Phoenix, Arizona

AFTER HE LEFT the office building, Morgan called Rodriguez and told her that a private contractor was holding unaccompanied minors in an office building that wasn't equipped to handle kids.

Her response was resignation. "That's outrageous, but is it more outrageous than everything that has happened so far?"

"We have to sue the government. There were more than twenty kids in the building. Four of our seven had already been transferred in the middle of the night, and the three I talked with this morning may well be on their way somewhere else too; that despite the fact that they have relatives near."

"If you have time, can you come to Tucson? We need to strategize. I'll bring Gloria in, too."

"Okay. First, I have to check in at my office and then I'll be on my way."

He reached Tucson in the early afternoon. He stopped at *Arizona Rescue*, where Rodriguez told him that Gloria couldn't meet until later, which made it a perfect time to invite her for a coffee. She seemed happy to have an excuse to leave the office. He could tell that she was suffering from the same weariness he was. After saving the report she'd been working on, the two got into Morgan's car.

A white 3 Series BMW was considered a modest car in his family's circles, but he could tell that Rodriguez didn't think so. Now that they finally were going somewhere together, he felt awkward and didn't know what to say. The easiest fallback was work, so he started to tell her about VNM and the office building.

"Let's not talk about work. That'll happen soon enough," Rodriguez said. "Tell me about yourself."

That was a surprise. On the phone Rodriguez had always sounded serious, focused on the job.

"There's not a lot to tell," he started out. "My parents are well-off and live just outside of Boston. That's where I grew up. Went to prep school, then to Yale and then to Harvard Law. I was a legacy since my father also went to Yale and Harvard Law. I got in even though my LSAT scores weren't that good. I did commercial law, because that's what my father did. He told me that it was the only way to make a living and I believed him. Bad advice all around. It was boring. I didn't make the law review, I didn't get to clerk for a judge. Just contracts. I got mediocre grades, so the firm in Phoenix was the best job I could find."

He thought that it sounded too rehearsed and wanted to lighten it up, but Rodriguez said, "What would you've rather done?"

"I dunno. Criminal law, or immigration law. I'm learning a lot now, and I'm glad I can do that pro bono work for my firm, but I wish I had been better prepared."

"Do you like handling immigration cases?"

"I'm not sure *like* is the right word. In the best of worlds, my services wouldn't be needed."

He saw the smile on Alma's face and was relieved that he'd found the right answer. "It's also very difficult. The stories I hear are just gut-wrenching. I could never have imagined what people go through. But it still is better than contracts. There are real people involved, people who are just looking for a safe place. It's really a privilege to be able to help them."

That sounded too over the top. He looked at her, but she showed no reaction.

"Where are we going?" he said.

"Oh, I thought you had a place in mind."

"Uh, no. I don't know Tucson at all."

"Okay, take a left at the next intersection."

She directed him to a coffee shop well south of the city center. It was a small, plain building, painted off-white. There was no awning, no store sign. Morgan parked the BMW. They got out. His car was the most expensive car in sight. He looked around, hesitating a moment.

"Don't worry," Rodriguez said. "Nobody's gonna steal it." She wasn't smiling.

He opened his mouth, trying to hide his embarrassment with a joke, but nothing came to mind, so he closed it again.

Inside, Rodriguez ordered *cafe mexicano* for both of them. He vaguely remembered something about coffee and liquor and was about to say that he still needed to drive, but he saw no bottles of booze anywhere and stayed silent. The shop was a simple rectangle, beige walls, a counter and a smattering of small tables. There were four other patrons.

Once seated, he watched the barista make the coffee. The process reminded him of making chai tea, something he'd seen in an Indian restaurant. The barista spooned ground coffee into a pan, added brown sugar, cinnamon sticks and orange peel, and poured boiling water over everything.

"It'll be a while," Rodriguez said. "You want any treats?"

"No thanks. I eat too much junk food at work. I need to cut that out and get in better shape if I hope to survive this job. But tell me about you."

"There's not much to tell," she started, a hint of a smile on her face. "Came to the US without documents over three decades ago. I was three then. My mom worked like a dog, cleaning houses in Paterson, New Jersey. After a decade or so, we got legal status. I was in and out of school, acting out, drove my mom crazy. Once I was eighteen, I moved to Newark. The usual dead-end jobs, booze, and pot. Then I saw how ICE grabbed someone right from the kitchen of the restaurant where I was working. It was awful. That's how I got into immigration work. Got my act together, studied human resource management. Got married, got a job. The job sucked, the marriage sucked. I got divorced, took my baby and moved to Tucson."

The barista brought the coffees and Morgan was grateful for the distraction. Whereas his life had been putting up with the boredom of having everything, hers had been a struggle from the get go. He resisted the urge to comment on that. What was there to say? Instead, he took a sip and told her that the coffee was delicious.

"I'm glad you like it. For me, it brings back memories of home. My mom used to make it and gave me a sip here and there."

"You in touch with your mom?"

"Not for a long time, but since Catalina was born,

we talk regularly. *Abuelas* don't let their *nietas* out of sight. If that's not possible, they call all the time. Catalina really brought us together again."

"Nice." He'd never been estranged from his parents because there was little to estrange. None of them were what you'd call close. He couldn't remember the last time he'd hugged his mother. He was pretty sure that hugs had never been part of his father's repertoire. All parties honored their obligations, as if his family was like those contracts his father negotiated in his law firm. Better to shift the conversation back to the developments of the day.

"Sorry, but I gotta talk about Phoenix," he said. "Those four kids that were transferred in the middle of the night? They are supposedly headed for Topeka, but I'm not sure, the ICE database doesn't have their new location yet. The three that are still in Phoenix could also be headed elsewhere, no idea if that's in Phoenix or not. Supposedly that office building is just for same-day transfers, but they told me that others had been there for a couple of days already. We can't let that continue. That's why I suggested the lawsuit."

"Arizona Rescue can't sue the government. We're too small and have no money."

"Well, somebody has to. I'll contact the ACLU. I wonder if any other lawyers have seen situations like this."

"It's the first time I heard that. An office building. Makes you want to scream."

"I know. I'll get the ball rolling on that. We have to think about a legal strategy for those three kids, too."

"How are we supposed to arrange legal representation if we don't know where they're going to be?"

"I think that's the point. The government moves them on purpose. They do a quick credible fear hearing when they arrest them, only because they have to. Afterwards, they shuffle them around until trial to make proper legal representation impossible. Without a lawyer, the immigration judge just hears the government's case and the kids are deported. It doesn't matter that they are returning to dangerous situations. The youngest of the three was a boy named Claudio. He's from San Salvador. He told me a harrowing story. Somewhere between Mexico City and the border, the truck he was riding in was hijacked by a cartel. They shot four people right there. He was totally traumatized."

"When did that happen?"

"I don't know. The poor boy looked like he'd walked in the desert for a long time. I'd say a couple or three weeks ago."

"He needs to talk to a therapist."

"I know, but I don't see that happening anytime soon. You know the strangest thing? He said there was a white man on the truck with them, who didn't speak Spanish or English. The cartel goons took him with them."

"A European?"

"The boy didn't know, all he said was that he didn't speak Spanish or English."

"I wonder..." Rodriguez stopped.

"What?"

"He could've been that skeleton."

"The skeleton? The one everyone is asking about? You think so?"

"Could be. I better call Valentin."

TWENTY-TWO

Sunday, October 21st,
Tucson, Arizona

RODRIGUEZ'S CALL ELECTRIFIED VERMEULEN. He was sitting in a coffee shop near their motel, wondering about the next steps. At last there was a clue. The European taken by the cartel had to be Luca. The chances of another European being smuggled across the border were tiny. He called Tessa who had gone to the university library for background research.

"I have news," he said when she answered. "A boy in detention recalls seeing a white man who was abducted by cartel members. He told Morgan, who told Alma. She just called me."

"Great, so we have a confirmation of my suspicion. Something to work with. I'm digging through analyses of the changing cartel landscape. It's constantly shifting. Old alliances become new conflicts. Makes your head spin."

"I can imagine. Loads of men with guns. When has that ever been a good thing? Do you think our stunt yesterday will have repercussions?"

"I don't think so," Tessa said. "The Agent in Charge would have to admit that we bamboozled him. His superiors won't look kindly on that. So wouldn't be a good career move."

"I guess you're right. Besides, as far as they are concerned, no harm was done. We went in, talked to a guy, and left again. Given the general chaos, it's the least of their worries. What do you want to do tonight?"

"Be done with the day. Let's eat dinner at a nice place."

"Great idea. I'll find something."

"With cloth napkins, please. Oh, tomorrow we're going into the desert."

"We are?" Vermeulen wasn't sure he liked that plan.

"Yes, I talked to Alain Ponce, the anthro prof whose students found the skeleton. He invited us to come along on one of their field trips tomorrow."

"The same place where they found the skeleton?"

"No, a different location. But I think experiencing the desert is important for my article."

"What about looking at the artifacts they collected when they found the skeleton?"

"We can look at them later. They're stored at the university and not going anywhere."

"Maybe I'll sit out the excursion. You go and I'll sort through those bags instead."

"What? You're chickening out?"

"Yes, trudging through the desert in ninety-degree weather isn't my idea of a good time. Besides, I won't learn anything useful. I need to get that county attorney off my back. Maybe if I bring him some info he'll leave me alone. Can you text me Ponce's number?"

"Your loss. See you later."

His phone dinged. *Ponce's number.* He dialed it.

Ponce answered after a long series of rings. He must've been taking Sunday off. Vermeulen introduced himself and asked if he could see the artifacts they collected at the skeleton site.

"Sure, anytime. I hear you're joining us tomorrow."

"About that, is it possible for me to examine the artifacts tomorrow?"

"Not up for a trip to the desert?"

"More like a division of labor."

"Hmm, let me check the schedule."

After a moment, Ponce was back. "Yes, one of my students is signed up to catalogue items. He'll be there from ten to noon and will be able to help you. Go to the anthro lab in the basement, Room 025. I heard they had you testify before a Cochise County grand jury."

"They did," Vermeulen said. "I'm the only lead the county attorney has. Seems like he's fixated on the idea that I know more about traffickers than I'm admitting. I don't know why."

"Carson MacMillan?"

"The very same."

"He dragged me in front of the grand jury too. I didn't know anything about the skeleton, but he grilled me as if I had shot the man. Wasted a whole afternoon. What are you looking for among the artifacts?"

"I'll know it when I see it."

THEY FOUND A decent restaurant closer to the downtown area. There was nothing special about the place—white walls, brown wainscoting, tables and chairs, but no booths. The menu, on the other hand, was outstanding. The array of southwestern, Californian and South East Asian dishes offered was surprising for such a nondescript place, and most likely the reason for the five star rating on the restaurant app. And they had cloth napkins.

"Let's make this a long and leisurely meal," Tessa said. "I want a cocktail, an appetizer, a main dish and dessert, and I want to be here at least two hours."

"You got it."

The waitress came and Tessa ordered a Negroni while Vermeulen chose an Old Fashioned.

The drinks came and the waitress hovered to take their appetizer orders.

"Just give us a minute," Vermeulen said. "We're taking it slowly."

The waitress gave them a 'whatever' glance and left again.

He turned to Tessa. "You want to talk business or not?"

Tessa pondered for a moment. "I guess so. It's not something we can just turn off. So tell me about Alma's call."

Vermeulen gave her a quick summary.

"It's good to know that our initial assumption was correct," she said. "One cartel agrees to ferry Luca to the US and another cartel cuts in and kidnaps him. What I don't understand is what they hope to gain from it."

"Ransom. What else?"

"I know, but how were they going about it? If the traffickers in Moldova speak Romanian how do they communicate? According to Alma, the rival cartel killed four men but only took Luca."

"Maybe it wasn't a random kidnapping."

"Really? That'd be something."

The waitress resumed her hovering and they ordered appetizers, Banh Xeo with spring onions and bean sprouts.

"If they really knew he was on that truck," he said. "And they kidnapped him, why did they kill him?"

"You don't know if they contacted the traffickers in Moldova first."

Vermeulen took a sip from his Old Fashioned. A beer drinker by habit, he rarely drank liquor, unless it was Genever from Antwerp, but this bourbon paired well with the bitters. The bartender knew what he was doing.

"True," he said. "But they probably didn't. How'd they know whom to contact? I don't think Luca had the phone number of the traffickers on him. That'd be a dumb idea from the traffickers' perspective."

"But he must've carried the contact info for his US destination. Maybe the second cartel contacted them."

"Or the second cartel kidnapped him to extort money from the first one. Like an internecine fight, not a trans-atlantic one."

The waitress brought a plate with the Banh Xeo and the dipping sauce to the table. The drink on an empty stomach had given Vermeulen a good appetite and he grabbed a pancake, dipped it in the sauce and devoured it. Tessa dug in as well.

"So much for taking our time," she said after they finished the Banh Xeo. "This was so good. Let's order dinner."

"Let me do the ordering. We'll have some nice East Asian dishes. Indonesian dishes are practically the Dutch national cuisine."

"Okay. I say this with some trepidation, but I should trust the man I love. Right?"

Vermeulen waved over the waitress. He checked the

menu and told the waitress to bring Banh It Tran and Rendang Sapi.

"What did you just order?" Tessa said.

"Something from Vietnam and something from Indonesia. You're going to like it."

"There better be meat in it."

"There is. Beef, Rendang style from Indonesia and Mung Bean dumplings from Vietnam. You're going to like it."

"You keep saying that."

"To come back to the extortion," Vermeulen said. "It might be an internecine fight, but it's also transatlantic. The traffickers in Moldova stood to make serious money off Luca. Enough to pay an advance to bring him to the US. Not only is the advance down the drain, but whatever they hoped to earn isn't going to materialize. So they're bound to be really pissed off."

"You think they want revenge?"

"I'd say. If we assume they trafficked Luca for the same purpose as before, we're talking six figure sums."

"Ugh." Tessa made a face. "We're here to have a nice dinner, let's talk about something else."

"What did you learn about the cartels?"

"That's not something else."

Vermeulen shrugged. "Sorry, I can't stop thinking about this case."

"I can see that. Anyway, the cartels pretty much control everything on the Mexican side and quite a bit on the US side. There's so much money involved they even have Border Patrol agents on their payroll. Finally, I was right. Ever since *El Chapo* was extradited there's been a lot more violence and fights over who controls what."

"So Luca could've been collateral damage of that infighting?"

"Yes..."

The waitress hadn't even reached their table yet, but the aroma of the dishes preceded her and made Tessa turn around. Her eyes widened and a big smile appeared on her face.

"You did good," she said. "If they taste half as good as they smell, you can order food for us from now on."

"Did you want any wine?" Vermeulen said.

"You're sweet to ask, but the Negroni was enough."

It was an amazing meal. The flavors of the Java Sea melding with those of the South China Sea ended all talk, except for the occasional sigh of pleasure.

After dinner, they considered dessert. The Lisbon Chocolate cake looked tempting. Tessa demurely asked if he wanted to share.

Vermeulen looked at her with raised eyebrows and said, "You're kidding, right?"

She broke out in laughter. They both knew she'd never share a piece of chocolate cake.

When they got back to their motel, they tumbled on the bed.

"That was a great meal," he said, lying on his back next to her. "I'm so glad you told me that you wanted a nice meal."

"It was wonderful. You know, we don't take enough time for us. Just us, no case, no job. Thanks for dropping all the talk once the main course came. It was worth it."

They dozed for a while, enjoying being satiated. A half hour later, he got up and got a glass of water. She'd rolled to her side and looked at him with soft eyes. He put the glass down and kissed her. She didn't hold back.

After the kiss, she mumbled something about being lucky to be in love with an amazing guy, and started unbuttoning his shirt. They kissed again and he pulled her close. He hadn't felt her body against his like this since coming to Arizona.

Her fingers slowly stroked his chest and sent shivers down his body. She pushed him onto his back and rolled on top of him. After another kiss, she sat up and pulled her top off. He reached behind her back to unhook her bra and let it slide off her shoulders. They kissed again. The feeling of skin against skin melted away what tensions were left in his body. She moved slowly against him until he said, "Let's get out of these clothes."

Which they did.

TWENTY-THREE

Monday, October 22nd,
Tucson, Arizona

THE NEXT MORNING, a taxi dropped Vermeulen at the Anthropology building on campus, a four-story brick and concrete structure. He enjoyed the cool morning air, the memory of the last night still lingering. This was the first time in a while that he and Tessa were working together. The last time had been in Mozambique, a few years back. He loved her, that was no question. But he also liked working with her. They fed off each other's ideas and he didn't have those moments when he saw no way forward. And making love was the icing on the cake.

He entered the building and found the storage room in the basement. It was a large room that contained two tables and old metal shelving units along all walls. Zip-tied plastic bags filled almost all the shelves.

A young man sat at the end of one of the tables. He had an open bag next to him and was typing something on his laptop. He looked up and said, "Hey."

Vermeulen returned the greeting and took in the space. Cramped was the only word that came to mind.

"Looks like you're running out of space to store your things," Vermeulen said.

"I know."

"I'm Valentin. Did Alain tell you I'm coming?"

"I'm Freddie. He did. Basic ground rules. Please open only one bag at a time and put everything back before opening the next one. And keep them in order, please. These zip ties can be opened again, just push the little thingy on the top and you can pull them apart."

"Which bags came from the site with the skeleton?"

Freddie got up and walked to the right wall. "The artifacts from site 1846 are on the bottom three shelves. They have green tags. We color-code each site. Knock yourself out."

Vermeulen wondered not for the first time what the detritus of migrants could tell about their experience.

"What do you enter when you catalog an item?" Vermeulen said.

"Name, category, date, time, GPS coordinates and tier."

"Tier?"

"Yeah, if it was on top of something else, below, in the middle, and so on."

Why would that even matter? But anthropologists probably had good reasons for their methods.

"Have you cataloged the items from the skeleton site yet?"

"Yes, do you want to see the entries?"

Freddie was obviously happy to have someone else to talk to. He typed on his laptop and waved Vermeulen over. On his screen was a spreadsheet layout with many rows.

"How many items did you collect there?"

"Exactly seventy-three."

"Was that all of them?"

"No, we try to collect a representative sample, emphasis being on *try*."

"Is there a way to narrow it to items that were close to the skeleton?"

"I can try. We all know the skeleton's coordinates by heart."

He typed something on his laptop, swiveled it to show the screen to Vermeulen and showed him the new list, now considerably shorter. It contained several gallon water containers, marked as black.

"Why are these water containers black?"

"The white containers are like beacons in the sunlight. A Border Patrol agent with binoculars can see them miles away. Once that news made the rounds in Mexico, the guys who supply the migrants switched to black plastic and charged more. The beauty of the market at work."

"You mean there are shops that supply migrants?"

"Not so much shops as open-air markets. In Altar or Fronteras, supplying migrants is a cottage industry. Backpacks, blankets, water containers, flashlights, batteries, cheap cellphones with American SIM cards, you name it."

Vermeulen checked the list again. There were several entries for 'Papers.'

"What are these?"

Frank looked at the lines. "Just papers we found. Might be a receipt, a list, whatever."

"Can I see these?"

"Sure, they're on the bottom shelf."

Vermeulen crouched down in front of the shelf and pulled out five small baggies. Each contained one piece of paper.

He didn't even have to open them. The first was a

cash register receipt from a Walmart in Mexico City. As far as he could make out it was for a backpack and energy bars he recognized from the US. The second bag contained a slip with a phone number. It began with two fives, a space and eight more numbers. That wasn't the pattern for US numbers.

"Did you check on this number?" He said.

Frank shook his head. "Nope. Nobody is working with these artifacts yet. So far, they are just stored. Eventually a graduate student will start working with these and write their thesis. What is it?"

"Looks like a phone number, but not a US number."

"Probably a Mexican one. Does it start with a double five?"

"It does."

"That's the area code for Mexico City."

Vermeulen sat up. If Luca flew into Mexico City, this number might be his contact there. It was a stretch, but not impossible. He copied the number into his notebook.

The third bag contained another receipt, this one impossible to decipher. In the fourth one, he found a piece of plasticized paper. It looked very much like the data page of a passport. Vermeulen examined it carefully. The paper had intricate pink markings. There were bite marks along the edges and just one bit of the machine-readable code: PAMDALUCA<<.

The final bag contained a piece of the same pink patterned paper. It wasn't plasticized, it could be from an inside page of a passport. All it showed was a stamped airplane icon in faded green, a red stamp "10 SEP" and, below that, a green "MéX."

"These are pieces of a passport. How come they weren't picked up by the sheriff's deputies?"

Frank shrugged. "No idea. The two deputies were a bit half-hearted about searching the site. I guess they figured it was just another dead migrant." He looked at the GPS coordinates on the tag. "According to the tag, this was found about a yard from the skeleton."

"And you didn't inform the sheriff that you found this?"

"Sorry, I wasn't part of the team that went to the site. They just bagged and tagged. Like I said, nobody has evaluated these artifacts yet."

Vermeulen took photos of all the documents he found and put the baggies back on the shelf. He thanked the student and called for a cab.

Back at his motel, he sat at the desk and stared at the images of the passport fragments. LUCA was obviously the last name. But the first five characters were a puzzle. A quick Wikipedia search solved that puzzle. MDA was the country code for Moldova and PA simply meant "passport."

The discovery was a bit of a downer. They knew already that the skeleton belonged to Luca and that he'd come from Moldova.

The other passport piece, however, provided new information. It looked like a visa stamp issued at an airport, most likely Mexico City. The red stamp was a date. He checked the Spanish spelling of the months of the year. Luca had entered Mexico on September 10. That was five weeks earlier.

Next, he called the Mexico City phone number he'd written into his notebook. He used the motel phone. Better to have that number show up than his own cellphone number. The phone rang for a few moments, then a male voice said, "*Bueno*?"

"Hello. Do you speak English?" he said.

There was a pause on the other end. Then the voice said, "Wait."

He waited until another male voice said, "Who are you?"

"I found this number and I want to know who it belongs to."

"You were not given this number?"

"No, I found it."

"Then we have no business."

"Wait," Vermeulen said. "Did Mihaly Luca from Moldova call this number?"

"We have no business."

The receiver was quiet.

Vermeulen stared at it; that was strange. It was not the reply he'd expected. If it was a regular number of a migrant's family, they would've wanted to talk to him. If it belonged to someone who was involved in ferrying Luca to the US, they would want to know how and where he got this number. But someone saying that they didn't have business with him didn't make sense. Not even an attempt to find out who he was; strange indeed.

TWENTY-FOUR

Monday, October 22nd,
Southern Arizona desert

TESSA BISHONGA SPENT the early part of her Monday morning in a cramped van full of students and their professor. She was sitting up front next to Ponce who was driving the van. Being the oldest person in the vehicle wasn't a big surprise. She rarely thought about her age, but sitting in close proximity to students less than half her age reminded her of the fact that she wasn't like them anymore. And she was glad about that. She also realized that being in a comfortable relationship and settled rather than jetting off to assignments felt good. She was still writing, she still had her finger on the pulse of social upheavals.

She didn't envy the students their youthful energy. So much of it ended up spent on worries and concerns that, years later, turned out to not matter all that much. A couple of them were staring at their phones, but the remaining five were talking to each other loud enough for her to hear the conversations. She remembered herself at that age. Her days at Mulungushi University in Kabwe seemed both long ago and only barely in the past. She remembered being homesick and quiet. Kabwe seemed far from her parent's home in Ndola. In reality it was only a little more than a hundred miles, but for a young woman who'd never been away from home it might as well have been a thousand miles.

These students didn't seem homesick. The loudness of their conversation wasn't an attempt to hide such anxieties. It was that odd combination of innocence and entitlement that made many American students want to save the world without ever asking if it needed saving in the first place. She'd seen plenty of them in the wild.

"Tell me about this article you're working on," Ponce said. He was a little shorter than Bishonga, had unruly black hair and a black full beard. Unlike some professors she had known, he didn't mingle with the students, at least not while they were in transit.

"Two colleagues and I are working on the militarization of borders worldwide. What that does to population movements and, as I'm beginning to see, how it influences the behavior of criminal organizations."

"You've come to the right place. Here criminality and hardening of the border are two sides of the same coin. Don't ask me which came first."

"Wouldn't it be the demand for drugs in the US?"

"It could be. There are also the repeated economic crises that cut into Mexican living standards. But whichever way you look at it, criminal organizations have always played a role."

"And now those cartels are global in reach and have relationships with each other."

Ponce quipped, "Like criminal diplomacy?"

She laughed. "Sort of. We don't usually use trust and criminality in the same sentence. Maybe we should. In diplomacy, there are meetings, memoranda and treaties to ensure mutual understanding and compliance. How does that work for criminal association working in different countries, how do they know that the agreement will be upheld?"

"Doesn't the mob usually break kneecaps if someone screws them?"

"That and worse, but how do you do that across borders?"

Ponce nodded. "Good point. How do you think it's done?"

"Probably reciprocity, you do me a good turn and I'll do you one."

"That doesn't solve the kneecapping problem, though."

"I guess hired muscle takes care of that. But how do you hire it?"

"Maybe the dark web," Ponce said. "From what I hear, you can buy everything there, why not an assassination team?"

"You may be right. What do you know about the cartels? Ever encounter them in your work?"

"This is the most unforgiving environment I know." Ponce shifted in his seat and pointed to the undulating desert landscape outside, its dryness masked by the shrubs that somehow found enough water to survive. "The cartels know that and don't hang out here. Sure, they control the guides and most everything else, but I haven't met any of them. By the time we show up, the migrants and whoever guides them are long gone. What do you hope to learn here?"

"Each desert has its own character. I want to get a sense of this one. I know it sounds superficial, but I want to get the setting right for this story."

The van hit a hole and shook the nine passengers to the bone.

"Hey Prof, look where you're driving," one of the male students yelled.

Ponce shouted back, "No complaints from the cheap seats. It's not like these potholes are marked."

The shakeup reminded Bishonga that they were in difficult territory. The track they were following was meant for four-wheel-drives, not an aging university van.

The laboring engine indicated that they were driving up an incline. She looked and out of nowhere, a mountain had appeared.

"Where did that come from?" she said.

"It's always there," Ponce said. "The vastness of the desert kind of plays tricks on your eyes. From the distance it just looks like a little berm to get over, but once you get there, you see that it's a couple of hundred feet higher."

They reached a plateau on the top and the van stopped. Bishonga saw a white/green Border Patrol SUV, a pickup with a trailer holding two ATVs, and a truck with a vaguely military-looking structure and a tall mast on its bed. Attached to the mast were several antennas. The high pitch rattle of a generator cut through the desert silence.

"A Border Patrol surveillance station," Ponce said. "They know we're coming."

An agent climbed from the SUV.

"Hey, Ponce, how many today?" he said.

"Seven students and one visitor."

"Who's the visitor?"

"A journalist interested in our work."

"She got ID?"

Bishonga stepped out of the van and said, "Sure do."

She handed the agent her green card and her Zambian passport. Although she was legally in the country and could go anywhere an American could, she held her breath while the agent inspected the documents. It was the same when she arrived at JFK. The agents had all the power and could refuse entry or detain you on some flimsy excuse or other.

The agent raised his eyebrows as he perused the passport. "Never seen a Zambian one." He flipped through the pages, looked at the photo, and checked the last entry stamps. "You been all over the place." He checked the ID page again. "You know it's gonna expire in eight months? Better get a new one soon." He handed back the documents and nodded to Ponce. Bishonga exhaled quietly.

"You're all set," the agent said. "I'll radio the patrols to tell them you folks are roaming in the area. Any specific destination?"

Ponce gave the agent a pair of coordinates and they got back into the van.

"How do you know where to go?" Bishonga said.

"I don't really. We've plotted all sites we've visited and that gives me a sense of the routes taken by migrants. The rest is speculation. The coordinates I gave the agent are my way of keeping them happy. They'd like to know who's messing about in their little corner of the borderlands."

The van stopped fifteen minutes later in a dry wash next to a lone shrub, maybe ten feet tall. A mess of leaves lay on the ground around it. They climbed from the van.

"This is a blue palo verde," Ponce said, pointing to

the shrub. "It leafs out after a rain and then loses all foliage again."

"How often does it rain here?" Bishonga said.

"We're actually just past monsoon season, but so far, we've only had a little moisture. The massive rainfalls haven't materialized."

"Monsoon? Really?"

"Yeah. You don't want to be caught in one out here. Flash floods, wind storms, you name it. You know it's coming when it gets humid."

"Wow, I didn't know."

The students gathered around.

"You know the drill," Ponce said. "Walk in a star pattern and keep your eyes open for artifacts. First finder gets the prize."

The students groaned. Bishonga smiled. Whatever the prize was, none of them wanted to win it. She participated in the exploration and walked away from the van.

Like everyone else, she'd covered all exposed skin and wore a hat. It was very hot, but she didn't sweat. It was too dry for that.

A hundred feet from the van, a deep silence enveloped her. As much as she strained to hear, there was no sound. She half expected a hawk screech, because every movie with a desert scene featured that. But this wasn't a movie.

A hundred feet further, that silence began to weigh on her. Her brain told her that the students were right behind her, but it didn't mask the pang of loneliness that pierced her heart. It came on fast and startled her enough to make her turn around and check that the others were still there.

They were.

She looked forward again. The vastness facing her had an aching, unnerving beauty. She was a mere speck in the landscape, inconsequential, mattering as little as the grains of sand under her boots. And if the desert had its way, she'd turn into sand too.

As quickly as the feeling of loss arose, it ebbed again. The heat replaced any sense of beauty. She thought of the migrants, who braved this landscape to get to a better place. She kicked a small rock. It tumbled a few feet. Wisps of dust drifted across the ground, like the souls of people who crossed here and lost their lives.

She was yanked from her morbid musings by a din that sounded like an outboard motor. She looked back again and saw three ATVs descend into the wash. They stopped at equidistant points around the van, like a posse circling outlaws. Six white men in camouflage outfits, carrying assault weapons, clambered to the ground. They approached Ponce.

The students had seen them too and walked back to the van. Bishonga stayed at her spot, leery. Better to assess a situation from a distance than to rush in. In this country, confrontations with armed white men generally didn't turn out well for dark-skinned people.

Ponce was talking to the men, looking all solicitous, at least that's what it looked like from where she stood. The students seemed to know the drill and didn't say anything. There was some gesturing by a couple of the armed men, but it seemed harmless. She started to walk back to the group.

One of the men took a look around and fixed his eyes on her as if he'd only just seen her. He stared a long moment as if a Black woman didn't belong in this desert. He yelled something she didn't understand. She slowed, her skin tightening. The man yelled again, something about hurrying up. Her mouth went dry. This wasn't going to be easy. She slowed even more. No reason to give him any satisfaction. Yes, escalation was often a bad idea, but for now respect trumped that, even if it made her heart beat against her rib cage.

"Hurry up, we ain't got all day," the man said and moved toward her. The words were innocuous enough, but his tone tightened her stomach.

"Then leave, nobody is stopping you," she said.

She saw Ponce making a face. He seemed anxious. "She's with us," he said.

The man ignored him. His assault rifle was slung over his shoulder, he also carried a pistol, holstered on his belt. He was in his late thirties, and a little bulky around the middle. She could see him laughing at a Saturday barbecue, a beer in his hands. Just as unnerving as those smiling white men posing on lynching postcards. Two of the other vigilantes had middle-age bulges, the rest looked leaner and restless, like discharged military unable to leave their wars behind—a strange image.

"You better behave, or you gonna be sorry," the man said.

His tone was sharper, nastier. Probably never had a black woman talk back to him. She said nothing. But her ears roared with rushing blood. He came closer and stopped six feet away from her.

"You one of those illegals from the Congo? Just rounded up some of those over the ridge yonder. Came with a large group of Hispanics. We held 'em until the Border Patrol could arrest them. Show me your ID, or I'll make a citizen's arrest and hold you for the authorities."

"Who are you?" Bishonga said, her voice much steadier than her composure.

"I'm Frank Welch, Commandant of this unit of the Arizona Border Protectors. Show me your ID." He unholstered his pistol.

"Nice to meet you, Mr. Welch. I'm Tessa Bishonga. May I see *your* ID, please?"

That caught Welch by surprise. Good. She'd put him off balance.

"I'm not gonna show you my ID," he said.

"Why not?"

"You ain't got no authority to demand it."

"Good point," Bishonga said, her knees feeling weak, but her face still firm. "I don't. And neither do you. So we're even."

Welch turned around to look at his fellow vigilantes. A couple of them smirked. This wasn't a good sign. He pulled the pistol from its holster.

"Don't mess with me," Welch said.

"You gonna let that black bitch talk back to you, Frankie," one of his men said.

She could tell by his clenched jaw that Welch wanted nothing more than prove his buddy wrong, to make an example of her. He was right on the edge, his gun pointing at her chest.

"Mr. Welch," she said, willing her voice calm. "We both know you're not going to shoot me. There are eight witnesses here. I'm pretty sure you're not going to kill all of them. The Border Patrol checked my ID about thirty minutes ago. They know we're here. So, let's just agree that neither one of us has the authority to demand the other's ID and be on our respective ways."

Welch opened his mouth and closed it again. A long

moment later, he holstered the pistol, raised his hand, made a circular motion and said, “Move out.” The vigilantes mounted their ATVs.

Moments later, the ATVs crested the rim of the wash and their roar was all that reminded them of the Arizona Border Protectors.

Bishonga exhaled violently, her heart racing now that the threat was gone. The students stood motionless. Ponce had an awkward grin on his face, as if trying to hide the fact that he hadn’t intervened. None of them had.

The student with red hair broke the spell when she stepped forward and said, “I’m Megan, and I want to thank you for showing me how to stand up to bullies.”

Bishonga couldn’t muster any sympathy. “Why didn’t you say anything? You don’t stand up to bullies by watching, you do that by acting.”

TWENTY-FIVE

Monday, October 22nd,
Ciudad Obregón, Sonora, Mexico

CAMILLE DELANO HAILED a ride to the Soriana supermarket at the southern edge of Ciudad Obregón. Soriana stores seemed brighter and friendlier than the Walmarts. Maybe it was simply the color scheme. Reds and yellows beat blues and grays any day. She found the pay phones near the snack area and the restrooms.

There was a new message. The same voice simply said that the *Cartel de Jalisco Nueva Generación* had agreed to her terms and that she should be at the discus thrower fountain by the Naigari Lagoon at five in the afternoon to take possession of the money.

She didn't fall for that. No negotiations, no threats? No cartel worth its name would choose that route. This was a setup. There would be no money. The CJNG thought she was some dumb blonde they could kill or worse to send a message.

After circling through the store, she went back to the pay phones and dialed the series of numbers from memory.

The voice at the other end said, "Management."

"I have an update on the Moldovan situation."

"One moment."

After the requisite number of clicks and hisses, another voice said, "What is the update?"

"As far as I could ascertain, the *Cartel de Jalisco Nueva Generación* was responsible for the death of the Moldovan. Through my contacts with the local cartel, I demanded the million dollars in payment. I just heard that they agreed."

"Why are you calling, then?"

She shook her head. Could they really be that stupid? Why'd she ever taken this job?

"This is a setup. There were no negotiations, no threats. They have no intention of paying. I think this may be a case for their Chechen hit squad."

"Are you sure?"

"Yes, I know as much about the cartels as an outsider can. They will not pay."

"We've charged the Moldovans for your double fee. They'll want more than just your gut feeling for that much money. Go to the meeting. Then report back. Or we'll take your fee back."

She put her hand over the receiver and took a deep breath. Her pulse ramped up in anger.

"You want me to walk into an ambush?" she said, her voice barely concealing her ire.

"Since you know about it, it won't be an ambush. You have a contractual obligation, which we will enforce."

Just as she'd thought, the Chechen hit squad was meant for her too. That answer shouldn't have felt like a slap in the face. She was a professional, she knew the rules. Nevertheless it did. She should've said no when management first contacted her. It was too late now. She'd agreed, thinking it'd be a one-off matter. That turned out to be a bad miscalculation.

"There's another development," the voice on the phone said.

"What now?"

"It appears that Valentin Vermeulen has become involved."

Her skin tingled as if struck by lightning. Vermeulen?

"How?" she said.

"We don't know, but he testified before a grand jury in Bisbee in relation to the Moldovan's skeleton."

"Where's that?"

"A couple of hours from Tucson. But we understand he's staying in Tucson."

She was quiet. Vermeulen in Tucson? Her mind reeled. She had to steady herself against the wall next to the phone. All those revenge fantasies she'd nurtured over the past six years? They stood a chance to become real. The man she hated most was only half a day's drive away.

"Are you still there?" the voice said.

"Yes. Processing this information."

Going after Vermeulen meant going back to the US. And that would make her life trickier. For one, Management had more of a sway north of the border. Her contract would be a lot more enforceable there. She'd also have to use her last clean identity—not a good strategy, unless she had a way of getting a new one. She didn't. Those connections had disappeared when she ran seven years ago.

But all that paled when put against the chance of getting even with Vermeulen.

"Okay," she said. "I'm going to the meeting, but I can tell you already there won't be a million dollars to be had."

"If that's how it unfolds, so be it. We need you to try so we can keep the Moldovans on board. After that, we've fulfilled our obligations and they can pursue whatever they want."

She pulled her card from the phone and left the supermarket.

Outside she paused.

The odds weren't good. She'd been to the lagoon a few times. It was a popular weekend spot. Food and ice cream vendors, all kinds of rides for kids, and a zip-line for the adventurous folks. During the week it might be less busy, although it was a warm day and by five in the afternoon there might be a good-sized crowd. More possibilities for collateral damage, but also a better opportunity for her to disappear fast.

The outlines of a plan began to emerge.

Yeah, this was doable. She felt energized. The thought of confronting Vermeulen was fuel to her mind.

She hailed another ride to the Chapultepec district of the city, asked the driver to stop two blocks short of her destination and walked in the opposite direction to a hair salon she used before. The cartels probably hadn't yet infiltrated the ride-sharing companies, but better to be safe than sorry.

She was lucky and only had to wait twenty minutes. When it was her turn, she asked for a cut and coloring. The stylist told her that her blonde hair was *muy lindo*, and was she sure she wanted to dye it brown; she was.

An hour and a half later, Delano left the salon with a brown pixie bob, looking both like herself and not. The cut accentuated her chin and lengthened her face. It made her lips look thinner. An acquaintance would have to look twice to make sure it was her. Anyone having just her old picture wouldn't even stop to look.

Next, she hailed a ride to a car rental place. For this job and the getaway, she needed her own car. She rented a small blue four-wheel-drive—some forgettable Korean brand—which could handle at least some difficult terrain. Her rapid exit might well involve rough roads.

The city had been a good home for the last years. As long as she managed her affairs quietly, she was safe. Now that she'd outed herself, she couldn't stay. The pressure to ally with one or the other cartels would be immense. And when it came to clubs, she was a strong believer in the Groucho Marx rule. Seven years outside the US—was that long enough? It probably wasn't. She wouldn't be on top of the wanted list, but that didn't mean that the authorities had lost interest in her.

She drove to her apartment and lugged her suitcase to the car. The last time she had to skip town, all she could take was her go-bag. Being able to pack and take her clothes felt like a small luxury. On the way to the Naigari Lagoon, she stopped at a small grocery store and bought five large potatoes.

TWENTY-SIX

Monday, October 22nd,
Ciudad Obregón, Sonora, Mexico

SHE ARRIVED AT the lake a couple of hours before the appointed time. She wore jeans, a short-sleeved shirt and sturdy sneakers, a casual look that fit the location. She drove around the fountain once, taking in the area around it. The most convenient parking lay to its west. Toward the south, a wooded area extended to an amusement park and toward the zip-line. A small gelato stand stood just to the north.

The discus thrower on the plinth was a replica of the ancient Greek discobolus. A nude guy, twisted tight, ready to explode and hurl the disc in his hand. The statue was surrounded by twelve columns that supported a dome-shaped structure of steel rods. The street circled around it as if it were a tiny Arc De Triomphe.

The fountain part of the discóbolus was turned off. The basins were empty. The columns were made of solid stone. They would protect her from bullets, but also shield potential opponents.

There were more people around than she'd expected. Lovers strolled by the lake, kids were on rides in a small amusement park, thrill seekers were lining up for the zip-line. A big pier jutted out into the lake some forty yards. It had attracted a few visitors as well.

The statue was the worst possible place to conduct this transaction. She entertained no illusion that the CJNG would just drive up and hand her a briefcase with money. There'd be a confrontation. Guns would be fired. She had three extra magazines in her purse just for that eventuality.

Ordinarily, crowded places would rein in potential shooters, but the cartels were notorious for acting without regard for innocent bystanders. The amount of collateral damage would be through the roof, which would get the police involved. They would have to, even if they'd been paid off—not that she'd planned on a shootout. Her Glock was no match against the firepower the cartels usually deployed.

She needed a diversion and an escape route. The zip-line looked promising. She could melt into the crowd and zip across the lake to her parked car. It would take binoculars to recognize her in the harness hanging from the steel rope. And, if they recognized her, she'd still be a moving target. The downside of escaping via the zip-line was the fixed destination. She couldn't change her mind. If they recognized her on the line, they would be waiting for her by the time she arrived at the other side of the lake.

As it turned out, the zip-line was a non-starter. There was a line to get on. Even though the crowd could've served as a cover, she still had to climb up a narrow steel tower, fully visible from the ground, a perfect target.

She drove around the southern edge of the lagoon, past the wooded area, and parked at a different, smaller lot across from a baseball diamond. As much as she believed in careful planning, there were too many unknowns in this scenario. She didn't know how many men would show up. Her only real advantage was that they wouldn't recognize her. She had to capitalize on that.

The little amusement park was a big hit. There were kids on the merry-go-round, on the little Ferris wheel, and waiting in line at a large slide to get their mat to glide down the four undulating lanes to the bottom.

Delano sat in one of the canvas gazebos sprinkled around the grounds. Two boys, maybe twelve or thirteen, were lurking near the entrance to the slide. They seemed alone, and by the looks of it, they had no money. They tried to sneak in behind a couple of other kids, but the woman taking the money had their number and yelled at them to get lost. They waited, their faces scared and upset.

Delano got up and walked over to them. Their clothes looked raggedy, their black hair messy—kids from the wrong side of the tracks. One was a little taller than the other, both had an expectant smile on their face as they watched her approach. Delano didn't disappoint.

"You want to slide," she said.

They noted her accent and smiled. A *gringa* tourist. It was their lucky day. She gave them a couple of bills, which they proudly presented to the woman at the slide. They got multiple tickets and had a great time zooming down the lane, racing each other. After three rides, their money was gone. They came back to her. If she was good for one round, why not another?

"I have a little job for you," she said.

"For money?" the taller one said.

"Yes, for money, two hundred pesos."

"For each one?"

"Yes, for each of you."

"What job?"

She checked her watch. It was four twenty. She took the potatoes from her bag.

"In forty minutes, some black SUVs will pull up here." It was a guess, but black SUVs were the standard transport of the cartels. The CJNG wouldn't be different. "After the passengers get out, sneak behind the SUVs and stick these potatoes into the exhaust pipes."

"Secretly?"

"Yes."

"Four hundred pesos."

She couldn't help but smile. The little sneak had just doubled the fee. She shook her head and said, "Three hundred." He nodded with a big smile. "Make sure nobody sees you or catches you," she said. The kid laughed. They were street kids, nobody ever saw them and if someone did they weren't going to get caught.

She gave each two hundred pesos and pointed to the empty bench where she'd been sitting and told them the remaining money would be there afterwards. Worst case scenario, they took the money and ran. Best case scenario, she'd get away.

She walked to the gelato shop to the north of the fountain. Two young couples, maybe eighteen or so, had just bought cones and were taking selfies. She'd picked them because they, too, looked like they could use some money. She said hello and showed them a fake ID from a US university that didn't exist. Would they like to earn two thousand pesos each? They would. *Good.*

"At five after five, I'd like you to pretend you fight with each other. Very loud. Keep it up for ten to fifteen minutes, then you can stop."

"Why?"

"I'm an American professor and I'm studying crowd behavior. Will people walk away? Will they try to intervene, mediate? I've done this in many other countries."

The couples nodded—the white-coat effect. If it was university research, it was legit. They checked their watches.

"Where will you be?" one girl said.

"Over there, filming it on my phone." She pointed at the bench by the trees where she'd been waiting. She gave each couple their money and went back to her bench.

At a quarter to five, three black SUVs circled the discobolus and parked in the "No Parking" zone just south of the legal parking area. It was a perfect spot. The drivers were seeking the shade of the trees, but those same trees also gave cover to the two boys with the potatoes. She nodded at them and they hustled into the woods. She put two one-hundred peso notes under a rock under the bench.

The next phase was about to begin.

TWENTY-SEVEN

Monday, October 22nd,
Ciudad Obregón

FOUR MEN WEARING black jeans, polo shirts and baseball caps got out. Although the polo shirts varied in color, the men clearly were on the same team. They were all armed; their holsters were unmistakable.

Two headed for the fountain, the other two spread out, checking out the people in the vicinity. They didn't bother with subterfuge. Everybody knew what was going on. The advance commando making sure the place was safe for a cartel bigwig. Laguna Naigari was popular with *narcos* too. Only a few visitors looked up.

Delano belonged to that group. She glanced up from her phone and met the eyes of one of the men surveying this section of the area; there was no sign of recognition. She sat about fifty feet south of the fountain and had a clear view of it.

The sweep of the surroundings complete, one of the men reported back to the last of the SUVs. The remaining crew took up positions on the outside of the fountain, roughly at the compass points with the fountain as the center. They faced away from the statue, a very defensible position.

The door of the third SUV opened and a young man in a lightweight suit stepped out. He carried a black briefcase. It was five o'clock. All the players were on the field now. Briefcase man and his driver brought the total to six. The driver remained by the car. Briefcase man walked to the statue of the discus thrower.

From where Delano sat, the columns concealed three of the four gun men. The biggest obstacle was the guy standing between her and briefcase man. He was older than the others and faced south, looking into her direction. He would see her walk to the fountain, would stop her, and tell her to go elsewhere.

At five minutes after five, shouting sounded from the direction of the gelato shop, a bit timid at first, then with more gusto. The girls were yelling at the guys at the top of their voices. Those kids were veritable actors, ready for the stage, that was for sure.

The guy facing Delano heard the clamor. He turned to briefcase man, eyebrows raised. Briefcase man nodded. The guy went to investigate. That left the path clear for her.

The other men's attention wavered. The couples were putting their all into the fight. They could have filled an auditorium with their voices.

The square formed by the bodyguards was losing its shape. They drifted toward the fight. A couple of them looked at each other, knowingly. Maybe they were married and knew that sound well. Or they were getting ready to marry and having second thoughts.

When all eyes were focused on the sparring couples, Delano got up and walked to the fountain, not straight to briefcase man but the left edge of the plinth. Briefcase man eyed her, didn't see anything to worry about and turned back to the screaming. Delano sped up; three steps straight, then two to the right. Briefcase man looked again, but he was too late. She slipped between him and the plinth, her Glock pushing hard into his lower back.

"Walk with me. No sudden moves, you know the drill."

Briefcase man did as he was told. She pulled him past the columns and marched backwards towards the trees. His men quickly realized what was going on but couldn't do much. She made sure to keep behind briefcase man so he became a shield against his goons.

Delano had figured him for a hard man. You didn't become a cartel money man being soft. But the guy felt flabby, not just his body—squishy as if he still had his baby fat—but also in his demeanor. The muzzle of the Glock in his back had taken the wind out of him. He let her pull him backward without any resistance. Maybe he was the son of a boss—a bit pampered, the apple of daddy's eye, having advanced to this position without paying his dues.

The two couples had done their job and were looking for her, checking to see how she liked their performance. They'd worked hard, like an audition. Seeing her dragging a cartel goon must've told them that she wasn't your standard American professor. They melted into the crowd.

The goons, on the other hand, came after Delano and briefcase man.

"Tell your men to stop where they are," Delano said and jabbed briefcase man with her Glock, like an exclamation point.

He did, a bit halfheartedly.

The goons listened, a bit halfheartedly.

It was more of a slowing than a stopping. Maybe

briefcase man's dad was a hard-ass boss, who would hold them responsible for his son's wellbeing.

Delano had no intention of dragging out this slow-motion pursuit. "Open the briefcase," she said. The briefcase man hesitated. She raised the Glock and stuck its muzzle into his right ear. She worked the trigger just a little bit. To his ear it must've sounded like someone loading a piece of artillery. He flipped the two clasps; the briefcase flew open and spilled fat bundles of cut newspapers.

There was no surprise there. What cartel would bring a million bucks to some unknown woman because of some vague threat of a death squad? Delano wasn't angry. A little prep, five potatoes and twenty-four hundred pesos were a small price to pay for telling the CJNG that the Moldovans were very unhappy with their actions.

She dragged briefcase man deeper into the trees, turned her head to the right and pulled the trigger. The left side of his skull blew out. She was sprinting to her car before he hit the ground.

The first return shots weren't far behind, too far off to be a threat. She heard a bullet smash into a tree four feet away. A small dust cloud bloomed a couple of yards ahead of her, but no real danger. Even good shooters miss at ten feet, standing still. Five guys shooting while running were odds she liked.

She ducked behind a tree. Two of the men were getting close. Maybe they'd been sprinters in high school, who'd stayed in shape. She steadied her arm against the tree trunk, grabbed the Glock with both hands, aimed, fired, fired again, aimed at the second guy, fired and fired again; two double-taps. Both went down. The remaining three dropped as if tripped by an invisible wire.

She'd had her own crew, back in Newark: some Eastern Europeans, who were hard as hammers, and just as dumb. So she knew what the three were thinking. Briefcase man was dead; they were still alive. No use getting shot after the guy they were to protect had already been offed. Sure, the boss would be pissed, but he's the one who made the mistake of underestimating that *chica*. There'd be a big funeral and then everybody went back to business, because Americans bought drugs like every day was Black Friday.

She got into her small SUV, fired up the engine, backed out of her spot and shot into the street with a squeal. It was tempting to drive past the fountain and see the guys staring at their SUVs, wondering why they didn't start. But she wasn't vain enough to be stupid. She drove city streets in a random pattern until she was out of town and took highway fifteen to Hermosillo and onward to Nogales.

It was midnight when she reached the border in Nogales. She parked the rented SUV on Calle Internacional, a few hundred yards from the border crossing. Stashed inside the lining of her suitcase was a sealed plastic bag. She used her nail file to extract a passport, a Delaware driver's license and two credit cards in the name of Sophie Tate, her last set of fake papers.

She destroyed the Vivian Beltrán papers with a pang of regret. They'd served her well and getting another clean set of papers like that was difficult and would cost a lot.

Drivers licenses were easy, if all you wanted to do

was fool a bouncer at a club. Getting one that held up at a traffic stop, required a bent DMV employee. And they weren't cheap.

The bottleneck for a passport was the birth certificate. Even a county clerk in Podunk, Kansas, didn't mail you the birth certificate for a name you got off a dead infant's tombstone anymore. There were checks and questions all along the way these days. The short of it was that getting a watertight new ID involved a lot of moving parts, most of which she didn't have access to at the moment.

At least the credit cards were no problem. Her bank on Grand Turk Island gave her what she wanted as long as her lawyer there filed the proper names with the shell company she set up to control her assets.

She dumped the scraps of her old passport, driver's license and credit cards into the sewer, grabbed her suitcase and headed for the pedestrian entrance of the border post. The line wasn't long. The female officer behind the computer did a double-take comparing her blonde hair on the photo with her new color and cut. She shrugged and slid the passport through the scanner.

"How long have you been in Mexico?"

"Nine months."

"Business or pleasure?"

"Pleasure."

"How did you enter Mexico?"

"Oh, it was a pleasant trip. I started in the US Virgin Islands, from there to a couple of other islands, and then to the Yucatan."

"Did you go by air?"

"No, by boat. Much more memorable that way."

She'd created that scenario on the way to the border

because the system wouldn't show a departure for her passport. It must've worked because she saw the beginning of a smile forming on the officer's face, who probably dreamt of such a trip.

"Anything to declare?"

"Nope."

"Welcome home."

Delano passed through the custom area and was back in the US for the first time in seven years. She found a cab and asked the driver to take her to a rental car office. Only one was open twenty-four hours. She rented a beige sedan with her new credit card and drove to Tucson.

Along the way, she tried to assess how vulnerable she was. Luca's bones in the hands of the authorities was bad news. It wouldn't take long before they connected him to the previous episode seven years ago in New Jersey. All it took was a call to the right department, and they'd dig up the old case file and her name would be back on the front burner. Whatever happened to Camille Delano? Was she still a fugitive?

Now that Vermeulen was involved, that would happen sooner than later. He could get the whole case reopened. Before you knew it, New Jersey police and the FBI and the whole alphabet soup of agencies would have her on their radar.

As far as she knew, that hadn't happened yet. And the only way to keep that from happening was to eliminate Vermeulen. By the time she'd reasoned herself to that conclusion, she'd reached Tucson, where she pulled into the lot of a chain motel off Speedway Boulevard at two in the morning.

TWENTY-EIGHT

Tuesday, October 23rd,
Bisbee, Arizona

AT 9A.M. VERMEULEN walked into the county attorney's building in Bisbee. He was miffed about having to do the drive again, but MacMillan had reminded him that the subpoena was still active. So he got into his car early and set off. Tessa had still been in bed by the time he left. The encounter with the Arizona Border Protectors had rattled her. He'd asked about it, but she didn't want to talk.

The administrative assistant tried to tell him that MacMillan was busy, but he walked right into his office anyway. MacMillan sat behind his desk, holding a cup of coffee in one hand and a cookie in the other.

"Can I be done with this?" Vermeulen said.

"The investigation is still ongoing. We're pursuing all leads. You are still a material witness."

"And what leads are you pursuing?"

"I'm not going to tell you what's happening with the investigation."

"Why not? I'm a witness, not a suspect."

MacMillan squirmed a little and put down the coffee cup.

"What?" Vermeulen said. "I've told you all I know."

"Yeah, so you say, but I still think you haven't told us everything."

"Don't be ridiculous. You got some notion that I know something about the traffickers. I don't know what your game is. Are you hoping to make a big bust and become famous?"

MacMillan looked at the cookie in his hand as if he'd just been caught taking it.

"You've got to be kidding," Vermeulen said. "You better do some real investigating instead of sitting around and drinking coffee. If you did that, you would have found out that Mr. Luca entered Mexico on September tenth. That's about five weeks ago. Enough time to be trafficked, kidnapped, killed and left to rot in the desert."

MacMillan put down the cookie.

"How'd you find that out?"

"By following the leads, not something I can say about you or the sheriff. There were fragments of Luca's passport among the detritus collected by Ponce's students. If I were you, I'd check with the Mexican authorities and get the flight information. Did he come straight from Moldova? Did he need a visa? If so, did he apply or did someone else? If you want to get to the bottom of this case, you've got to do the work."

MacMillan looked flustered.

"You don't even know where to begin, do you?" Vermeulen said. "There's got to be a Mexican consulate in Arizona, check with them. Make it an official request. Tell them it's urgent. Put it in writing. Have someone hand deliver it."

"There's a consulate in Douglas."

"That might just be a branch. Do they have one in Tucson?"

MacMillan nodded. "A Consulate-General."

"Well, there you go. Draft the request and be nice about it."

MacMillan pushed himself up from his chair. "Mister Vermeulen, you don't tell me how to do my job."

He wasn't as tall as Vermeulen. His attempt to radiate resolve came off a bit pathetic.

"Somebody has to," Vermeulen said. "Because you're not doing it."

"I take exception to that."

Vermeulen had the next retort on his tongue, but held back.

"Okay, MacMillan, we're on the same side here. But it would help to know who applied for his visa."

"Did he even need one? I think Mexico lets Europeans in without visas."

"That's easy to find out." Vermeulen pulled out his phone and tapped the search request. A minute later, he smiled. "There we go. Yes, Moldova is one of a handful of European countries of which Mexico requires visas. Hang on." He tapped more. "Oh, there isn't a Mexican embassy in Moldova. That means they must've applied for the visa elsewhere. Probably Romania. It's next door."

Vermeulen looked up from his phone. "Okay, contact the consulate-general about the visa. This is one thing you can do today that would help your investigation."

"Do you think the traffickers applied for his visa?"

"I'm almost certain. The last time I spoke with him, seven years ago, he didn't seem like he had the wherewithal to organize such elaborate travel on his own.

Besides the traffickers would want control over his movements."

MacMillan nodded in agreement. "Good, I'll pursue that. And I'd really appreciate your help."

"What's in it for you?" Vermeulen said. "I mean it's not the first dead migrant you came across. I can't imagine you mounting this kind of investigation for every dead person found in the desert."

"It's a murder case."

"I know, but is this your first murdered migrant case?"

MacMillan looked away.

"I didn't think so. Why are you pushing this one?"

MacMillan coughed. "I wasn't going to, but Deputy Perez made a big stink about it. He thought the New York number was the crucial difference. He hates traffickers and thought the number belonged to the American part of the trafficking network. I agreed and thought it was a good case to pursue."

"Well, I have testified. You know that I'm not a trafficker. So we better be done. I'm leaving in two days."

"But you continue to provide valuable information."

Vermeulen shook his head. "I'm not your investigator. Use the Deputies."

"I guess you're right. So, yes, we are done. You're free to go home."

Vermeulen left the office, got back into his car and drove back to Tucson. Good to have one thing out of his hair.

AROUND THE SAME time William Morgan the Third checked the ICE website for the A-numbers of the three boys he'd interviewed at the office building in Tucson.

He was prepared to see them transported to faraway places, and was surprised that they were being held at a shelter in Tucson.

He picked up his phone and called Alma Rodriguez.

"I have some good news," he said. "The three boys I spoke with last Friday have been transferred to a shelter in Tucson. I can represent them during their trials. At least they'll get a proper hearing."

"That is really good news." He could hear the relief in her voice.

"I know. All this moving around of children leaves them totally disoriented. Without representation, they don't even know how to state their case. On the other hand, Western Refuge is not a place for kids. But at least I'm close by and can represent them."

"Thanks for letting me know. My morning is a little brighter."

"What's happening over in your shop?"

"We've organized another volunteer mission to drop water and food in the desert. The van is about to leave."

"Are you going?"

"No, somebody's got to do the paperwork. Our volunteer coordinator is leading the drop."

"Are they still being hassled about dropping supplies?"

"Yeah, on and off. The militias are a pain. Men who hate foreigners, and guns. A terrible combination."

"How about the Border Patrol?"

"The volunteers run into them occasionally, but the encounters are usually civil. On the other hand, I've seen video of Border Patrol agents destroying the supplies we and others leave. So it's not clear cut."

"Nothing is these days, is it? Well, I'm going to visit

those boys around noon and see how they are doing. Contact with the outside is always important."

"Would you like some company?" she said.

He couldn't believe his ears. "You want to come?"

She must've heard the excitement in his voice. "Sorry, not me. I was thinking Valentin and Tessa. You know she's writing about what's happening here. I'm thinking getting inside a shelter and publicizing how we treat the weakest of the weak would help our cause."

"Oh. I guess so."

"Let me call them and give them your number."

Morgan wasn't sure he liked that suggestion. He'd have preferred Rodriguez. Unlike her, he didn't think additional publicity would make any difference. Those who hated the current administration already knew what was going on, and those who adored it weren't going to be swayed by more information.

What a crazy world, he thought.

Growing up he thought of his father when he thought of the Republican party, well-to-do people, who wanted low taxes and a strong military. Advocates of the night watchman state, keep our stuff safe but stay out of our business. Sure there had been the abortion fanatics, but they weren't part of his family's circle. Watching the faces at the president's rallies now, he realized that a massive shift had happened. Those weren't your country club Republicans anymore, more a mob whose adulations had turned a con artist into a messiah beckoning everyone to a crude and mean future.

His phone rang. It was Tessa Bishonga, asking to come along.

TWENTY-NINE

Tuesday, October 23rd,
Tucson, Arizona

BISHONGA ARRIVED IN the parking lot of Western Refuge at ten sharp. She'd always thought of a shelter as something temporary, something built for emergency housing, and she remembered the pictures of tents and kids walking in lines between them. This building was large and looked solid, permanent. It could've been a motel at one point. The arrangement of windows and the concrete dividers between them looked like the divisions between rooms. The structure enclosed an interior area that was not visible from the street.

Morgan was waiting for her at the entrance.

"Was this a motel once?" Bishonga said.

"Close, it used to be college housing. It does have that look, doesn't it?"

"Have you been here before?"

"Yes, I had some clients here. There are about 300 children in this facility. Every room is used and some extra spaces have been converted into sleeping quarters."

"What happens here?"

"The kids eat and sleep, get what the authorities consider education, and wait. The lucky ones are placed with relatives or in foster homes. The others stay here while they wait for their trial."

"Hmm. This is a bit different from what I expected. I remember those pictures of tents."

"Yeah, those were Border Patrol shelters. When the administration suddenly decided to put the parents in prison for crossing the border, they had to separate the children, but they had no place to put them. They change policies all the time, and every time they do, it's a brand new mess. Unbelievable."

They walked into the building and stopped at a reception desk. He explained to the woman behind the desk that he was the attorney of three minors and that Bishonga was his assistant. The woman didn't make eye contact as she wrote down their particulars and tossed them two visitor passes.

Bishonga kept her head down and followed Morgan's lead. If the outside looked like a motel, the inside had a different vibe. She could tell that people were locked up in here. The solid doors were an obvious sign, and there was something sad in the atmosphere, like a suppressed yearning. It made her skin clammy despite the air conditioning. An employee took them from the reception area through one of those solid doors to another part of the administrative building. They passed a medical clinic and arrived at another door. The walls were painted in bright colors and there were cartoon characters on windows that offered a glimpse at classrooms, but those didn't make up for the weight she felt walking through this space.

Their guide opened the door. Another employee waited on the other side. Their guide said, "attorney visit."

"No, it ain't," a voice said. Bishonga had heard this voice before.

She was standing behind Morgan and looked past him. The blood in her veins thickened as if she'd been thrown into an ice bath. She closed her eyes. Was this a mirage, an image transported from the desert and put in front of her? Was it a trick of nature? She looked again. No, it was no mirage, no trick of nature. The face was still there.

It was the face of Frank Welch, commandant of the Arizona Border Protectors. Instead of wearing desert fatigues, he wore a green polo shirt with the Western Refuge logo and tan pants. His face, though, wore the same sneer she'd last seen in the desert.

"She ain't no attorney," Welch said.

"I'm the attorney," Morgan said, a confused look on his face. "She's my assistant."

"She ain't your assistant either."

"I'm not sure what your problem is…" Morgan leaned closer to read the name tag, "…Mr. Welch. But I know my assistant. We're here to consult with my clients. I'm sure you don't want to obstruct that visit."

"She was in the desert yesterday with a bunch of students."

Bishonga had finally wrapped her mind around the fact that the man who accosted her in the desert was working for a private shelter company.

"What I do in my spare time doesn't interfere with my job, Mr. Welch," she said. "Apparently neither do your extra-curricular activities. Or do your employers approve of your illegally rounding up people in the desert?"

"I'm the director of this facility," Welch said, as if that obviated an answer to her question.

She turned to Morgan. "Mr. Welch here is the commandant of the Arizona Border Protectors. On the weekend he and his fellow goons round up migrants in the desert and turn them over to the border patrol. While they're at it, they also harass people who don't look like them."

Morgan looked at Welch, at Bishonga, then at Welch again. He opened his mouth, hesitated a moment, then closed it again.

Bishonga fixed Welch with a hard stare. "Do you also round up kids in the desert?"

"What if I do?"

"So you are handing children to the Border Patrol, who are then sent to this shelter?" She turned to Morgan and said, "Talk about job security. He's creating his own source of profit. That's privatization for you. To me it looks like conflict of interest. Is that something your law firm can do something about?"

Morgan had that deer-in-the-headlight look. He must've been aware of it because he roused himself and said, "We're here to see my clients." He gave Welch the paper with the three names on it. "Please bring them to a private room."

He stepped past Welch.

"Not gonna happen," Welch said.

Morgan spun around. "And why not?" His voice with an edge now that Bishonga hadn't expected.

"You can go in, but not her. She needs to be vetted before she's allowed contact with minors."

"Surely that doesn't apply to attorney consultations."

"It does if I say so," Welch said, the sneer turning into a mean grin.

Morgan didn't have a reply ready for that.

Bishonga, hand in her pocket, said, "I'm sorry, what did you say?"

"It does if I say so." The grin on Welch's face was getting broader.

"What does?"

"That you can't come in here."

"Thank for repeating that so clearly," Bishonga said. "I recorded it. We'll see how the Department of Health and Human Services feels about your interfering with attorney privileges. And while we're at it, let's see if their background check also included your racist activities on the weekends."

Welch's face froze into a grimace, the smirk half replaced by furrows of anger.

Morgan said, "So, what's it going to be?"

Welch turned around. The employee led them to an empty classroom. Bishonga could feel the wake of the anger boiling inside Welch.

Bishonga and Morgan waited for the boys in a room that could've been in any elementary school. A map of the world hung above a white board and flags from many countries were tacked to other walls.

She could tell that Morgan wasn't happy about the confrontation between herself and Welch.

"Sorry, I guess there was no way to avoid this," she said.

"Not your fault. I just try to avoid making waves. It's easier to get my job done that way. It's appalling that the director of the shelter is a white supremacist, but

I've got to focus on the kids." He looked at her. "Wait. Did he harass you in the desert?"

"He did." She didn't want to say anything else.

"Oh man, that must've been scary. A bunch of guys with guns? And here he is running a shelter. That's just nuts. But we got to focus on the clients. Believe me, I've heard more nasty comments going in and out of immigrant detention facilities than anywhere else in my short legal career. I swallow it and focus on the clients. They're the ones who'll suffer if my ego gets in the way."

"So you want me to just shut up when a racist militia guy messes with me?" Bishonga felt a wave of fatigue wash over her. What would it take?

"I don't know," he said. "My job is hard enough as it is. If the staff want to make my job difficult, they can do so easily. All it takes is one misplaced letter in a name. They tell me that the person isn't here, or that I'm not properly registered as their legal representation, stuff like that. I'd drive here, be turned away, a whole morning wasted. I'm at their mercy and therefore I make as few waves as possible."

She saw the same fatigue in him that she felt herself. She swallowed her anger and said, "Of course. You have to deal with them every day. I'm here only once. I understand."

He gave her a grateful smile, but didn't say anything.

They waited until Welch brought the three boys. The sour expression on his face didn't leave any doubt as to his mood.

The two García boys seemed to be in pretty good shape. They smiled when they saw him and plopped into their chairs. Claudio López lagged behind a bit, cautious, checking out what was next in store. His face lit up when he saw Morgan, then he noticed Bishonga, and his smile was replaced by suspicion.

Once all three were settled, Morgan introduced Bishonga as a journalist who was interested in their plight. The conversation that followed was slow. Since Bishonga's Spanish was spotty, Morgan translated for her. Manuel García seemed to be the one more comfortable in English and filled in where he could.

Apart from being locked up, which none of them liked, they seemed healthy. The staff treated them okay, the food was better than the cheese sandwiches they'd gotten in Phoenix, but still bad. They hadn't gotten their phones back from the Border Patrol, but they could make phone calls once a week.

Did they contact relatives in the US? The García boys nodded. Their uncle was coming to get them in a few days. He first needed to pass the vetting by the authorities. Claudio López said he'd talked to his cousin, but the cousin couldn't take him yet. She was trying to work out something.

The classes offered some diversion, but they were boring. The teachers weren't good. They could play soccer once a day. The staff kept girls and boys separated except for class, recreation, and meal times. Milton García seemed most upset about it because there was this girl he liked a lot. His brother ribbed him, saying that she'd never even noticed him.

Did they get to speak to a social worker or a psychologist? Yes, they'd talked to someone, but it was in groups and the person's Spanish was hard to understand.

Any other troubles? Yes, some of the girls were talking about a male employee touching them. Morgan's ears pricked up.

"Which one?"

The boys shrugged.

"Did the girls complain?"

Manuel said, "Maybe. They scared. Don't want old man touch them."

Morgan made a note to follow up.

"Anything else?" There was one altercation. During soccer, one of the boys' shirt was pulled up. Those near him saw the tattoo "Mara 13" on his chest. Immediately several boys jumped him and started beating on him. The staff called some kind of code and a bunch of them flooded onto the field and stopped the fight. They weren't nice about it either.

"Kids is here 'cause they run from Mara 13," Manuel said. "They see Mara 13 tattoo, they want fight."

"Was the boy with the tattoo a member of Mara 13?" Bishonga said.

Manuel didn't believe so. "Mara 13 take kids and tattoo 'em. Kids no want to. Mara 13 no listen. After kid get tattoo, he can go home no more, he go to Mara 13."

The matter of fact manner with which Manuel relayed that story shook Bishonga. Those poor kids were scarred for life and didn't stand a chance of getting asylum. A gang tattoo on their body was considered evidence of membership and that meant a very short trial and deportation. It didn't matter how much they protested that they had been forcibly tattooed.

She looked at Morgan and saw that his face was a rigid façade. Maybe such stories didn't shock him anymore. Would her heart become as calloused doing this job every day? She couldn't imagine it but she could also imagine that becoming too involved would lead to a quick burnout. That wouldn't help anyone either. What a messed-up system it was.

Since no date had been set for the trial, there was little else to discuss. Morgan promised to come back in a week, or sooner if there was a possibility for release.

Back in the car, Bishonga said, "What are you going to do about the staff member touching girls?"

"I'll file a Freedom of Information request for any paperwork regarding sexual harassment complaints. Then I'll inform the ACLU."

"How long will that take?"

"Your guess is as good as mine."

"What about the kid with the tattoo?"

"His chances are lousy. The proceedings are so fast, there's no way to explain the context of El Salvador or Honduras, the power of the gangs there and the fear the kids have. He'll be deported back to the very place he fled."

"How can you stand to do this work?"

"Somebody has to do it."

Bishonga looked him in the eyes. He tried to look away, but couldn't. She'd found that fenced-off part deep inside him. He had to rub his eyes.

She put a hand on his shoulder.

"You are a good and brave man. I can't say that strongly enough. But I beg you to talk to a trusted friend or a therapist. Do it sooner than later. Your survival depends on it."

THIRTY

Tuesday, October 23rd,
Tucson, Arizona

THE DRIVE ON I-10 had become boring, nothing but dry desert, hot asphalt, and, as Vermeulen neared Tucson, tract housing as monotonous as the yellow stripes spooling off in the middle of the road. It was about noon when he took the Speedway exit and stopped at a light. He sent a quick text to Tessa, telling her he was almost there, then nosed the car east toward their motel.

He had just turned onto Stone Avenue when he heard the first shot. It was a gun shot, not a car backfiring. Cars didn't backfire anymore, just like they didn't have carburetors anymore.

He slowed. To his left was a city park. Was it a drug deal gone sour? He craned his neck, didn't see anyone in the park. No surprise, it was kind of hot.

Maybe it was some wiseass squeezing off a round. From what he remembered, anyone could carry a gun in Arizona, openly or concealed, no license required.

Next thing, he saw a beige sedan shoot out of the parking lot of the chain motel at the end of the block. The sedan cornered hard and zoomed toward him. Seconds behind it came a large black SUV. A man was leaning out of the passenger window and fired a long salvo from a submachine gun. The rear window of the sedan exploded as did those of two cars parked on the street.

The sound of automatic weapons fire triggered Vermeulen's war zone memories. His reflexes kicked in immediately. He screeched to a stop and folded his six-foot frame across the middle console, pressing down as deep as he could. The engine block was his best shield against stray bullets.

The Doppler effect told him when both cars had passed him. He raised his head and looked back. The sedan swerved back and forth. That didn't deter the guy in the black SUV from firing again. Vermeulen saw the rear tires of the sedan disintegrate. It drove on its rims for a few yards, then stopped. The black SUV stopped as well.

The guy came out of the passenger side door, holding his automatic weapon like a commando, and approached the sedan. He was about twenty feet away when the driver's door of the car flew open. A woman rolled out on the street, pistol in hand, and fired three shots in rapid succession. The gunman went down hard.

The driver of the black SUV jumped out, also carrying a submachine gun. He sprayed the space in front of him with a hail of bullets. Like most untrained men, he was enamored with the full-auto setting on his gun, unaware that pulling the trigger in full-auto pulled the muzzle of the gun up. The thirty or so bullets he'd fired missed the woman.

She, in turn, adjusted her prone position, held her pistol in both hands and fired twice. The driver joined his pal on the asphalt.

The silence that followed was eerie. Even more so because nobody ran out on the street, nobody stood in doors, nobody screamed. Maybe automatic weapons fire was not uncommon in Tucson and people knew to stay low and inside. Or it was that time of day when people were engaged elsewhere.

Vermeulen opened the door of his car and surveyed the vista of wreckage. The sedan was shot to pieces, it wasn't going anywhere. At least three parked vehicles were shot to pieces. The black SUV stood there, doors open, engine running. It had Arizona plates.

The woman got up. She had short brown hair and looked no worse for wear. He thought of asking if she was okay, but decided against it. She had a gun and knew how to use it. The sound of sirens echoed from the distance. Somebody in the surrounding houses had made a call.

She must've decided that being the survivor of a massive gun fight wasn't a role she wanted to play for the police. The cops would be here soon. She grabbed two bags from the sedan, hurried to the black SUV, put one foot on the running board and glanced at Vermeulen. For a second, their eyes locked. She did a double take, hesitated, then got inside and drove away as if she had no worry in the world. She turned a left at the next intersection.

Vermeulen sat still, but his heart was beating against a rib cage that felt too small. He'd seen that face before. The hair was shorter and the wrong color, and, yes, it had been seven years since he'd last seen it. But it wasn't a face he was liable to forget. Certainly not in the current context.

What the hell was the Broker doing in Tucson?

VERMEULEN HEARD THE sirens and drove the one block to his motel. He didn't want to be the sole witness to a shootout. If the interactions with the Cochise County attorney taught him anything, it was to not get involved. The police would question him, get every detail, ask again…and again. The same question would just be posed in new ways. He knew the routine.

He drove the block to his motel, pulled into the parking lot, parked the car away from the street and strolled up to his room as if nothing had happened.

Inside, Tessa waited for him. She pulled him into a tender embrace before the door had a chance to close.

"Are you okay?" she whispered into his ear as if afraid the shooters could hear her.

He returned the embrace with equal tenderness and said, "I am. I'm fine. Nothing to worry about."

They held each other for a minute longer then let go.

"What happened?" she said. "I got your text, next thing it sounds like a war zone out there. Who was shooting?"

"A couple of guys in a black SUV, mostly. Could've been cartel goons. They sure had the kind of weapons cartel guys use."

"They weren't after you, were they?"

"No, but you'd never believe who they were after."

She eyed him with a raised eyebrow.

He told about the woman in the beige sedan, the gunfight, and her escape after killing the two goons.

"And you recognized her?" she said.

"Yup. The hair was different, but the face was the same. That was Camille Delano, the Broker from Newark. Can you believe it? First Luca, now the Broker. The gang's all here."

Tessa had started pacing. Vermeulen could tell that her mind was trying out puzzle pieces to see which ones fit.

"You think the discovery of Luca's skeleton and her appearance are related?" she said.

"If they aren't, then it has to be the most unlikely coincidence in recent history."

"But how?"

"I need some caffeine to answer that question." He went to the coffee maker on the desk.

"Sorry," Tessa said. "I used the last of the bags the room service left. But there's coffee at the reception. Bring me one too."

He opened the door just a crack. Their room on the second floor had a perfect view of the street where the gunfight had happened. Sure enough, several police cars had arrived on the scene. The officers had cordoned off the entire block and two of them were busy establishing the perimeter around the shot-up sedan with yellow tape. Two more were scanning the street for evidence. A third was bagging items, most likely the cartridges from the submachine gun. The street had to be littered with brass. It was a good thing he hadn't waited.

When Vermeulen opened the door to the motel office, he saw a man talking with the attendant. If he wasn't a police detective, he'd be the perfect actor to play one on TV. He had the long-suffering face of a cop who'd seen it all but was still a few years from retirement. His clothes only emphasized that appearance. Vermeulen hesitated a moment, but it was too late. Backtracking would only raise suspicions. He marched on to the thermos, pumped coffee into two cups, put lids on them and carried them back to the door. He'd almost made it when a gravelly voice behind him said, "A moment of your time, please."

Vermeulen turned. "Who's asking?" he said.

"Detective Barney Gumble, Tucson PD. Did you hear anything on the street over the past hour?"

Vermeulen didn't have to ponder his answer for a second. "I only just got here a few minutes ago, sorry. What's the commotion about?"

"An incident on Stone Avenue. We're canvassing for witnesses."

"Oh. Sorry, can't help you there."

He turned and took a step toward the door.

"You sure you didn't see anything, a car driving away at high speed, for example?"

Vermeulen shrugged and gave Gumble the "I'm sorry" face and walked outside. He took the steps to the room two at a time, hurried inside, put the coffees on the table and plopped into the second chair.

"There's a detective downstairs, canvassing. I told him I only got here a few minutes ago."

Tessa pursed her lips. "Are you sure that's a good idea?"

"If I tell them what I saw, we'll be stuck here and won't make our flight back."

"I guess you're right. By the way, I went to a shelter with William Morgan the Third."

"Oh."

"I wanted to see how the most vulnerable victims of the border politics fared."

"I can imagine it was horrifying."

"Outrageous would be a more appropriate description."

He shook his head, "Sadly, I'm not surprised."

"And not just the situation of the children. The commander of the Arizona border protectors is the director of the shelter."

Vermeulen sat up. “He is? That’s crazy.”

Tessa started pacing again. “He was there, smug as only white men can be and refused to let me in. I threatened him with exposure of his border raids and he finally let me in.”

“What a jerk.”

“He’s way more than that.” The way Tessa looked at him told him that his choice of words bothered her.

“What?” he said.

“Forget it. Two more days and we’ll be on our way. I better put those to good use. This state gives me the creeps.”

Vermeulen raised his eyebrows. “The entire state?”

Tessa nodded. “Okay, not the Grand Canyon. But the rest I can do without.”

“Welch and his gang really got under your skin, didn’t they?”

“I don’t want to talk about it.”

“But you’ve been in far dicier situations. And those didn’t spook you.”

“It’s different. Just leave it.”

She turned, sat down at the desk and opened her laptop. Vermeulen could see the document that she’d been working on. Vermeulen knew her well enough to hear the slight change in tone that signaled, “Don’t push me.” But he didn’t heed the warning.

“How is it different?”

“It just is. If you don’t understand that, it’s your problem. Not mine.”

“But you’ve been surrounded by armed men in Darfur. You were held hostage in Maputo. It’s not like you’ve never confronted men with guns.”

She turned, her eyes flashing a warning. "Just leave it." She sat down in the chair facing the laptop.

"Let's talk about it. Tell me what's going on."

Her head swiveled toward him. Her face had turned into a mask. "You don't really want to hear what's going on. You've already made up your mind. You've been downplaying what happened ever since I told you."

"I have not. I'm just surprised. I've seen you face really dangerous situations. I don't see how a posse of weekend warriors would surpass those."

"You're doing it right now. Calling them weekend warriors. That's why I'm not interested in talking any more about it."

"Come on..." He stopped abruptly. The depth of the hole he'd dug himself appeared with startling clarity. Oh man. His stomach clenched at the thought of how big he'd screwed up this time.

Listen first, don't assume.

She'd told him a hundred times. Each time, he promised, but then his impatience or his certainty or his stubbornness would push those words aside like a breeze would a tossed wrapper.

He took a deep breath—then exhaled. Took another breath and said, "Yes, you're right. I'm sorry. I think I'm ready to listen now."

She didn't react. Vermeulen said nothing more. The prickly silence lasted for a long time. He was about to say something because he couldn't stand the leaden atmosphere in the room any longer, but he held his tongue until he saw her face soften.

"Yes, I've faced men with guns all over Africa," she said. "I've been in danger because I put myself in these situations. I knew the risks. I had some degree of control. This was different. You weren't there, you can't know how it felt. This time, I did not purposely put myself in a dangerous situation. I ended up in danger because of something I have no control over, the color of my skin. A man threatened me with a gun because of how I looked. And he would've killed me if there hadn't been eight witnesses."

She took a deep breath and exhaled slowly.

"Ponce said I was with the group, but Welch ignored him. After that, Ponce remained silent and the students just stood by. I've never felt so alone in my life. It took all my strength to keep my composure. That man didn't know me, but I saw a deep hatred in his eyes. He didn't hate me personally, how could he? He hated me for belonging to a group of beings he considers subhuman. That's why this was different. White people like you will never understand what that feels like."

Vermeulen didn't say anything. The urge to apologize again came on strong, but he resisted. The truth of what she said stood on its own. Anything he could say would diminish it.

The silence continued, not prickly anymore, but exhausted, as if Tessa telling her truth had used up all the energy left in the room.

THIRTY-ONE

Tuesday, October 23rd,
Tucson, Arizona

THERE WAS A knock at the door. Vermeulen and Tessa looked at each other. The lodgings weren't secret but nobody knew they were staying here.

Vermeulen said, "Who's there?"

"Detective Gumble."

Vermeulen opened the door.

"Sorry, but I have a couple more questions. Is that green car down there yours?"

"Yes, we rented it."

"Okay. You told me downstairs that you had just arrived and hadn't seen what happened on Stone Avenue. Is that correct?"

Vermeulen's skin tingled. Better be cautious. "Well, the word 'just' may have been an exaggeration. I got to the motel, parked, walked up to my room. The two of us talked about our day so far and then I went down to get coffee. So maybe five, ten minutes had elapsed."

"Sure, we're not quibbling over a few minutes. But either way, you didn't see or hear an exchange of gunfire on Stone Avenue. Is that correct?"

Vermeulen shrugged. "I don't think so. I had the car radio on, playing music. Some satellite station."

"And you didn't see a black SUV, you didn't see men

with submachine guns firing on full auto, or someone else killing said men?"

The moment of truth. Obviously, a witness had seen his car and described it to the police—probably even told them that it drove to the motel.

"No, not exactly."

"How about inexactly?"

"As I said, I was listening to the radio. I heard something that might have been a shot. I stopped and ducked as low as I could. I saw nobody doing anything. I dove for cover and waited for it to stop. Once the shooting stopped, I got out of there."

"But you saw the black SUV, I mean, before the shooting started."

"I saw a big black SUV as I drove away. I couldn't tell you a make or model."

"Okay, a big black SUV. We're getting somewhere. And you didn't see anyone. Because you were smart and ducked for cover."

"Right."

"And you, Miss?" Gumble said. "Where were you? Also in the car?"

"No, I was in the room. I heard some popping sounds, but didn't pay much attention to it."

"Where're you folks from, if I may ask?"

"New York City," Vermeulen said.

Gumble nodded. "Long way from home. Here on business? I reckon it's not for pleasure. Tourists don't come until November."

"Yes, on business," Vermeulen said.

"What kind of business, if I may ask."

"I'm a journalist," Tessa said. "I'm working on a piece about borders."

"You a journalist too?" he said to Vermeulen.

"Uh, no. I'm just tagging along."

"What do you do?"

"I work for the United Nations."

"You don't say. Never met anyone who did that. Well, you folks have a nice day." He turned and walked away.

Vermeulen closed the door, exhaling with relief.

"Do you think we got rid of him?" Tessa said.

"I hope so, but don't count on it. He struck me like the kind of detective who's been on the force for a while, who's methodical, and who's used to digging. If there are other witnesses who saw me, he's sure to come back."

He sat on the bed and leaned against the headboard.

Tessa sat down at the laptop to select their seats on the return flights. It took longer than she'd thought, because the flight departure time had changed. That made their layover in Dallas rather tight. She finally found two seats next to each other on both flights.

"Are you sure Camille Delano recognized you?" Tessa said after she closed her laptop.

"I'm pretty sure she did."

"And is that going to be a problem?"

"What do you mean?"

"You rolled up whatever operation she had back in New Jersey. She might've nursed revenge fantasies over the past seven years. Now that she's seen you, those fantasies could become reality."

"You think so?"

"I don't know the woman. You interacted with her, did she strike you like someone who'd hold a grudge?"

Vermeulen tried to remember the events seven years earlier. He'd first seen her after he met with Jackson at a bar. She was cool and ruthless then, threatening him. He was an obstacle, she needed to get rid of that obstacle. The next meeting was at that doctor's home. There she displayed the same transactional manner. She had her objectives, he was in the way, so he needed to go. He didn't remember her being emotional. The speed with which she'd disappeared told him that she had few if any emotional attachments. If one door closed, she opened another one and went on to the next project. No need to cry over spilled milk or hold a grudge.

"No," he said. "She didn't strike me like someone who'd hold a grudge. For her it was all business. Her crew consisted of hired hands, not very good at their job, if you ask me. She could pick up the few marbles she owned at any moment and move to a different place."

"Why would she show up here, in a shootout with a narco cartel?"

That was the big question. Vermeulen got up and finger-combed his hair. "It has to be related to Luca."

"Nothing else makes sense. But how would she know that Luca's skeleton was found in the desert?"

"Let's think this through." He leaned against the bathroom door. "Luca was trafficked to the US seven years ago. He got caught and was deported. The Moldovan traffickers lost whatever money they had invested in him plus their cut from the unrealized profits. They wouldn't just let him get on with his life."

Tessa nodded. "Remember, Kaminsky said he was tortured. The traffickers wanted their money."

"That's it. They forced him to come back to the US, this time via Mexico. Same deal. They must've contracted with a cartel to ferry him across the border. If the party on the US side was the same, it stands to reason that Delano was involved in this deal."

"Yes. But then another cartel kidnapped him."

"Would that get Delano involved?" Vermeulen said. "She disappeared seven years ago. The FBI couldn't find her. They suspected that she'd left the country."

"Maybe she disappeared in Mexico."

"That's a possibility."

"And now she's here," Tessa said. "I suggest we lay low 'til Thursday and get ourselves to the airport before she gets any ideas."

Vermeulen nodded. He opened his mouth, but a knock on the door interrupted him. He got up and said, "Who's there?"

"Detective Gumble."

Vermeulen sighed and opened the door. Gumble came inside the room this time.

"Sorry to bother you again," Gumble said. "But you weren't quite straightforward with me earlier. A witness told us that she saw you open your car door and surveil the scene, that you were looking quite intently at the aftermath of the shootout. I suggest we start over again, and this time you tell me the whole story."

Vermeulen sighed. This wasn't going well. The worst part? He knew better than to lie to the police. He'd interviewed enough people to know that the truth will come out eventually. Best to make a clean breast of it from the get-go.

"I apologize, Detective. I should've been more forthcoming from the beginning. My only excuse was that I didn't want to get involved because we have tickets to go home in two days."

"And why would you think you couldn't leave town? Are you involved in this shootout?"

A hot flash of anger shot through Vermeulen. How

stupid was he? Why didn't he just stick to the known facts?

"Of course not. I just know that the wheels of justice turn slowly. This had nothing to do with me, with us. That's all."

"Okay, let's start from the beginning. Can I see your IDs?"

Gumble took out his notebook and wrote down their particulars. After that he took notes as Vermeulen told the story exactly as it happened, from the first shot, the small blue SUV zooming out of the parking lot, to the woman getting into the black SUV and driving off.

"Did you see the woman?"

"Yes, but not her face. I wasn't that close, but she had short brown hair, wore jeans and a long sleeved shirt."

"Did she check on the men she killed?"

"No. She just got in their car and drove off. Who were the men anyway?"

"We haven't identified them yet. Their IDs were false, probably Mexican cartel members. Who else drives around with a folding stock AK-47?"

"Wow, that's what they were using?"

"Yeah, you must've seen all that brass littering the street. A fat lot of good it did them. One got killed by two 9mm rounds, the other by three. Whoever that woman was, she knew how to shoot. You sure you didn't see her face? Anything distinguishing besides short brown hair?"

"Sorry, I didn't."

"Anything else you noticed?"

"Yeah, nobody came running to see what's happening. Are people in Tucson used to small arms fire like that?"

"I wouldn't say that, but the cartels are here, that's for sure. People know that and curb their curiosity."

Gumble added a couple more scribbles to his notepad.

"And you were inside the whole time?" he said to Tessa. "No peeking through the blinds? Or stepping out on the balcony?"

"No. I've been to enough war zones to know that bullets travel far."

"You're a war reporter?"

"Yeah, used to be, not anymore, though. I'm choosing more sedate topics."

Gumble made a sound that was half laugh and half snort. "As if immigration is a sedate topic."

He put his notepad away and made for the door. He opened it and, halfway outside, turned.

"What color shirt was the woman wearing?"

Vermeulen, startled, frowned. "You know, I couldn't tell you. All I remember is that it had long sleeves. I thought it looked hot for the weather here."

Gumble nodded. "And you never saw her before?"

"Nope."

"The name Sophie Tate ring a bell?"

"Can't say that it does. Was that her name?"

"It might be, it might not. When are you leaving?"

"Thursday," Tessa said.

"So you'd be here until then, if I had more questions?"

"Sure," Vermeulen said.

"Okay. Next time just tell the truth from the get go. It'd save us both time and trouble."

THIRTY-TWO

Tuesday, October 23rd,
Tucson, Arizona

ABOUT THAT TIME, Camille Delano ditched the black SUV in the long-term parking lot of the Tucson airport and hailed a ride back to town. Standing there, waiting for the car to come, she ran through what had just happened. That the cartel goons were out for blood was no surprise. Killing the guy with the briefcase couldn't go unpunished. Doubly so if his father was high up in the CJNG.

What baffled her was how fast they found her. Crossing the border on foot and renting a new car under a new name on the US side should've interrupted the trail. Why didn't it?

Okay, it didn't take a lot of guesswork to assume that she'd head for the US. Nogales was the closest major crossing, much easier to reach than a California crossing. So it made sense to check there first. The timing wasn't too hard to guess either. A single woman with brown hair coming through on foot after midnight would be memorable.

Getting her name took a little more doing, like finding a bent border official, someone already on the cartel payroll. The CJNG had their established sources. A couple of phone calls and her new name would be in the cartel's hands. The rest was simply a question of access to data and the cartels in Mexico had all the access they wanted.

The only reason she wasn't dead yet was because she never parked in front of her room but two or three rooms away. She'd woken up when someone kicked in the door two rooms to her left. No thinking necessary; grab the go-bag, worm through the tiny bathroom window onto the empty lot behind the motel, and sneak around to the front.

The black SUV was a dead give-away.

She waited until the two goons kicked in the next door and made a run for her car. She'd have gotten away without trouble too, except that room was empty, they came out sooner and saw her drive away.

What a disaster. Way too many bullets fired. Her rental destroyed, and two bodies on the street. Her new identity compromised before she even had a chance to use it properly. The cops would be on this like flies on shit.

And worst of all, Vermeulen had seen her.

The revenge plan she'd hammered out in her head on the drive north depended on surprising him, seeing the fear in his eyes before she put a bullet between them. Now he knew she was in town. The last thing she wanted was a cat-and-mouse game.

But first things first. She needed a place to stay that didn't care too much about IDs and she needed a ride. She asked the driver if he could recommend a place to stay that wasn't part of some national chain with computerized check-ins.

The man thought for a moment and said, "I think I know just the right place."

He took I-10 north, past downtown and past Speedway Boulevard. Several miles further he took the exit and a few turns later pulled into the parking lot of the Orinoco Motel. The place wasn't much to look at, but he assured her that it was nicer on the inside. He was right. She was shown a surprisingly attractive room on the first floor. The bed was decent and the bathroom clean. She filled out the registration slip and paid with cash for two nights. The kid behind the counter—barely twenty and more interested in his phone than his job—did ask for her driver's license, but only shrugged when she told him that her wallet had been stolen.

After showering and putting on what clean clothes she had left, she went to the front desk and asked about a used car lot in the area, intimating that she'd pay cash. The kid shrugged and pulled out the yellow pages.

"Help yourself, I wouldn't know where to send you."

She looked through the pages and focused on the ads that touted a variation of "Bad Credit? No Problem," took a photo of two that seemed right and went back to her room.

She called for another ride and two hours later she was behind the wheel of an eight-year-old Toyota sporting a dealer's plate. The extra five-hundred to let her keep the plate for a couple of days was not too bad for getting wheels without leaving a trail.

Back at her motel room she sat down to make a plan. Vermeulen was a danger to her, not only here but also in the future. Now that he'd seen her, she had no doubt he'd continue the trouble he started seven years ago.

Back then it had taken three days of being on the move, switching from planes to boats, to cars, and back to planes to hide her tracks. She'd killed one boat operator who'd ferried her from St. John in the US Virgin Islands to Tortola in the British Virgin Islands. From there, she had taken a flight to Saint Martin, then to Santo Domingo and finally the Grand Turk Island. On Grand Turk, she had crashed and slept for twenty-four hours. She bought new clothes and got her finances re-jiggered for a life on the run.

In the seven years since, the hatred she'd felt then continued to smolder. Sometimes deep down, other times it flared up. It wasn't the fact that he'd beat her. Hey, you win some, you lose some. That's how it was in the life she chose. What irked her was that he wasn't better or smarter. She could accept defeat at the hand of a better opponent. But Vermeulen wasn't that. She'd nailed him back then. He was locked away and on his way out of the country. And then it fell apart: all because he could call on a bunch of activists to block the street and get the FBI involved.

In her life, no one was ever on the right side. She managed transactions between criminals. As long as she covered her ass, she couldn't care less which one of her clients won or lost. Everybody had a racket going and most could be bought for the right sum. Vermeulen didn't have a racket. That made him such an unpredictable opponent. He'd do things nobody in their right mind would. By the time she understood that, it had been too late.

Seven years later, and here she was on the run again.

Or was she still on the run?

Her left hand had balled into a fist.

The smoldering fire burst into a bright flame.

THIRTY-THREE

Tuesday, October 23rd,
Tucson, Arizona

THE MEMORY OF their fight and the interrogation by Detective Gumble had left both Tessa and Vermeulen deflated. She sat on the bed, and he leaned against the wall by the door.

"What are you going to do about Welch?" Vermeulen said.

"I'm going to expose Welch and his racist militia. I'm going to expose that company for employing him."

"What have you got to do that?"

She grimaced. "Not much, just a recorded snippet of him telling us that he was calling the shots about meeting with detained kids."

He nodded. "I think you should go about this methodically. Is Welch just one case, or is there a pattern? What was this outfit called again?"

"The Arizona Border Protectors."

"Well, you are the online research whiz, there's got to be plenty to uncover. If you want to get started, I'll get us some food. You haven't eaten yet, have you?"

"I'm not hungry. But you're right, let's use the days we have left here to show Welch that he can't harass innocent people with impunity. You can get yourself something, I'll get started."

Vermeulen smiled. That was the Tessa he knew. He also knew she'd want food the moment he'd walk in the room with his lunch. So he set out to get a nice meal for both of them.

TESSA OPENED HER laptop and started with a search for Arizona Border Protectors. In the Trump era, organizations that previously only existed in the shadows felt emboldened to come out into the open. So, of course, the Arizona Border Protectors had a web presence. The site spouted the usual nonsensical mix of incorrect readings of the constitution, blatantly racist venom, and a highly selective history of the Arizona border region. She found no membership list, but there were plenty of photos, showing members strutting with their automatic weapons, sitting on ATVs, patrolling a piece of desert. A particularly galling photo showed three men in fatigues, big smiles on their faces, combat knives in their hands, pointing at gallon containers of water they had sabotaged.

As she searched for more images, she found one that made the blood in her veins boil. It showed five members, fully armed, surrounding a group of eight border crossers. The Border Protectors were pointing their rifles at them. The migrants were huddled together in a scared clump, the women pulling their children close, the men attempting to shield them.

She knew they rounded up migrants and then called the border patrol to arrest them. Welch had admitted that. But seeing it in action was much worse. She wasn't a lawyer, but this looked very much like unlawful detention and impersonating an officer of the law, maybe even kidnapping. She enlarged the image and identified

Welch in it. If nothing else, that should be of interest to the corporation that employed him.

Vermeulen walked in with bags of food and the smell of cumin and smoked peppers filled the hotel room. Her stomach immediately growled. It must have been loud enough to echo across the room, because Vermeulen said, "Sounds like you changed your mind about not being hungry."

"And if I know you, you brought two lunches, right?"

"Yeah, because I know you."

He spread the chipotle chicken tacos on two paper plates, put out a container of beans and rice, adding two bottles of Modelo Negra.

Over lunch she told him what she'd found out so far. He was impressed.

"That photo of them rounding up migrants could really be important. They have no right to detain anyone. Have you been able to identify any of the other members?"

"Not yet, it's not hard though, an online reverse image search usually does the trick. I'll get to that after lunch. It will be harder to find out if any of them work for private contractors. So far I only know about Welch."

"You'll figure that out. Even if you don't, you can point out to them that Welch has broken the law. The thing with private contractors is that many of them are publicly traded companies. They have to maintain a proper image. They don't want to scare off investors. I can imagine that their contract with the Federal Government requires certain minimum standards in terms of employee vetting."

"Even under this administration?"

Vermeulen made a face. "I guess you're right about that. For all we know, there are folks like Welch working for the Border Patrol."

It took another half hour and Tessa had identified all six of the men who'd been in the desert on Saturday. That was the easy part. The hard part was linking them to any particular job. Searching for the names alone was totally unproductive. She narrowed the search by adding qualifiers like the state and the cities around Tucson. Next, she searched for the names in connection with Western Refuge. That also generated too many hits. Limiting the search by location gave her a shorter list. It was still a slog through press releases, employee updates, volunteer opportunities, the usual corporate stuff one finds on their websites. An hour later, all she could confirm was that Welch and one other member of the militia worked for Western Refuge—not a rousing success, but better than nothing.

She decided to expand her search to include all private contractors of ICE. There were about fifty of them, handling everything from incarceration to food service to mental health counseling to tech support. Although the dollar figures were vague, the total contracts amounted to billions of dollars. Just Western Refuge took in upward of a half a billion dollars for shelter services all over the Southwest. A couple of hours later, she had confirmations for four of the six men.

"Here's what I have," she said. "Two of the men, including Welch, work for Western Refuge, and two work for LaPointe Corrections Corporation. What's the next move?"

Vermeulen, who'd just come in with a coffee from downstairs, and was reading news updates on his phone, perked up. "Just call them and ask for comments on their employment of militia members."

"This is going to be a sidebar to the main project on militarization of borders. Something along the lines of *America's war on immigrants has been farmed out to the private sector.*"

Vermeulen smiled. "That ought to get a response."

"There's another angle, even more worrisome. According to the boys Morgan spoke with, some girls have complained about unwanted touching by a male staff member. I guess I can ask them about their background checks. I'm not sure if that will generate any results. I'll just get the standard corporate reply. I think I should go back and follow some of the female staff when they come off work. Ask them informally if they heard something."

"Or you could file a Freedom of Information request about any information to that effect."

"You're right. Morgan is already doing that. I'll wait to see what he gets."

THIRTY-FOUR

Tuesday, October 23rd,
Tucson, Arizona

At mid-afternoon Camille Delano found a salon and had her hair bleached. She wouldn't look like her old self until it all grew out, but at least she got rid of the brown. Afterwards, she drove back to where she'd seen Vermeulen last, the site of the attack. She passed Stone Avenue, which was still blocked off. She could tell that the wreck of her rental had been removed. Two cruisers still stood there. The cops must've canvassed the entire area and gathered every one of the spent cartridges on the tarmac.

The fact that her last identity was now revealed made disappearing harder, but not impossible. Tomorrow Vermeulen would meet his fate. All she had to do was find him.

After that she'd disappear again. The Caribbean was nice in October.

Why had Vermeulen been in this neighborhood? He'd been driving south on Stone Avenue, the opposite direction of her escape route from the motel. Theoretically, there were hundreds of reasons, but most of those could be eliminated easily. The Stone Avenue wasn't a major thoroughfare, but not a side street either. Locals would use it as an alternative to Main Street or

Sixth Avenue to get downtown, but visitors like Vermeulen wouldn't know that. He might have been lost, but who got lost these days with a navigation app on every phone? Chances were he'd been at this spot for a specific reason.

She didn't know why he was in Tucson. If he still worked for the UN, he had no reason to be here. Maybe he had a new job. Or perhaps he was on a vacation trip? Somehow, she couldn't imagine Vermeulen going on holiday, certainly not in Tucson.

The UN would be the first lead. She looked up the OIOS number on her phone and called.

"Office of Internal Oversight Services, how may I direct your call?"

"Hello, I'm trying to reach Valentin Vermeulen, one of your investigators. Could you connect me?"

"One moment."

She'd reached an internal phone. After three rings, she was dumped into a voicemail system, asking her to leave a message or press zero for further options. She did that and ended up with the voice who'd answered the phone.

"Hello again," Delano said. "Mister Vermeulen isn't answering, and I have an urgent message. Can you tell me if he's in. If not, I'll call the other number I have."

"One moment."

A second voice answered. "Investigations?"

"Hello, I'm trying to reach Valentin Vermeulen. He doesn't answer his phone. I just want to know if he's in before I leave a message. It's rather urgent."

"May I ask who's calling?"

"I'm Vivian Beltrán. We worked together on a case a few years ago." Even though the Beltrán identity was useless in Tucson, the receptionist at the UN wouldn't know that.

"Mister Vermeulen isn't in his office. But he checks his voicemail regularly. Leaving a message is fine. Do you want me to connect you?"

"Do you know if he'll be back today?"

"I'll connect you."

"Wait, is he in town or away on an assignment?"

"I can't disclose that information."

"Can you tell me when he'll be back?"

"No, sorry. I'll connect you to his voicemail now."

"Thank you."

Delano waited until Vermeulen's phone rang again and ended the call before the voicemail system started. So he still worked at the UN—which made his presence in Tucson odd. He had no business here or any other place in the US.

Maybe it was simply a vacation.

But why this neighborhood?

She checked the map on her phone. There were no tourist attractions here, nor any restaurants beyond the usual fast food chains or tiny hole-in-the-wall places. That left accommodation. On her phone she only saw one motel, just a block south of the place from which she'd escaped.

She drove past the other motel, checking the parking lot. He'd driven a green sedan. There wasn't one on this side. She circled around the block and got a different view of the lot. And there it stood; a green metallic sedan.

She pulled over a block away and dialed the motel's number. A man answered and she asked to be connected to Mr. Vermeulen.

"Just a moment." A couple of seconds later, he added, "Please hold."

Delano hung up as soon as she heard the second ring.

It seemed too easy. She could have taken any motel room in the city, so could he. At the same time, her choice wasn't random. She wanted an anonymous chain, not located near obvious places like the airport or the bus station. Near the city center, but off the main streets was a logical choice.

As she looked at the motel, she saw a man coming up the stairs and walking along the second story balcony. That man had the height and stature of Vermeulen. She counted the number of doors from the staircase—seven. That was the last bit of information she needed.

She drove back to the Orinoco motel.

Now that she'd found Vermeulen, the energy that had kept her going through the past couple of days faded. The hunt was over. The next thing was making a plan. And for that she needed a clear mind. She took a hot shower, dried off, and slid under the covers. Five minutes later she was asleep.

TWO HOURS LATER, she woke up refreshed and got dressed.

Part of her just wanted to drive to Vermeulen's motel, knock on his door and shoot the bastard. Get it over with, then she would drive to the airport, fly to Puerto Rico and from there to Grand Turk Island. The left side of her brain nixed that idea; better to have a plan, how to get in, how to get out. If there was one thing she learned about Vermeulen, it was not to make any assumptions. Things had a way of going sideways when he was around, and she needed to be prepared for that.

The best time would be early in the morning—four or five, before he was awake. Drive up, kick in the door, kill him and get out; easy plan.

What if the door frame was too solid? It's not much of a surprise if you're kicking the door but the frame didn't give way. Vermeulen would be awake and she'd hurt her ankle.

Okay, drive up, bang against the door, yell, "Police. Open up." The door opens, kill him, get out.

What if he didn't open the door? He was a suspicious character. He'd want to see an ID. No problem, shoot him through the peephole. That should do it; nah, too iffy.

Wait outside in the car until he leaves. Kill him as he gets into the car. Nope, it could be broad daylight then. Witnesses would be everywhere.

Rig his car to blow up. That would be neat—except she hadn't got the material or expertise to do that; too late to hire local muscle. Besides, that'd be expensive.

She circled back to banging on the door. The police had probably talked to him about the cartel shooting. They must've canvassed the neighborhood. There might be witnesses who saw him. So an early morning visit from the police might not be totally unexpected.

She needed to be facing him as she pulled the trigger. What good was revenge if you didn't see the terror in his eyes, the recognition that his life was about to be extinguished? That's why the sniper approach was out of the question.

Five in the morning, either kick in the door or do the police routine, then watch him die.

There was also the question of getting out of town. Flying out of Tucson was iffy. The Sophie Tate ID was associated with the shot up car. The cops were looking for her. They might not get the airlines to report her, but there'd be foot patrols about with her photo in their pocket.

One option would be to drive to Albuquerque or San Antonio, catch a flight there. It definitely would be safer, but also a long drive.

The second option would be a private air charter. She pulled up a website, checked several listings and found a perfect solution: an empty-leg flight from Marana regional airport to Dallas/Fort Worth. No cop would be looking for her there.

It was time for a nice dinner.

THIRTY-FIVE

Tuesday, October 23rd,
Tucson, Arizona

VERMEULEN, NOT HAVING anything else to do, was feeling antsy. Tessa was drafting the article that highlighted both the pervasive use of private contractors and the fact that members of anti-immigrant militia groups worked for them. It was three in the afternoon and he didn't have any plans.

The fate of Luca and hearing about the three kids in detention in a shelter had made the entire refugee crisis snap into sharp relief. At first glance, it seemed overwhelming, the new policies so heinous, they defied any sense of decency. At the same time, it wasn't unique. He'd experienced the crisis surrounding the Syrian refugees first hand and despite the efforts of many to take care of fleeing Syrians, the attitudes of many European countries turned negative. Walls, fences, armed soldiers had become routine in Southeastern Europe. The rhetoric of the governments here and there were depressingly similar. Tessa's general theme, the militarization of borders, applied all over the world.

He felt the urge to do something. There were people needing help and he sat in a motel room bellyaching about terrible policies. Alma Rodriguez was doing something. Her work made a direct difference in the lives of the asylum seekers and border crossers. He picked up his phone to call her and see if he could be of help.

Before he could dial her number, the phone rang. It was the OIOS office in Manhattan. He answered.

"Valentin?" It was Jenna Sibinski, the office manager at OIOS. She'd been managing the investigations office for as long as Vermeulen could remember.

"Yes, Jenna. What's up?"

Jenna paused briefly.

"Just checking in to see when you're coming back."

"We'll be in town very late on Thursday evening. Why?"

"Well, work is piling up. We need you back. Suarez has been asking about you."

"Suarez has?" Vermeulen had an ambivalent relationship with his boss. Although he cleared his cases and helped generate the positive results that sometimes featured in OIOS's annual reports, Suarez could never get used to the unorthodox methods Vermeulen employed. Suarez was usually happy if he didn't hear Vermeulen's name. The fact that he'd been asking about Vermeulen could only mean that his name had come up somehow.

"Yes, he has. I'll tell him you'll be back Friday. Bye now."

Vermeulen stared at his phone. What a strange call. He and Jenna had a good relationship and they usually chatted for a while when on the phone. This call seemed abrupt and just plain weird.

A moment later, his phone rang again. It was a Manhattan number he hadn't seen before.

"Yes," he said.

"Valentin, it's Jenna again. I'm calling from my own cell."

"What's going on? Your last call was a bit strange."

"I know, I just wanted to make sure you were available. I'm outside the office now. I wanted to warn you. A complaint has been lodged against you. Suarez is livid."

"A complaint? I haven't been in the field for over five months. I've been behind my desk. How can anyone complain about me doing paperwork?"

"It's a complaint from the Department of Homeland Security. I overheard the phone conversation because Suarez didn't close his office door. Did you bamboozle your way into a federal facility claiming to be a UN inspector?"

Vermeulen swallowed, his throat suddenly feeling tight.

"Uh, yes, last week. I needed to speak with an asylum-seeker. It was important and it lasted less than an hour."

"Good grief. You should know better."

"It was so fast, nobody thought there was anything wrong with it. I played my role very well."

"Not well enough. Whoever was in charge of that facility called DC to make sure your visit was on the up-and-up. He talked to some muckety-muck in Homeland Security, one of Trump's appointees, who called the Secretary-General complaining about illegal interference with the territorial integrity of the United States. Once he had your name, the Secretary-General called Suarez directly. I don't have to tell you how that went."

Vermeulen's stomach had clenched as tight as a fist. "So Suarez is pissed off?"

"To put it mildly. From what I heard, he promised to

take decisive action to safeguard the image of the institution in the eyes of the Trump administration. So be prepared for serious fallout when you come back."

"Thanks for the warning. It's always good to know when you're about to walk into a buzz saw. Did he say what decisive action he was planning to take?"

"Nope. He was blindsided and you know how he hates that. I guess he's still figuring out what to do with you. Anyway, I gotta go."

"Thanks again, you're the best."

"Oh, I almost forgot, a woman called for you, she seemed keen to know where you were. All I said was that you were out for the day and that she should leave a message. It felt a little weird. Maybe check your office voicemail to see who that was."

"Thanks, Jenna. I'll check."

He ended the call and stared at his phone.

"Bad news?" Tessa said.

"Sounds like it. Our visit to the Border Patrol detention facility didn't remain a local news item. The Agent in Charge there didn't call his superior, he skipped a few rungs in the ladder and went straight to Washington, DC, where he asked about our little visit. They got all territorial and called the Secretary-General, who called my boss."

"And?"

"Suarez wasn't happy; he promised decisive action. I assume he means me."

"Really? Any idea what he means by decisive action?"

"None. It could be another reprimand for my file. I've gotten a couple of those. Or it could be more severe. It'll probably just be a slap on the wrist."

"Don't be so sure," Tessa said. "This administration is run by people who nurture a deep sense of affront, of having long been disregarded. Now it's their time to get even. They'll demand something visible, something they can use to show their supporters that nobody is going to mess with them anymore."

"Yeah, but the UN isn't going to play that game."

"Don't be so sure. US money is still the single largest slice of annual dues."

Vermeulen shook his head. "Not what I need to hear right now."

"Just preparing you for the fact that you might be a sacrificial lamb."

"That's not a role I'm going to play. I'm not going to be trussed on a platter with an apple in my mouth to be presented to Trump."

"That's the Valentin I love."

He got up and gave her a kiss. "How far are you on your research?" he said. "Ready for a break. Dinner?"

"I'm almost done, I haven't got all the information I wanted, but I have enough. I called and emailed Western Refuge for comment and didn't get a reply. Just a few finishing touches. Could you give it a read?"

"Sure. Let me order some Chinese take-out first."

"Great."

He found the menu of the Chinese restaurant someone had pushed under the door, selected the dishes he knew they liked and called to order. The man on the phone told him it'd be delivered in a half hour.

Vermeulen spent that time proofing Tessa's article. It was good. He told her so.

Tessa whooped after she clicked the 'Send' button of her email app. "There. That's done. By tomorrow morning, the world will not only know that white supremacists are working for private contractors that deal with minors and other migrants, but that these men are actively engaged in rounding up those migrants."

There was a knock at the door and their dinner arrived. Vermeulen paid and tipped the delivery man and Tessa cleared the desk to create a semblance of a dining table. Vermeulen always ordered General Tso's chicken from Chinese take-outs, which amused Tessa to no end. "Don't you ever get tired of that? Be more adventuresome, try something new." His reply was always, "Why mess with something that works." Although he'd ended up with some pretty awful General Tso's on occasion, it was a dish that was hard to mess up.

As they were eating he remembered that he'd forgotten to tell her the rest of Jenna's message.

"Oh, one more thing. Jenna told me that a woman called who was eager to talk to me and, when I wasn't there, wanting to know when I'd be back."

"So?"

"I'm pretty sure that was Delano. She played that trick seven years ago. But I don't know why she called. She saw me."

"I told you that woman holds a grudge. Damn, you better keep your eyes open."

THIRTY-SIX

Tuesday, October 23rd,
Tucson, Arizona

It was around five-thirty when Alma Rodriguez called Benita López, Claudio's cousin. She'd gotten the number from Morgan. Thinking that the woman would likely be at work during the day, she'd waited until the early evening. Even then she half expected the call to go to voicemail. To her surprise, a woman answered.

"Benita López?" Rodriguez said.

"Who wants to know?"

"This is Alma Rodriguez. I'm with Arizona Rescue and I'm calling about your cousin Claudio. He's still at the Western Refuge shelter and I'm checking to see if you are going to pick him up."

"Yeah, that lawyer called me about it too. I'm working on it."

"Can you tell me what that means? Do you have a timeline? He's locked up with three-hundred other kids. It's not a good place for him to be."

"I'm not legal. I heard that ICE arrest people who come to pick up kids at the shelter. I can't do that."

Rodriguez sighed. It was true that Health and Human Services, the agency in charge of the kids after they were arrested by the Border Patrol, had shared sponsor information with ICE. Extreme vetting was supposed to weed out child traffickers, but the safety of the kids seemed less important than upping the deportation numbers.

"I understand," Rodriguez said. "But ICE doesn't do that anymore, so you could go and pick him up."

"I don't know who you are or why you're bothering me. I gotta sort out a few things before I can take care of him."

"Do you need any help? There are services available."

"I'm not gonna let anyone snoop around my house."

Rodriguez hadn't expected that level of hostility.

"That's not what I meant," she said. "Claudio had your name and phone number in his shoe when he was taken by Border Patrol. Clearly his parents thought you'd help him. Were they wrong?"

"Just leave me alone."

"But time is of the essence. Being in the shelter damages kids. They think of it as prison. They wonder why they are there. They didn't do anything bad. It's really important."

"Listen, I didn't invite him, I didn't ask for him to come. I don't even know him. I barely remember my aunt in San Salvador. She sure had a nerve to put my number in his shoe. Everybody back home thinks that once you're here, you're living the high life. I got two rooms, I got a live-in boyfriend, who keeps promising me that he'll hit the big times any day now, I got a shitty job cleaning offices every evening. I don't have money to get a bigger place. You want him to sleep in the bathtub?"

Rodriguez swallowed. Just as she'd suspected. She knew that when border crossers contact relatives, the extended family ties usually overrode whatever misgivings the extra mouth at the table might cause. It's an imposition, but it's family. And then, at times, the family ties were so tenuous, the situation so difficult, that there was no space. It happened less often than she thought it might. But it did happen.

"I'm sorry, Ms. López, I understand. I didn't mean to push you into a corner. How would you feel if I contacted a service and found a foster home for Claudio? Maybe just for a while until you get things sorted out?"

The silence at the other end lasted so long, she thought the cousin had hung up. Then she heard quiet sobs becoming louder.

"Ms. López? I'm so sorry. I didn't mean to cause you sorrow. It's okay."

"No," López said between sobs. "It's not okay. My life is so fucked up. I can't even take care of my cousin. My *tía* will tell my mom. I'm so embarrassed. *Dios mío.* How did things get so bad?"

Rodriguez hesitated. There was nothing she could say to make Benita's situation better. But she couldn't just hang up. "Nothing is ever quite as bad as it seems when we feel down," she said. "Let me make a few calls. I'll see if I can find a temporary place for Claudio. If that doesn't work, there are a few resources you can tap into even if you don't have papers. I'll be in touch. I'll call you tomorrow, okay?"

There was more sniveling on the other end, then a loud honk. "Yes, and thank you, Miss."

"Call me Alma. What time do you go to work?"

"I gotta leave in a few minutes to catch the bus."

"I'll call earlier tomorrow."

Rodriguez ended the call. Without warning, she was

reliving the days in Paterson, when her mom was struggling and she was acting out, having all that anger. She had no knowledge of Benita's life, or why she was struggling. But that sentence about everybody back home thinking that living in the US was the high life stuck with her. She remembered her mom's crappy jobs. She remembered her mom talking on the phone, telling her family in Guadalajara she was doing well. It was a lie. But who wanted to admit to being a failure?

She stared out the window. All the crappy jobs she herself had taken. Eventually, she got back on her feet, but it took a while. Would Benita make it?

The reality of the present moment pulled her back. Claudio needed to get out of the shelter as soon as possible. No matter how many colorful images of happy kids Western Refuge had on its website, it was a prison. The kids weren't free to go. They weren't allowed to touch or comfort each other. The damage to young minds was incalculable. All this was known, but it was allowed to continue.

Someday there would be a reckoning. The damage caused by these policies would be tallied, fingers would be pointed, hearings held, and nobody would be held responsible.

It was enough to bring tears to her eyes again. She wiped her eyes and sat up. The present had no time for tears. There were hardly any left.

She opened her contacts app. Claudio needed to go to a foster home, at least until Benita had gotten to a better place. Rodriguez contacted Catholic Charities and inquired about a family who could foster Claudio, a fourteen year-old refugee from San Salvador. She told them that he was staying at the Western Refuge shelter in Tucson. They said they'd do what they could, but didn't sound encouraging. She called Lutheran Services, she called Jewish Family services, all with the same reply. She called Child and Family services. Their answer was even starker. Arizona didn't have enough foster families for its own kids in trouble, never mind refugee kids.

THIRTY-SEVEN

Tuesday, October 23rd,
Tucson, Arizona

CAMILLE DELANO DIDN'T quite have the clothes to go to an upscale restaurant. Getting out of the first motel in Tucson with her go-bag meant carrying the essentials and little else. She rummaged through the bag—mostly dirty clothes. She could really use an extended shopping trip for some decent clothes, but that was out of the question at the moment. Her little black dress that never showed any wrinkles no matter where it was stuffed was the best she could do. It was a bit passé, but so what? She wasn't planning on impressing anyone.

She put on her only non-sports bra, slipped the dress over her head, and tugged a little here and there. The woman in the mirror staring back still surprised her. The bobbed bleached hair just wasn't her at all. Ah, but who cares?

Her go-bag safely stored in the trunk of her car, she drove to a restaurant that had a rating of plenty of stars and looked decidedly not flashy. She wasn't in the mood for stainless steel, birch plywood and halogen lights.

The place was almost like a throwback to old New Jersey. Smallish, dark-paneled, and decidedly male in its atmosphere, a place where old rich men brought the young women who either were their third wives or aspired to become one. Her first instinct was to back out—she didn't need guys leering at her—until she remembered that a benefit of middle age was that the leering eyes would pass right over her and fixate on the twenty-somethings. And this didn't look like a place where older women went to pick up boy toys.

The maitre d' looked at her with one eyebrow raised, "Table for one, Madam?"

She nodded with a benevolent smile. Might as well let him know that she didn't talk to just anyone. He led her into the dim dining area. There was a bar in the rear, where two solitary men sat on stools and nursed their drinks. Either they were early or stood up. About half the tables were occupied. Just as she'd expected, most of the patrons were older men and young women. A few male heads looked up when she walked by, but, also as she'd predicted, they turned back to the younger women at their tables. A few old couples completed the clientele. There were no children in the restaurant. That alone was a good reason to stay.

The maitre d' seated her at a decent table and, before he could glide back to his position near the door, she asked him to bring her a glass of Dalwhinnie, neat, with water on the side. It's all about letting the people around you know who's the boss. He raised the same eyebrow again, but didn't say anything.

A waiter appeared rather quickly with the drinks. She added a couple of splashes of water to the liquor, swirled her glass and took a sip. Ahh—still the smoothest scotch she knew; a nice change from vodka. The menu fit the atmosphere of the place: lots of red meat. It went with the oak paneling. Or was it the other way around? She ordered a small ribeye with potato à la Hasselbacken and braised leeks.

When she finished her whisky, she ordered a glass of Pinot Noir. She let her gaze wander to the other tables, never resting long enough to attract attention. There was a stuffy sadness in the room. The two old couples looked like they hadn't spoken with each other in a long time, probably had separate bedrooms and were disappointed in their kids. The tables with the old men and the young women looked equally sad. The men half-scared their Viagra would let them down that night. The women wondering whether they had to spend the whole night or could slip out early.

There was only one table that intrigued her. The man was maybe sixty, but he could also be ten years older and in great shape. He had a full head of white hair and enough laugh wrinkles on his face to let everyone know that he didn't spend his life fretting about things he couldn't change. The woman was in her late twenties or early thirties and wasn't nearly as dolled up as her counterparts at the other tables. Maybe it was father and daughter or uncle and niece. They seemed be having a genuinely good time.

Good for them; Delano wanted to have those laugh lines when she was sixty or seventy.

Her dinner came and it was excellent. The stars of the online reviews were very much deserved. She settled in for a leisurely meal.

When she got back to the Orinoco motel she felt mellow, a feeling she hadn't experienced in a long while. Gone was that sense of being on edge that never left her during those years she spent in Mexico. The cause wasn't being outside of the US, it was the unfinished business she'd left behind. Now that she had Vermeulen in the cross hairs, that tension disappeared. Funny how the mind worked.

As usual, she parked her car three spots away from her door, although that precaution seemed superfluous. A car with a dealer's plate, no way anyone would link it to her. She sat in the car with the lights off. No matter how nice the meal, she was back on the street. That meant knowing your environs.

The motel was quiet. A few windows were lit up. Most were dark, their curtains drawn. Nobody was out or about. The office was lit up. She could see a woman working the night shift. She got out. The air was warm and didn't smell of anything in particular. A train whistle blew in the distance.

She turned around once. Nothing of importance stood out. Parked cars were in the lot and on the street beyond. A rather massive pickup truck—Whatever had happened to pickups? Had male egos really become that fragile?—stood near the exit of the parking lot. It was one of the four-door types, basically an SUV with a short bed behind it. It was black.

She hesitated. Big black truck—enough to make the hairs at her neck stand up. Her hand slid into the outside pocket of her handbag to made sure the Glock was still there. She walked to the office.

"Hi, could you give me an extra bath towel? I took a bath and used up the supply in the room."

The woman shrugged and went into the back. She came back with the towel. Delano looked out the window at the pickup and said, "That's one hell of a truck."

The woman looked in the same direction and nodded, "Sure is. I'd need a step stool to get inside."

"They staying here?"

"Not as far as I know. Sometimes people park here and go to the bar across the street. The manager doesn't like it, but I'm not going to make a stink about it."

"Right you are. And thanks for the towel."

She left the office and didn't go to her room. Instead, she went to the truck, stepped on the running board and gave it a good shake. Instantly, the car alarm kicked in, lights flashing and horn screaming. She hurried to the back, stepped on the hitch and climbed into the bed, the one occasion where the little black dress didn't serve her well. If the owners of the truck really were in the bar across the street, it would be a while before they'd notice.

As it turned out, the owner arrived much faster because he didn't have to cross the street, only the narrow parking lot between the motel room and the truck. The room he came from happened to be hers. The cartel had caught up with her again.

She had no idea how they'd found her. She'd used a random name at the motel and the clerk hadn't checked her ID. The car title was in her name, but there was no way it could've already been registered in the DMV computer. She'd put a new SIM card into her phone. She knew that each phone had its unique identifier, but that didn't ping cell towers. Or did it? In any case, here they were.

Cartel guy pushed a button on the remote and the alarm died away with a sigh. The cause for the alarm not clear, he came closer to inspect the car. The doors were locked. The bed being high off the ground, he probably had to stand on his tiptoes and hold on to the sidewall to see inside.

Just as he did so, Delano rose from the bed. She would never know what he was thinking. Maybe he was superstitious and thought she was a ghost. That would explain why he remained standing on his tiptoes rather than dropping to the ground. Maybe he didn't see her clearly, what with her black dress blending into the night. She pressed the rolled-up towel against his forehead, like a bolster for a head stand. The man still didn't react. Those cartels really needed to train their men better. Not every occasion was suited to using an AK-47 on full auto. She pressed the Glock against the towel and pulled the trigger.

The towel muffled the report of the gun enough to avoid the attention gun shots usually attracted in a dense urban area. She climbed out of the bed again via the hitch in the back and waited. There was at least one more gunman waiting for her. She took the towel, now singed with powder burns on one side and blood on the other.

What to do next? Wait for the second guy to come and check on his buddy? It was tempting since the trick had worked once already. But she knew better than to go for a repetition. The second guy would be careful when his buddy didn't respond. He might not even come to the truck.

So, go to the door and wait beside it until he came out? Not a good idea, either. She'd be standing in the light and visible not just to the guy, but also anyone else passing by. Driving away was always an option. She could get a new toothbrush anywhere. But she also wanted to send a message to the cartel. Tell them it was too expensive to continue to pursue her. To do that, she needed to kill the second guy.

Her handbag in the left hand and the Glock in the right, she sauntered to the door. It wasn't closed, the latch bolt just resting against the strike plate. *Good.* She visualized the room. The entrance on the left side of the wall, a table and two chairs under the window, the bed against the right wall. She heard no sound, no TV. Where was the other guy? Sitting on a chair? Or lying on the bed?

The bed would be easy; walk in, aim, shoot. The chair was harder because it was covered by the open door. The door wouldn't shield her against bullets but it also hid her, thus giving her a chance to surprise the guy. Chances were, the guy was lying on the bed. Isn't that what guys always did? Not even taking their shoes off?

She eased the door open a little. She saw a TV on the wall, a dark screen with some of that new high-tech coating that doesn't reflect a damn thing. She put her bag on the concrete path.

Okay, here goes nothing. She opened the door slowly with the muzzle of her gun until the gap was wide enough to step through. Weird that the guy on the bed didn't notice the door moving. Maybe he was asleep. That'd be best. She grabbed the Glock with both hands and stepped into the room. She swiveled, arms outstretched, finger on the trigger, aiming for the guy on the bed.

Except there was no guy on the bed. There was no guy in the chair.

Only one guy? That wasn't cartel policy. Arms still outstretched, she turned slowly, rechecking the room, as if she somehow had missed the guy. The room was still empty.

Then the toilet flushed.

She took a quick step toward the bathroom door. Arms and finger still in the same position.

The faucet ran.

Jeez, a fastidious crook. What next?

The faucet stopped running.

The door opened. The guy looking down as he zipped his fly. He looked up. The expression on his face mirrored a brain that couldn't make sense of what his eyes saw:

A woman in a sexy black dress?

A woman with a gun?

Was this a movie?

He didn't get to answer those questions because Delano pulled the trigger. The guy was dead before he hit the floor.

Delano grabbed her tooth brush and snatched up her handbag by the door. She got into her car, tossed everything inside and pulled out of the lot without screeching tires.

Goddamn it. She was ready for a place where she could stay a while.

She drove five miles until she saw a sign for a large chain motel off the freeway. She parked, took her go-bag, went inside, looking like she was a customer. She found a bathroom off past the registration desk, went in and changed back into clothing that would be more appropriate for her next task.

THIRTY-EIGHT

Wednesday, October 24th,
Tucson, Arizona

A LOUD KNOCK on the door woke Vermeulen. He checked his watch. It was almost one in the morning. He glanced at Tessa next to him. Her gentle snore told him that she was fast asleep. He rubbed his eyes and wondered if he'd dreamed the whole thing. He'd been in the middle of a strange dream.

Another knock followed. It was not a dream after all.

A voice followed. "Mister Vermeulen, this is Detective Gumble, there's been another incident, open up."

Vermeulen padded to the door and checked the peephole. It was indeed Gumble.

"What kind of incident," he said, not eager to have Gumble come inside.

"Another shootout. Two more cartel hitmen dead. You wouldn't know anything about that, would you?"

Vermeulen opened the door and slipped outside so as to not wake Tessa. It was chillier than he expected, standing there in his boxers and T-shirt. A uniformed officer stood behind Gumble.

"Did I wake you up?" Gumble said.

"What's it look like?"

"Sorry. It looks like the Tate woman struck again."

"More cartel goons dead?"

Gumble nodded. "And you were here all evening?"

"Yes, we got take-out for dinner. We've been in the room most of the day."

"So you didn't drive up North and check out the Orinoco Motel?"

"The what? No. I told you we didn't leave the room all afternoon and evening. Call the China Express. They brought our food right here. The damn cartons are in the trashcan. You want to check?"

"No, I believe you. And you have no idea who this Sophie Tate could be?"

"No. I don't. Never heard that name." He was as convincing as he could be. Being in his shorts and sleepy helped. "How do you know it was her?"

Gumble gave him a stony look. "The room was registered to a Daisy Miller, but it's one of those places that rents by the hour and they don't really check ID. The clerk said she was good looking and had short bleached hair."

"Didn't this Sophie Tate have brown hair?"

"Yes, but I figure she had it bleached after the last encounter. Ask yourself, how many women can there be in Tucson that escape cartel hitmen with such ease? It had to be her."

Vermeulen shrugged. "Can I go back to bed?"

He half turned to go back inside. But Gumble said, "One more question. You said your partner is writing an article on border issues. She get in touch with the cartels or ask about them?"

"She's writing about them but she got the info from the Border Patrol. She certainly didn't interview cartel members if that's what you are implying."

"Any idea why the cartel is out for Sophie Tate?"

Vermeulen exhaled noisily. "I don't know a Sophie

Tate. How often do I have to tell you. I have no idea why some cartel goons are after a woman I don't know. I wish you'd finally believe me."

"Okay. You'll be sure to call me if you remember anything else, right?"

"Sure."

"Good night."

Vermeulen went back inside and closed the door.

"Everything okay?" Tessa said. She was propped up on her elbows.

"Gumble again. Looks like Delano's had another run in with a cartel. Two more hitmen dead. I assured him that we hadn't left the motel all afternoon or evening. He seemed satisfied. He did ask about your articles and if you'd interviewed cartel members. I told him that your information came from the Border Patrol. I think he's out of our hair."

"I'm not worried about Gumble. I'm worried about Delano. She's left four people dead in a couple of days and she called your office and asked about you. I don't think she's done yet. We should get out of here."

Vermeulen came to her side of the bed and sat on the edge. "I think you're overreacting."

He saw the look on Tessa's face and said, "Sorry, bad choice of words. We're leaving Tucson in less than thirty-six hours. She doesn't know where we're staying. It's really a lot of hassle for what seems like a minute possibility of her finding us."

Tessa shook her head. "And I think you underestimate her. Remember, hell hath no fury like a woman scorned."

"Wow, talk about using the wrong adage. I got between her and her business. It wasn't anything personal."

"Good grief. Sometimes you really are the stereotypical male. All I'm saying is that she might not compartmentalize her feelings like you do. You forced her into exile. Don't you think that might bring up some anger?"

Vermeulen wanted to roll his eyes, but thought better of it. "And I'm saying she didn't strike me like the kind of woman who would do that."

"Ah, and what kind of woman would do that? Are you the expert on women now?"

"That's not..."

He stopped. They'd argued twenty-four hours ago, and he was about to repeat his performance.

"What's the worst case scenario?" he said, hoping that approaching the question with reason would defuse the situation.

"She shows up here in the middle of the night and kills you."

"How would she know where we're staying?"

"Really, Valentin? This woman killed four hitmen in two days and you think she couldn't figure this out. You didn't just happen to drive through this part of town because it's so picturesque. She'll know you were here for a reason and a motel is as good a reason as any. She's seen your car. Now it's parked outside our room."

"That's a stretch, but, okay, I grant you that. Let's take care of it in the morning. I'm tired."

"No, let's do it now."

Vermeulen knew that look on Tessa's face. There was no budging her.

"Okay. But let me at least take a shower. Is there any coffee left?"

Tessa shook her head. "No coffee and no shower. We need to get out of here now."

Vermeulen acquiesced, his mood sour. He went to the closet, yanked out his carry-on. He stopped, went to the bathroom, washed his face, brushed his teeth and stuffed his bathroom items into his dopp kit. Back in the room, he saw that Tessa was almost packed.

She gave him a look that said, "Hurry up."

He didn't respond and began stuffing his things into the carry-on. By the time he finished, she was already at the door waiting.

He pushed his case shut a little more vehemently than the situation demanded. "There, happy?"

"You got everything?" she said.

He padded his pants pockets and said, "Wait, my keys. Where are they?"

"On the desk."

He pocketed them and joined her at the door.

She opened it and said, "Don't forget your jacket."

"Jeez." He turned around and took it from the coat rack.

"And where are we going?"

"There must be plenty of motels by the airport."

They walked down the stairs to the parking lot. Tessa shoved her bag onto the rear seat and got in the driver's seat while Vermeulen did the same with his, got in and slammed the door shut.

There was no traffic on the street. Vermeulen looked around and saw nothing. The neighborhood was quiet. Even the traffic on Speedway Boulevard a block away, sounded muted.

Nearly two in the morning, he thought. Crazy, they could've stayed until the rest of the night and gotten some sleep. Tessa backed away from the building and nosed the car towards the Stone Avenue exit where she turned south.

THIRTY-NINE

Wednesday, October 24th,
Tucson, Arizona

DELANO APPROACHED VERMEULEN'S motel on East First Street. She slowed down. The lot was illuminated by security lights and she saw right away that the green car wasn't where she'd expected. She stopped. Where did he go? It was just past two in the morning. He should be in bed.

He hadn't left, had he?

The pleasure part of her brain had anticipated killing Vermeulen with so much fervor, the rational part hadn't gotten a word in edgewise. The shock of not seeing their car gave the neglected lobes a chance to chime in.

She didn't know the first thing about why he was in Tucson or for how long. Of course he could've left. Whatever his job was, he got it done and flew back to NYC.

She'd missed her chance.

Goddamn it.

The disappointment left her feeling deflated. Oh, fuck it all. Just get the hell out of this rotten town. In twenty-four hours she'd be on her way to San Juan. Forget Vermeulen. She'd never see him again.

She saw a couple brake lights flash under the porte-cochere, then a blinker signaling a left turn. As the car emerged from the shadow, she saw it was metallic green.

Vermeulen.

She stepped on the gas, raced to the intersection with Stone Avenue and turned south. The green car was a block away.

TESSA HEADED SOUTH on Stone Avenue, keeping to the speed limit. Good thing they got out when they did. Unlike Vermeulen, her stomach had felt queasy at the news of Delano's clashes with the cartel hitmen. A killer so brutally efficient was a threat to Vermeulen, even if he didn't want to admit that. She was glad they were out of their motel.

As she approached the intersection of University Boulevard she saw lights in the rearview mirror. A car had just turned onto Stone Avenue and was following them at a high speed. Her stomach clenched again. This wasn't good.

She sped up and took the next right at high speed.

"Why'd you do that?" Vermeulen said.

She didn't answer but made a hard right turn onto Ash Street heading north.

"I saw a car following us. I'm not taking any chances."

She turned off the lights and rolled along Ash Street. There was lots of covered parking but not really a place to hide.

"Pull in here?" Vermeulen said, pointing to an empty slot.

At least he didn't challenge her instincts, but the spot he pointed out was no good. "She'll see us right away. We need a place that hides us from the street."

She sped up again and turned left onto Second Street. Tucson's city planners had installed small roundabouts at residential intersections to slow down traffic. The centers were planted with shrubs, many of which had grown tall enough to provide good cover, as long as she was at least a block ahead of her pursuer.

The residential area had lots of driveways and garages, but all of them open to the street. She turned into Queen Avenue, which, despite the grandiose name, was basically an alley with garages and trash cans. She saw a small opening between a garage and ratty fence and pulled into it.

"You think this is safe?" he said.

"I hope so. Unless she drives past us, she won't see the car."

"That's assuming it was her driving that other car."

"I think she was; my gut is rarely wrong when it comes to danger. Why else would that car have sped up and gone after us. And if I'm wrong we'll just sit here for a while. No place else we have to be."

"Might as well turn the car off."

She did so and they sat and waited.

"When do we know it's safe to leave?" he said.

"I don't know. If I were her, I'd loop around looking for a green car. We're easy to spot."

"So we should stay here until there's more traffic on the road?"

"Yup. Unless you have a better idea."

DELANO HAD RACED after the green car, its paint shimmering metallic, reflecting the light from the street lamps. She hadn't made the driver, but who else would be leaving the motel at this hour of the morning?

Speeding up, she had seen two silhouettes in the car. A taller one in the passenger seat and one not quite as tall driving. Who was the driver?

The green car had accelerated suddenly. Did they recognize her? That was impossible. They didn't know what color car she was driving. Still, the other car raced south on Stone Avenue, and cornered hard at the next intersection. She followed at speed, turned the corner with a squeal, but saw only the empty cross-street.

The other driver was definitely trying to shake her. No doubt about it. Definitely Vermeulen, but how did he recognize her?

She inched forward. To the left a narrow street, lots of cars parked under corrugated iron carports. To the right a big apartment building. Its lot was about two-thirds filled with parked cars.

Damn. She didn't have time to search every parking spot. If it really had been Vermeulen, he could be anywhere by now.

She continued on to the next intersection and circled the roundabout once and looked: no cars driving anywhere, no pedestrians, just the light cones radiating from the street lights. She drove past houses, hidden behind vegetation. She got to the next roundabout: nothing.

She stopped. The best course of action would be to get a room somewhere, sleep the rest of the day, then get on her plane tomorrow.

She couldn't make herself do that, not yet. Vermeulen was like an itch she couldn't quite reach to scratch.

She drove for half an hour, randomly turning left and right. One car drove toward her. It was a pickup, someone going to work. She pulled over again. What next? It was past three in the morning. She drove back to Vermeulen's motel to check once more. Who knew?

TESSA AND VERMEULEN waited in the car. They sat quietly. After twenty minutes, Vermeulen reached back to take his jacket that was draped over his bag. He padded its pockets, padded them again and shook his head.

"What's the matter?" Tessa said.

"My phone isn't in my jacket."

"It's probably in your bag."

"I don't think so, I wouldn't pack it in my bag."

"Look away."

He squirmed in the seat until he could reach back and started digging through his carry-on. His search grew more exasperated.

"It's not in my bag."

"Where did you have it last?"

"In the room. I usually put it with my keys."

"You took your keys but not your phone?" The incredulity in her voice made him cringe.

"Well, you were the one who was hurrying us out of there."

"Come on, don't blame me for your forgetfulness."

"Damn it, damn it. I need my phone."

"Does she know me?" Tessa said.

"No, she's never seen you, she doesn't know you're here."

"Let's drive back to the motel. If everything is clear, I'll just dash up, get your phone and we're off."

"And if the coast isn't clear?"

"Then I'll step on it and we'll drive to the next police station and call Gumble."

"Okay."

Vermeulen didn't sound terribly convinced, but she didn't have time to worry about that. She started the car and backed out into the street. She took Ninth Avenue, south to University, took a left, and then took the alley between Stone and Seventh to their motel. The motel was an L-shaped building with rear walls facing south and east. She stopped short of First Street along the motel's eastern wall, and kept the car running.

"Okay, I'm going to check. If it's clear I'll run upstairs. Get in the driver's seat and be ready to get us out of here when I come back."

She got out and walked toward First Street. At the corner of the building, she inched toward the parking lot. She lingered at the next corner and let her gaze wander: parked cars, a solitary light in the manager's office, the pool. All was quiet. She walked along the fence to the parking lot entrance, turned toward the coke machine and the staircase to the second floor. Why had they chosen a second floor room?

Upstairs, she stayed close to the wall and hurried to their room. At the door, she stopped and looked around. The parking lot was still quiet, no cars passed on the street.

She opened the door and slipped inside. The phone wasn't on the dresser where Vermeulen had put his keys. She scanned the room, then the bathroom. Where could it be? She pulled the blanket and then the sheet from the bed. The phone tumbled onto the carpet. Of course. She grabbed it and opened the door again.

FORTY

Wednesday, October 24th,
Tucson, Arizona

DELANO PARKED HER car a block away from Vermeulen's motel on Stone Avenue. There were more cars on the street now. The evasive maneuvers taken by Vermeulen told her that he knew she was following him. Better to approach on foot. Only a gut feeling, but she done well trusting those.

She took her Glock and walked across the empty parking lot of a bank branch toward the alley that ran between Stone and Seventh Avenue.

In the shadow of the south wall of the motel, she lingered a moment and inspected the alley. It looked like alleys all over the US, three parked cars and a couple of blue recycle bins lying on their sides; a rummage closet guests will never have to see.

She dropped into a crouch and peeked around the corner.

A car stood near the mouth of the alley—a green metallic car.

She pulled her head back.

She looked again, more careful this time. Against the street light on First Street, she saw someone sitting in the driver's seat. *Vermeulen?* She couldn't tell from where she crouched. It was two-forty-five. The sky was dark. Dawn was a few hours off still, but her time was running out. If it wasn't Vermeulen in the car, it was someone waiting for him—no difference.

The alley wasn't dark enough to hide her figure approaching the car. Staying close to the wall was her least bad option. Whoever sat inside would focus forward. No reason to expect someone to come from behind. It was all she could hope for. She got up, inched around the corner and pressed her back against the wall. It was gritty and she could smell the dust baked into the paint by the relentless heat. Her clothes would look like shit after this. Once it was done, she'd splurge on a new wardrobe.

The stink of exhaust told her the car was running. Nobody kept their car running in an alley unless they planned on a fast getaway. It had to be Vermeulen. He was waiting for someone, but for whom?

There was only one way to find out.

She took three fast steps, yanked open the passenger door, dropped into the seat and shoved her Glock into the side of the person in the driver's seat.

It was Vermeulen.

"Thought you'd get away?" she said.

Vermeulen said nothing.

"Who are you waiting for? A girl friend?"

No word from Vermeulen. He looked straight ahead.

"You ruined a good thing I had going in Newark. You drove me out of the country. You're responsible for my living in Mexico all these years. Now you're the one who can link me to that old case."

She prodded him with the muzzle of the gun. "What? Cat got your tongue?"

Before Vermeulen could answer, the inside of the car

was flooded with bright lights coming from a car that had pulled up behind them.

"The fuck?" Delano said.

A loudspeaker behind them barked, "Police, turn off the car."

"Ignore that," she said to Vermeulen.

They waited.

The loudspeaker came on again. "Both of you, get out of the car. Nice and slow."

"We're not going to do that," she said.

She raised the hand with her Glock and pushed it against the side of his head. Whoever was watching in the police car had to understand what the situation was.

"Okay," she said. "Start driving."

JUST OUTSIDE THEIR ROOM, Tessa heard the loudspeaker. She knew it meant trouble. Did the cops find out that Vermeulen had lied to them about knowing Delano or whatever her name was these days? She could well imagine Vermeulen getting angry and then doing something stupid. She hurried down the stairs.

Once at street level, she saw bright lights shining in the alley. Just as she'd suspected. A police cruiser had pulled right behind their car. She hurried to the First Street exit of the lot and around the fence to the alley.

Vermeulen sat in the car, a police car stood behind him, its search lights framing the scene in unnatural clarity.

The loudspeaker blared again, "Drop the weapon out the window."

Weapon? Vermeulen didn't have a weapon.

That's when she saw that Vermeulen wasn't alone.

There was someone in the passenger seat pointing a gun at his head. *Delano?*

Where'd she come from, and why were the cops here? Delano was trying to keep the cops at bay by pointing the weapon at Vermeulen's head. That only made sense if she planned for him to drive away. She could not let that happen.

Tessa hurried to their car and stepped right in front of it. There wasn't going to be an escape.

DELANO SAW THE black woman appear in the headlights of Vermeulen's car, stopping right in front of the car.

"Who the fuck is she?" Delano said.

"That's Tessa Bishonga."

"She's what? Your girlfriend?"

"She's been my partner of eight years."

"Wow. A committed relationship? Aren't you a model of domesticity."

That quip barely covered up the seething rage that made her blood roar in her ears. Seven years on the run, seven years of random sex with strangers because she couldn't ever trust anyone. And Vermeulen, who put her in that situation? He's got a partner and was playing house with her. The urge to shoot the woman right then was almost overwhelming.

Keep calm. This situation was dicey enough.

"Tell her to get out of the way."

"She won't. No use trying," Vermeulen said.

"Too bad for her."

Delano pointed the gun at Tessa, still standing in front of the car. Just as she pulled the trigger, Vermeulen pushed her arm to the right. The bullet shattered the right side of the windshield. Delano didn't hear that because the bang of the shot had left her deaf and disoriented. She shook her head and squeezed her eyes shut for a second. The black woman was still standing in front of the car. *Damn.*

She aimed again. This time, Vermeulen grabbed her arm, his hand like a vise, and pushed the gun up. She boxed his ear with her left hand. It wasn't a strong enough blow. She used her elbow. He didn't let go of her arm. She forced her arm down, but Vermeulen kept pushing it to the right side, away from the woman and himself. The goddamn mechanics of sitting in the passenger seat gave her little leverage to counteract his strength.

When her door opened suddenly, she half tumbled onto the street. A cop must've run up and opened it.

Vermeulen lost hold of her arm. This was her chance.

Somebody else grabbed it.

She squeezed the trigger. Another shot echoed through the narrow alley like a cannon.

There was a scream.

Her arm was free again. She scrambled outside. Vermeulen had to pay. She turned and crouched. Vermeulen was staring at her. The black woman was coming around the front of the car.

In the glare of the searchlight, Vermeulen's face was as pale as a ghost.

Good.

He was ready for his new role. She raised her arm and aimed.

The gun seemed heavier than it should. That was because whoever had grabbed her arm before was grabbing it again, pulling it down. She threw her elbow. *Let go of me.* It must've connected. The hand disappeared.

A third shot echoed through the alley. It seemed much louder than the first two. It startled her. She didn't remember pulling the trigger. There was a faint sensation of something liquid running over her skin. She couldn't quite tell where. Had she been shot? Odd. There wasn't any pain. Shouldn't it hurt? The lights around her grew dimmer and dimmer until everything was dark.

VERMEULEN CRAWLED OUT of the car, his head still reeling from the explosion of the gun in a small space. He saw Tessa running toward him. He stumbled in her direction. She embraced him with such force, he had difficulty breathing.

"Are you okay?" She repeated the phrase over and over like a mantra to conjure up the reality she hoped for.

It took a moment before he could croak that he was. She held him at arm's length. Tears were running down her cheeks but she smiled. His head was still buzzing and sounds seemed muffled.

Someone spoke behind him. He turned. It was Detective Gumble. His expression wasn't nearly as concerned as that of Tessa. He said something. Vermeulen pointed to his ear and shrugged. Gumble leaned closer.

"I thought you didn't know Sophie Tate."

Vermeulen took a breath to compose himself.

"I know this woman, but I know her as Camille Delano. Sophie Tate meant nothing to me."

"Camille with two L's? And Delano as it sounds?"

Vermeulen nodded. Gumble went back to the police car and said something to the officer, who typed on his laptop. When he came back, Gumble looked impressed.

"Man, that's one rap sheet. You dealt with her back in 2012 before she disappeared from the radar?"

Vermeulen nodded.

"Good thing I didn't trust you," Gumble said. "I knew that there was some connection between you and her. Got here just in time."

"Why did you come?"

"A hunch. You're not very convincing when you lie."

"I wasn't lying. I didn't know she used Tate as a name."

"Whatever, I figured a professional hit woman who iced four cartel hitmen would not leave you alone either. When I didn't see your car in the lot, I thought we'd go around the block. Good thing we did."

"Thank you, Detective. I'm very much in your debt. Was one of the officers wounded?"

"Yes, the second bullet grazed his leg. An ambulance is on its way. He'll be okay. You'll need to come to the station for the report."

Vermeulen sighed. Just what he didn't need.

FORTY-ONE

Wednesday, October 24th,
Tucson, Arizona

It was six o'clock in the morning when Vermeulen and Tessa finally were done with the interviews at the police station. Since Delano was dead, they went back to their motel, bone tired and riled up at the same time. Sleep was out of the question.

They sat on the edge of the bed. Vermeulen's mind was a jumble of adrenaline, delayed fear and chagrin for having downplayed the danger posed by Delano.

Finally, he took a deep breath and said, "I'm sorry about being such a jerk earlier. I'm glad I listened to you."

Tessa didn't look at him and remained silent.

The minutes crept as slowly as cold molasses.

After an eternity, Tessa said, "Thanks for saving my life."

"Does that mean we're even?"

She punched him once more in the shoulder, hard. "Now we are."

They fell back onto the bed, too tired to stay upright and too tense to sleep.

A ping from her phone roused her. She got up and checked. A smile appeared on her face.

"My piece about private contractors employing the

white supremacists is live. My colleague edited it a bit for clarity and put it up right away. He thought it was timely and important. It's even got Welch's picture."

"That's great. Congrats."

"They sent the link to the Western Refuge head office, HHS and the local media."

"Let's hope that generates some action. I can't believe for a moment that Welch is a trained child care worker."

"Let's face it," Tessa said. "This night is over, whether we like it or not. When are we supposed to show up at the police station to sign the statements?"

"I think Gumble said at nine-thirty."

"Plenty of time for breakfast. Maybe some eggs and toast will revive me."

THE TIME AT the police station was as dull as Vermeulen expected it to be. Gumble read them the report, asked if there was more, grilling them over and over for more details and background. They went over the same events three times before Gumble was satisfied. Vermeulen wanted to tell him to be happy. After all, the detective had cleared four homicides in a couple of days and taken out a professional killer. He didn't. Smart aleck comments like that just annoy the cops and that's the last thing Vermeulen needed. He was pretty sure that Gumble didn't buy his explanation that he'd known the Broker only under the name of Delano. At noon they were free to go.

"I wonder what's going to happen to Delano's money," Vermeulen said, as they sat in the rental car. "She must've accumulated quite a tidy sum from all her illegal transactions. She had no partner or children."

Tessa looked at him with a frown. "Why are you even thinking about that? She tried to kill us."

"You're right. Just wondering. She didn't plan on her life ending here."

"Crooks never do, that's why they're crooks. For all we know she's endowed a college fund somewhere. Who cares? Honestly, I'm starting to wonder about you. Did you have a thing for her?"

"What? Me? Of course not. All I'm saying is that she was smart and resourceful. She could've been successful in the world."

"But she wasn't, so let's drop it."

They drove back to their motel.

On the second floor, a woman was standing in front of their door. When she saw them come up the stairs, she came towards them.

"Hi, I'm Christie Diller with the Tucson Examiner. Are you Tessa Bishonga? I'd like to ask you a few questions about your piece on white supremacists working for HSS contractors."

Tessa seemed taken aback. Vermeulen noticed and said, "Can this wait? It's been a long day already."

He turned to open the door.

Diller wasn't taking no for an answer. "Where did you meet the Arizona Border Protectors? How did you find out about their employment? What do you hope to achieve with this report?"

Vermeulen let Tessa enter, then turned to the reporter to repeat what he'd said before and closed the door after them.

The reporter knocked on the door, repeated her questions. Tessa looked at Vermeulen and said that she wasn't in the mood for an interview.

"It looks like your article hit a nerve in Tucson," Vermeulen said.

"As well it should, it's unbelievable that men who illegally detain border crossers should work for contractors who house them. I hope the article causes enough of a stir that Welch and the others get fired."

There was another knock on the door. "It's Christie again," the reporter shouted. "What's your reaction to the statement the Arizona Border Protectors just issued?"

That got their attention. Tessa grabbed her phone and navigated to the website of the Tucson Examiner. There it was, a bold headline, *Arizona Border Protectors Threaten Consequences*. She skimmed the article.

"Should you be worried?" Vermeulen said.

Tessa shrugged. "It's hard to tell. Their statement is part rant, part threat. The rant is about the invasion of brown people, the threat is to anyone who obstructs their efforts to uphold the US Constitution."

"What are they threatening?"

"Consequences."

"That's a bit vague. Are you worried?" Vermeulen said.

"I don't know. Men with guns are always worrisome. Especially if you meet them in the desert. I don't know what they can do in the city. Welch needed his posse, without them he was just a guy with a belly approaching middle age. I don't think he'll come and confront me. Besides, he doesn't know where we're staying."

"The reporter found out, I bet Welch can too."

Vermeulen opened the door. Diller was still standing there, an expectant smile on her face.

"How did you know we were staying at this motel?"

"Well, I normally don't reveal my sources, but in this case, you'll find out anyway. I called the website office, introduced myself and asked to speak to the editor."

"And he told you we were staying here?"

"Yup."

"Hang on a second."

He closed the door again. "You better tell your editor not to give out your whereabouts."

"He did?"

"Yes, according to Christie outside."

Tessa grabbed her phone again and tapped furiously. The conversation that followed was short and angry. She ended the call. "That idiot. As long as someone told him they were press, he told them where I was staying. He thought it'd be great publicity and would lead to more subscribers."

"How many did he tell?"

"Four people called to talk to me."

Vermeulen took a deep breath. "That means Welch and his warriors could be on their way here."

FORTY-TWO

Wednesday, October 24th,
Tucson, Arizona

ALMA RODRIGUEZ CAME to work almost as tired as she'd been the evening before. She hadn't slept much. The worry about Claudio had kept her awake. She didn't blame his cousin Benita. She knew how hard it was to get by. But something had to be done about Claudio. Since there weren't any foster spots available, her only option was making it possible for López to take Claudio.

The first issue was housing. A fourteen-year-old boy needed his own room. She didn't know how much Benita spent but she could imagine the rough amount. She left several messages with acquaintances who often knew someone who knew someone who had an apartment for rent.

Next, she focused on food. Since López had no papers, food stamps were out of the question. That left the community food bank. But instead of just signing Claudio up for after school meals, she checked to see if the community kitchen had an opening in its culinary arts certification program. If López could take the course during the day while working at night, she could get the skills for a better paying job.

That call brought the first good news of the day. There was a spot open starting in a week. She signed

López up. She could always cancel it. The community garden was also an option, but there were no open spots.

Gloria Fuentes came into her office with a manila folder of papers. She overheard the last bit of the conversation.

"Are you planning on becoming a gardener?" she said.

Rodriguez shook her head. "No, as much as I like the idea, I don't have a green thumb. I can't even keep a houseplant alive, never mind a garden. I was calling for someone else."

Fuentes raised her eyebrows.

Rodriguez sighed. "It's about one of the boys at Western Refuge. His cousin says she can't take him. None of the agencies have a foster space for him and I want to get him out of the shelter. So I'm trying to figure out something that would help the cousin take the boy in."

"You can't let yourself be pulled in. You know better."

"I know too much about that boy and what he went through. I can't just let him languish in the shelter."

Fuentes shook her head. "I know it's impossible, and yet we have to try to focus on the larger picture. I'm not saying you shouldn't care about this boy, but not at the expense of all the other boys who need help."

A flash of anger shot through Rodriguez. "How long have you known me, Gloria?"

Fuentes didn't answer.

"Have you ever seen me ignore any of the people we try to help?"

Fuentes shook her head.

"Then don't assume that I'm going to start doing it

now. This boy Claudio deserves my attention. But I'm not going to ignore my job."

Fuentes raised a hand, trying to assuage Rodriguez. "I'm not suggesting that you're not doing your work, Alma. Believe me. I'm only concerned about you. The work we do wears away whatever protective shield we have. It's bound to. Who can look at all the misery and not despair? We need to control how much of our shield we compromise. And we need to replenish it. Otherwise this world will grind us up and spit us out."

Rodriguez made a dismissive sound. "Sometimes, we haven't got time to replenish our shield. We need to act. This is one of those times."

"And what happens when you wear out? What happens when all this misery swamps you like a tidal wave? Think of Catalina. You want to be there for her."

Rodriguez stood up. "My daughter has nothing to do with this."

"Of course she does. You can't be a mother to all the kids who are caught up in this terrible attack against children."

"I'm not trying to, just this one. And I'm not trying to be his mom. I'm just trying to help his cousin step up and help him. She wants to, I heard that last night, but she doesn't know how. Her life feels like a failure, she sees no way out. All I'm trying to do is show her that she can do what, deep down, she wants to do."

Fuentes took a deep breath.

"Good, I understand now. What have you done so far?"

"I've put the word out for a larger apartment and I got her registered for the culinary arts program at the community food bank. I'll get the boy registered for the after school meal. So the missing piece is the apartment. And maybe her boyfriend, who doesn't sound like he contributes all that much."

"Okay, I'll leave you to it. I hope you know that I wasn't criticizing you. I'm only concerned about your well-being. We need you here."

Rodriguez's face softened. "I know. Thanks. Sorry for being so abrupt."

After Fuentes left her office, Rodriguez calmed and called López. A lot was riding on how this call went. It was tempting to take charge. She had done that on a number of occasions and, on balance, it worked.

It was also tricky. A couple of wrong words and López would refuse further contact. She sounded as if life had kicked her enough and coming on strong could be that one kick that would cause her to shut down.

"*Hola*, Benita. It's Alma Rodriguez from Arizona Rescue. I'm calling again about your cousin Claudio. I made a lot of calls yesterday to find someone who could take care of Claudio until his asylum hearing." She paused, looking for the right words. "It doesn't look good. All the agencies are swamped and there aren't enough families in the foster system."

"I told you, I can't do it." López sounded a lot less distraught than the day before. This might not work out.

"Yes," Rodriguez said. "I heard you last night. You haven't got the space, your job isn't paying enough, and you have a boyfriend. I know all that. It sounded to me that your living space and work seemed to be the biggest problem. What if we could help with that?"

There was a pause on the other end. Rodriguez spun a pen in her left hand, a nervous habit she'd acquired in college.

"For example, we could find you a larger place to live," Rodriguez said. Better to get her argument in while she could. "There are programs that help with job training for a better paying job. We can help with that."

"A larger place would be nice, but I gotta be able to pay for it. And job training? I got no money for school."

"I understand. Do you like cooking?"

"Cooking? Why do you ask?"

"There's a ten week program in culinary arts offered by the community food bank. You learn cooking, food safety and everything you need to get a job in a restaurant."

"How much does it cost?"

"You pay twenty-five dollars at the beginning and if you complete it you get fifty dollars back."

That must've sounded enticing to López because she started reminiscing about helping her mom in the kitchen back in San Salvador. "They need a cheap Salvadoran restaurant in this town. Enough with the tacos already. I haven't found a decent *pupusa* anywhere."

Rodriguez exhaled with relief. The spinning pen slowed down a bit. "The course is five days a week morning to afternoon. You'd still have time to work your night job. Once you complete the program you can find a better paying job."

"What about a bigger apartment?"

"I put the word out this morning, so we'll have to wait. Claudio can participate in the community food bank after school meals. That way he'd get at least one square meal."

"Oh, I didn't know about that. What is this food bank thing?"

"That organization has been around for a while. It

works on making sure that people have access to food. On Mondays, you can get fresh produce."

Rodriguez sensed that she had hit the right note about the opportunities available. Time to bring it back to Claudio.

"If you are available one of the next few mornings," Rodriguez said. "I'd love to take you to the shelter where they keep Claudio. It'd be a chance to meet your cousin."

The silence on the other end told her that the excitement she'd created about opportunities had moved to the background. She held her breath. This was it. If López declined, it'd be the end of the conversation and her plan. Her left hand stopped spinning the pen. Her heart beat so loud, she was afraid it could be heard over the phone.

López had every reason to say no, except one. Claudio was family. Would that outweigh all the reasons against? Rodriguez had never faced such a decision. Part of her said, *Sure, I'd take my cousin in.* But there was that other part, that part that had acted out and had driven her mother crazy. That part would've said, *Hell no!*

When López finally answered, it was with a small voice, very tentative, as if she were finding her way in a dark room, hands outstretched, unsure what she would encounter.

"Okay, I'll go with you. I could go Friday morning."

Rodriguez lowered the phone so she could exhale. She lifted it again quickly. "That's wonderful. Tell me where you live and I'll pick you up around ten."

She had no clue if she could get in at Western Refuge at that time, or if William Morgan the Third could meet her there. It didn't matter, Benita López had said *yes*. The rest were details.

FORTY-THREE

Wednesday, October 24th,
Tucson, Arizona

THE VISION OF a bunch of angry militia members showing up at their motel room spooked Vermeulen. A bunch of volatile white supremacists with guns? The number of ways this could go sideways was too scary to imagine. He'd downplayed the danger they were in before. He wasn't going to make that mistake again and put Tessa through a repeat of the harrowing encounter she'd had.

"Let's get out of here," he said. "We can return the car and get a room at some airport hotel that has a shuttle."

Tessa had no objections. He was still grateful that she hadn't rubbed in his boneheadedness of the night before. They packed what they'd taken out that morning, and did one last scan of the room to make sure nothing—especially his phone—was left behind.

Vermeulen put his bag out on the balcony, stepped to the railing and scanned the parking lot. He figured militia men would come in pickup trucks, but who knew? None of the parked cars looked like vehicles that matched the toxic combination of wounded pride and testosterone he assumed to be at the core of the militia's psyche.

There was a large black SUV parked by the office

of the type favored by the FBI and the cartels. Vermeulen did a double take. He couldn't fathom why the FBI or any of the other federal agencies should come to their motel. Were they cartel goons? Again, no reason to come here. That left Welch and his militia buddies. Maybe it was just someone with a black SUV.

Tessa handed him her bag. He put it next to his.

"I guess we're ready to go," she said, the room key in her hand.

He heard a sound. He turned.

The expression on Tessa's face told him she'd heard it too.

The sound came from the office. Like a balloon popping a couple of rooms away, muffled by all that drywall, lumber and glass.

Except, it couldn't be a balloon popping. He'd heard that sound often enough to know it was a gunshot. His whole body tensed.

The silence that followed was long enough to make him think that maybe it had been a balloon after all.

Almost.

Still standing near the railing, he heard a squeak, turned again, and saw a man in a dark suit come out of the office. He stepped backward immediately, pushing Tessa inside the room, and closed the door.

"A man with a gun," he said. "Dark suit, black SUV. He looks like a hitman. Could he be with the Arizona Border Protectors?"

"Is he alone?"

"I don't know, but I doubt it."

"They're after me," Tessa said.

"Maybe, although that hitman didn't look like a militia member."

"Maybe they hired someone? You know, deniability."

"Then why are they at the office?"

Tessa rolled her eyes. "To get our room number."

"But we assumed the militia has our room number. They called your editor."

Tessa raised her eyebrows. "You're right."

Why did they hit the motel office? There was no money. All bills were paid by credit card. What else was there to have at a motel? The computer that had all the guest information. That insight rattled loose a crucial bit of memory he'd almost forgotten. Once it had moved to the foreground, he froze.

"I hope I'm wrong," he said. "But I think they're here for me."

Tessa looked at him, eyes wide. "Why?"

His blood turned from ice to red hot in a flash. Calling that number in Mexico City; how stupid!

"What have you done?" Tessa said.

"Among the artifacts the students found near Luca's skeleton was a piece of paper with a Mexico City phone number written on it. I thought it might be Luca's contact in Mexico."

"And you called it?" Incredulity was written all over her face.

"I did. Not much happened. A man who spoke English asked me where I got that number. I told him that I'd found it. He said that if it hadn't been given to me, we had no business. It was a strange call, I gave it no more thought."

"Did you give them your name?"

"No, I'm not totally daft."

"Which phone did you use?"

"The motel phone, I didn't want them to get my cell phone number."

She shook her head. "This is a landline. Anyone who has the number can look up the address in a reverse directory. You've put the Sinaloa Cartel on our tail."

He hadn't thought about that at all. But there was a silver lining. He relaxed. "Since they don't have my name, they don't know which room to look for."

"But you called Mexico. The motel must log all long distance and international calls. How else are they going to charge us for them?"

"That's why they stopped at the office," Vermeulen said.

"The shot we heard could've been a warning."

What had Olga Kaminski said back at the dive bar? *Leave this alone, the cartels operate on both sides of the border.* His palms got sweaty.

"We need to move now," he said. "They don't know what I look like and they don't know about you. I think we can make it to the car."

"Okay. We better leave the bags here. Makes us look like we're just out for a tourist adventure. Let's use the other staircase."

He eased the door open a crack. Nobody was on the second floor balcony. This far from the railing, he couldn't see the lookout either. So far so good. He handed the bags to Tessa who tossed them inside. She inched outside and clicked the door shut. Staying close to the wall and windows, they eased in the opposite direction of the office toward the corner of the building and the second staircase.

They heard another popping sound. A squeak followed. The second man had left the office. The killers had found out their room number. Vermeulen resisted the temptation of looking back and moved steadily toward the staircase.

He heard someone running below them. His pulse started hammering in his temples. The hopes of a clean getaway were fading fast. At the top of the staircase stood a soda machine, bulky and humming. Vermeulen thought of hiding behind it, but there was no time to move the thing. The steps below were getting close to the bottom stair.

"Let's go, we gotta pretend," he whispered, willing himself calm.

Much louder, he said, "So, where do you want to go this afternoon? We could go see the mission of San Xavier del Bac."

Tessa, picking up her role immediately, said, "I don't know. It's too beautiful to be inside. How about the Sonora Desert Museum instead?"

They'd reached the top of the stairs.

The growling of big engines in the parking lot stopped them. Vermeulen looked and saw two large pickup trucks pull into the lot. They stopped and four men in camouflage, carrying assault rifles stepped onto the tarmac. The steps below them stopped instantly.

"Uh oh," Vermeulen said. "It looks like the militia has arrived."

He pulled Tessa down to a landing halfway between the top and ground floors. Not much cover but at least they couldn't be seen from the parking lot.

"What should we do?" Tessa said.

Vermeulen leaned forward and peered at the ground level. The hitman stood, gun in hand, and stared in the direction of where the militia men had to be standing.

For a moment the only sounds Vermeulen heard was the traffic on Speedway Boulevard.

The hitman must've decided to get the drop on the militia guys. He raised his gun and fired. The response was a volley of automatic weapons fire that pocked the stuccoed wall. A cloud of cement dust swirled like an evil fog. The hitman at the other end of the building must've followed his partner's example. In seconds, the parking lot had turned into a battle zone. The cracks of guns and the whine of ricochets were deafening.

The first scream pierced the din. Vermeulen couldn't tell whose it was.

Tessa was crouching behind Vermeulen. "Can you see who was hit?" She had to speak loudly over the guns' clamor.

"It wasn't the hitman. He's taken cover behind a car and is still shooting."

"We can't stay here," she said. "It's four against two. The cartel hitmen will end up dead and then we'll face Welch and his killers."

"I agree, but we can't go anywhere else. For now, this is it. And the cartel guys are well covered. There's no telling who'll come out alive. I'm calling Gumble."

He pulled out his phone and Gumble's card, dialed his number. When the detective identified himself Vermeulen told him what was happening.

"Man, are you a magnet for trouble or what? We're on our way."

Tessa tugged at Vermeulen's sleeve and pointed down. The cartel hitman inched backward from behind the car toward the staircase. Maybe he thought this was better cover. Since he was focused on his opponents in the parking lot, he hadn't seen Vermeulen or Tessa crouching on the landing above him.

Vermeulen looked at Tessa, eyebrows raised. She shook her head and pointed up. It was his turn to shake his head. Upstairs wasn't any safer. A fire extinguisher hung on a hook of the wall. Vermeulen lifted it off and inched downward.

The gun battle continued, albeit at a slower clip. Both sides had probably come to the conclusion that conserving ammo was better than a free for all.

Vermeulen sneaked up behind the cartel hitman, who was peering around the corner to squeeze off a round. As he pulled back behind the edge, Vermeulen smashed the fire extinguisher against the man's head. The hitman collapsed, dropping his gun as he fell. Vermeulen pulled him back, kicked the gun toward the stairs and went through the man's pockets. He found a spare magazine, a wallet and car keys. He pulled the man's belt from his pants and used it to tie the arms behind his body.

Tessa had joined him and said, "This isn't making it any better for us. Now the militia men can get us."

"This guy would've noticed us before long and then we'd be his hostages. Besides, they don't know he's out of commission."

"What's our next step, then?"

"We'll wait for the cavalry."

There was a lull in the shooting. Vermeulen knelt down and peered around the corner. He could see the two pickups, but not any of the militia members. He could see the second cartel man kneeling behind a car at the other end of the motel.

"I'm going upstairs, I got to see how many militia guys are still there," he said.

Tessa shook her head, but he climbed upstairs and then crawled to the edge of the railing. That spot gave him a clear view of the parking lot. One of the militia shooters was in position covering the hitman near the motel office. Another one was kneeling next to a prone body and was talking; a body lay to the side not moving.

He moved back to the landing.

"Looks like two of the militia men are down."

The remaining militia men fired again. Not full auto, but a steady hail of bullets, almost like covering fire. Maybe Tessa had been right. Vermeulen rolled the unconscious man forward. He'd be the first the militia man would see. Vermeulen picked up the pistol by the staircase and told Tessa to move upstairs. He pressed himself against the wall of the staircase.

Sure enough, a militia guy inched around the corner, assault rifle at the ready. He saw the unconscious hit man. He lowered the rifle and bent down to check on the man. Vermeulen took two steps and pressed the pistol against the man's back.

"Drop the rifle. Now!"

The militia man's position was awkward and his long gun the wrong weapon for a close quarter confrontation. He tried to rise, but Vermeulen jabbed the pistol in a way that left no ambiguity about his plans. The assault rifle clattered to the ground.

"On the ground. Face down."

The militia man hadn't met Vermeulen before. He couldn't know who he was and what he was capable of. He was still alive, which was more than two of his fellow fighters could say. He dropped to his knees and lay down splayed on the concrete. Vermeulen put his knee in the small of his back, and removed a pistol from the man's holster. Conveniently, the militia man was prepared to round up undocumented border crossers. A bundle of plastic handcuffs hung from a carabiner clip on his belt. Vermeulen loosened one of these, wrested the man's hands behind his back and zipped them tight.

DETECTIVE BARNEY GUMBLE seemed put out by the fact that he, yet again, had to question the two. Vermeulen felt the same. The dull institutional green of the police station walls was enough to induce nausea. A different detective had taken Tessa to a different room.

"What's your story this time?" Gumble said with barely disguised anger.

Vermeulen gave him a description of the events. Explaining the call to Mexico City meant explaining the story of Luca's skeleton, and that meant explaining the grand jury in Bisbee. Vermeulen cut that short by simply saying that he'd called Mexico City to help out Tessa in her investigation. Tessa's article had been in the news all morning. Gumble accepted that the publication of the identities of the militia men was sufficient reason for the appearance of their posse.

Gumble questioned him again on every detail. Vermeulen was sure Tessa wasn't undergoing the same ordeal. In the end, their stories matched and they were allowed to leave.

The police had found the office attendant dead at the office, so there was no doubt about the hitmen's intentions. Apparently, the screen of the computer still showed Tessa's guest folio when the detectives entered the office.

The second hitman had been killed by the police. The remaining militia man gave himself up. Welch had been killed early in the shootout. The wounded member was transported to a hospital.

Gumble told them that a grand jury would evaluate all the evidence and testimony. Vermeulen's heart sank at the thought they'd have to stick around for days until the grand jury met. But since they were only witnesses, they signed affidavits and were free to go.

"Mind you," Gumble said. "If the grand jury determines that the affidavits are not enough, they'll subpoena you to come back."

"Let's hope they don't"

It was nearing ten in the evening that Wednesday when they finally were allowed to leave. They drove back to the motel and got their luggage. Two hours later they had returned their car and settled into a room at one of the airport hotels.

"I'm done with this city," Vermeulen said.

"I was done with the whole state a while ago."

"I remember, except for the Grand Canyon."

She smiled. "Yup, except for the Grand Canyon. And the desert."

"The desert?" Vermeulen frowned. This whole mess had started in the desert.

"Yes, the desert, at least before Welch and his gang showed up. I don't think I've ever had an experience like the one I had there. I saw a haunting beauty and at the same time felt a deep loneliness. Standing away from the students and looking at the landscape, I finally understood Edmund Burke's distinction between the beautiful and the sublime. The desert isn't beautiful, it is sublime. Its beauty is wrapped up with its threat of death. The very thing that was so pleasing to my senses also had the power to kill me."

Vermeulen had never read Burke's essay on the sublime, but he understood right away.

"And it has killed so many already. When I first talked to Alma, she was writing letters to the families of the victims found in the desert. What a difficult task."

He paused. "You know, nobody is going to write such a letter to Mihali Luca's family. They'll never know what happened to him."

Tessa looked at him. "Why don't you write it?"

Vermeulen shook his head. "I don't know how to write that kind of letter."

"You still have their address?"

"It's on my phone."

"Don't think too much about it, just tell them what happened and send your condolences."

Vermeulen sighed and got up to sit down at the tiny desk. He tore a sheet from the hotel writing pad and started his note. He kept it simple, listed the date the skeleton had been found, that he had been identified by his notebook and that he had been buried in Tucson, Arizona. That last part he made up, but he assumed that the city had a place to bury unclaimed bodies. He expressed his condolences and ended the latter.

After addressing the envelope he got up. "I'm going down and get stamps."

"Thank you for thinking of that," Tessa said. "At least his family will know."

FORTY-FOUR

Thursday, October 25th,
Tucson, Arizona

VERMEULEN AND TESSA arrived at the airport much too early. As if there were an unspoken agreement between them, they preferred the commercial sterility of the airport instead of any more time in the city. They dropped off their luggage, passed through security and got to their gate with many hours to spare. It didn't matter. Sometimes boredom is a preferred state of being.

Tessa read the news on her phone and Vermeulen checked his email. Announcements droned over the PA systems in a predictable pattern. Every ten minutes something about not leaving luggage unattended. Every fifteen minutes a welcome from the mayor, and the non-smoking alerts at more random intervals. Did people really needed to be reminded that smoking was prohibited in airports?

They strolled next to each other the length of the terminal and back. They even splurged and had a fifteen minute shoulder massage each. They had an overpriced lunch. They went back to their gate and waited some more.

The flight prior to theirs was delayed. People were antsy. Urgent sounding staff called for Mister Marcus. Finally the plane arrived. People streamed in, relieved to be off the plane. The new passengers jostled for position. The flight boarded, the doors closed, Mister Marcus was still missing. The display behind the desk went blank, then rearranged itself to announce their flight to LaGuardia.

They looked at each other and smiled. He reached over the arm rest to touch her hand. She took and held his. The warmth of her hand in his felt good, the tension of the past week ebbing as she wove her fingers with his. He looked at her again. Her face was more relaxed. The smile had faded into a more content expression. He opened his mouth to say so, but decided not to. There was no need.

She leaned her head against his shoulder. He scooted closer to make it more comfortable for her.

"I've said some pretty harsh words the last few days," she said.

He said nothing.

"I was upset when I said them."

He let her words linger a while before saying, "I know you were. I was too caught up in myself to see that."

"Yes, you were, but so was I. I hope to handle such situations better in the future."

"But you were right. I should've seen that."

"I don't want to get caught up in right and wrong. I want to do what strengthens our relationship. That also means letting you know when I'm hurt, but I'll work on communicating that better in the future."

Vermeulen wiped his eyes with his other hand. "And I'll work on trusting you."

Tessa squeezed his hand. "We are a good team, though. Look at the last week. Despite the nightmare confrontations, I got a lot done and you played a big part in that. The way you got us into that Border Patrol lockup, that was classic Valentin."

He had to smile. That had been one of his classic moves. "Yes it was, but it will come back to haunt me."

"It doesn't matter. We have each other. That's the only thing that matters."

He squeezed her hand back. "Yup. We're a good team."

A half hour later, Vermeulen phone's buzzed to tell him that he'd received a new email. He checked. It came from a sender he didn't recognize: more spam. But boredom being what it was, he read it rather than delete it.

It turned out it was not on that promised millions of dollars, or penis enlargements, or whatever. The message came from Jenna, the office manager at his work. But she sent it using her personal email address. That could mean only one thing—more trouble.

He was right. In quick sentences, typos here and there—not at all like Jenna, she must have been in a hurry—Jenna informed him that she'd been told to draft a termination letter for Vermeulen. Something to the effect that the impersonation of a UN inspector at a US Border Patrol Station was an egregious violation of his terms of employment and the host agreement between the UN and US. The Secretary General personally had promised the US Secretary of State that the UN would take swift and serious action to remedy this situation.

"Just a heads-up," Jenna wrote.

Vermeulen showed the email to Tessa. She rolled her eyes.

"They can't be serious. Nothing happened. We walked in, we talked to three people and we walked out. What harm was done?"

Vermeulen sighed. "The principle. I violated the goddamn principle. In the end, that concept of sovereignty is more important than any deed that's committed in its name. Holding people crammed together in cells with only a mylar blanket is the real violation, but that's shoved aside because I violated some asinine principle."

Tessa took his hand. "I'm sorry, love. You don't deserve that. You've done too much good to be treated this way."

He tried a smile. It didn't quite materialize.

"Are you going to fight this?" she said.

"You bet. It's my job. What else am I going to do?"

Their plane arrived on time. More people were streaming into the terminal. The airline attendant at the desk called their flight and explained who all got to board first. Vermeulen didn't listen because they weren't on that list. His mind reeled with anger, pity and anxiety; anger that his boss Suarez had buckled under the pressure from above instead of protecting his investigator. Pity for himself, although he handled that feeling with care. It was too easy to fall into the self-pity hole. That wouldn't help anyone, least of all himself. And anxiety over how he would earn his income, the fate of his pension fund. Did you still get your pension if they fired you?

Most unexpected, but interesting, was that tinge of relief he noticed. He'd never admitted that to himself, but there was that tiny voice that said, "Good riddance. You never liked that job." He knew that voice was mostly wrong. He had liked the job. Well, maybe not the job, but the principles it stood for, the idea that a global organization pledged to create peace would do all it could to prevent those principles from being sabotaged by unscrupulous individuals only out for their personal gain.

The job itself was often tedious, tiresome both physically and emotionally, and, most of all, frustrating. He could still taste the anger he felt eight years ago over the failure of the UN to take meaningful steps to bar a gun runner from supplying UN Peacekeepers. That was just one example. Over the years, those had multiplied, the political power of the top member states trumping justice more often than not. That had always bugged the hell out of him.

Yes, there was that bit of relief. The sense that a new vista might open, that he, at age fifty, wasn't washed up. It was tenuous, but it was strong enough to keep him from despairing.

Their seats were finally called. They snaked their way to row thirty, way in the back of the plane, and promptly fell asleep.

THEY ARRIVED AT LaGuardia late that Thursday and decided to splurge for a cab rather than take the bus. The taxi dropped them in front of their building on West 199th Street. They climbed up two flights of stairs to their apartment. Once inside, they kicked off their shoes and fell on the sofa.

"Can you tell me what that last week was all about?" Vermeulen said.

"Yes and no. Yes, in the sense that we got a close-up of a terrible immigration system at work. No, in the sense that nothing has changed and everything will go on as before."

"A waste of time, then?"

"I don't think so. We outed some white supremacists working for ICE contractors, I gathered a lot of material for an article, and the Cochise County Attorney can closed the case of the skeleton."

"Not a lot to show for losing my job."

"Don't worry about the job. You'll keep it. Don't

they have a staff association? There's gotta be a grievance procedure. If I know anything about large organizations, it's that there are always options to explore. I don't think you'll be fired when it's all said and done."

Vermeulen didn't believe her. He knew the lines he could cross better than her. He'd overstepped a lot of them and gotten away with it. This time was different. To have the country that pays the largest share of the UN budget demand that an employee be fired, meant he was a goner. There was no way back from that.

He didn't tell Tessa all that. Instead, he said, "Maybe I'll beat them to the punch and resign."

Tessa leaned forward. "You what?"

"I've been thinking and I noticed that one of my reactions to Jenna's email was relief. Think about it. All those days and weeks away. The frustration of dealing with the bureaucracy. If I quit, I can leave without having a mark on my record. I think the office would like that, too."

Tessa's brow had turned all furrowed. "I can't believe I'm hearing right. You've never been one to throw in the towel."

"I know. But I've put in fifteen years at the UN. That's a lot."

"What are you going to do?"

"Maybe a consulting job. Vermeulen and Associates, Your Pathway to Success."

Tessa laughed out loud. "I can just see you, a fancy business card, a flashy website, all the while you hunker on the converted back porch and do internet searches, hoping that none of your clients ever want to meet you in your office."

Now Vermeulen laughed too. "That damn porch is drafty as hell. It was just an idea. There are plenty of firms who hire folks with expertise like mine. Or I could go back into law."

"Not in the US unless you pass the bar exam here. And I'm not so sure I want to move to Belgium."

"All I'm saying is that there are other opportunities. This job isn't my only option. And I really like the idea of quitting so they can't fire me."

He checked his watch. A little after nine.

"I think I'm going to call Gaby. Let her know we're back."

He dialed Gaby's number. This time she answered quickly.

"Wow, Dad, either it's midnight or its six in the morning."

"I didn't wake you, did I?"

"Nah. Don't worry. I was up. Are you back home?"

"Yes, I am. It was a crazy trip. But we're safe and sound."

"Don't tell me you can't even go on vacation without stepping into something."

"It's a long story, and totally crazy. Remember seven years ago when you were in the hospital in Vienna?"

"How can I forget?"

"One of the crooks back then was never caught by the authorities. And she found me."

"No way. If you're not looking for trouble it finds you anyway. What happened?"

"I'll tell you some other time. Just wanted to let you know we're back."

"At least your job isn't hanging in the balance."

"Uh, it may. I'll call you on Saturday and fill you in."

FORTY-FIVE

Friday, October 26th,
New York City, New York

THAT FRIDAY MORNING, as he'd done for many years, Vermeulen took public transit to the United Nations headquarters. He followed the usual path to his office, but made a short detour past Jenna's desk in the reception area of OIOS.

When she saw him, her face turned into a pained smile. "Good to see you, Valentin. I wish the circumstances were different."

"No change since yesterday?"

"None. He had me type the paperwork for the disciplinary procedure. There'll be a hearing and you can have a lawyer or a rep from the Staff Association present. Don't get your hopes up. Suarez is going through the motions. The outcome has already been determined."

"Have you written the dismissal letter yet?"

She put on a defiant grin. "No. Maybe there'll be a miracle."

"That's nice of you. I don't know what I would've done without you."

"For what it's worth, Suarez isn't happy about this either. They forced his hand."

"Did he put up a fight?"

"Sort of. You know him. He's not one to make waves.

I don't know what was said on the phone, but yesterday, his door was open again and I could hear him say that all you'd achieved should count more than a little transgression." She paused, then said, "What were you thinking, doing that inside the US?"

"We needed information and it was the only way to get it."

She shook her head as if to say, "When will you learn?"

"Don't worry," he said. "You won't have to write that letter."

She raised her eyebrows. "You have some secret get-out-of-jail card?"

He gave her a wan smile. "I'm afraid not. In my pocket is a letter of resignation. I quit. Admittedly, it's not of my free will, but that's always preferable to being fired."

Jenna opened, then closed her mouth.

"You have a cardboard box?"

She got up and went to the supply closet where she extracted an empty box that had once held copier paper. "I always have one handy. You never know."

He took the box to his office and filled it with the few personal belongings he kept there. He tried to shrug off the sadness that percolated through his body. It didn't work. Fifteen years. It had been a good run. Maybe the most important work he'd done in his life so far. Yes, he'd cut corners, but never for his personal benefit, only to get the job done. The Tucson affair wasn't strictly something to get the job done, but was that enough to wipe out everything else he'd accomplished?

His things barely filled a third of the box. There was nothing left to do but wait until Suarez was ready to see him.

The phone on his desk rang, he picked up the receiver. It was Jenna. Suarez was ready.

He went to Suarez's office. Jenna was standing outside. He looked at her, she shook her head. No, she hadn't told Suarez.

Inside, Suarez was sitting behind his desk, a folder, probably Vermeulen's personnel file, in front of him. He looked at Vermeulen with the pained expression of a father who'd finally given up on his wayward son.

"Really, Valentin? A Border Patrol detention facility? Quoting the goddamn Refugee Convention? What were you thinking?"

"It was necessary and I didn't think it'd go up the chain. I was wrong. But I'm here to save you a whole bunch of trouble." He put the envelope with his resignation letter on top of the folder. "I hereby resign from my position as investigator of the OIOS."

Suarez leaned back in his chair. "You're not going to fight this?"

Vermeulen shook his head. "Not this time. I went too far. It was the proverbial last straw. I know what I did and that it was important, but I also know that there are consequences. Besides, I understand that it's not even in the hands of this office anymore. So, please accept my resignation."

Suarez didn't make much of an effort to hide his relief. One headache less on his plate. "At least I don't have to have someone escort you off the premises. Thanks for all you've done over the years. You've tested my patience more than once, but you always knew you were right. We'll have a going away party soon. It's the least we can do. Check with Jenna about all the paperwork. And good luck. I'm glad I know you."

VERMEULEN STOOD ON First Avenue and 46th Street and took a deep breath. It was a typical New York City fall day. The temperature was lower than in Tucson, and the air felt crisp.

He looked out at the busy street, a sheen of sweat on his forehead, cabs, buses cars and a stream of people headed for the UN tour. It was a little bit like the scene in *North By Northwest*, when Cary Grant runs from the General Assembly building.

As trite as it sounded, this was the first day of the rest of his life. He had a few savings, but he couldn't afford not to work. Time to sort out what came next.

A black limo pulled up in front of him. He stepped back, expecting some VIP to exit the vehicle. Maybe an ambassador late for his speech. Was the General Assembly even in session? As always, he had no clue about the official goings on.

The driver of the limo had come around the front of the car. He opened the rear door, turned and said, "Mister Vermeulen? Please take a seat."

Vermeulen stared at him as if he were an apparition from a parallel world, someone looking like a chauffeur of this earth, but an alien nevertheless.

"You *are* Mister Valentin Vermeulen, right?"

"Uh, yes."

A voice came from the dark interior of the limo, "Come on in Mister Vermeulen. The police don't like limos standing here too long."

Vermeulen had never heard that voice before, he was sure of that. The only time he'd ever been picked up by a limo was a few years earlier, when a tech billionaire tried to bribe him to participate in his corrupt plot. He couldn't imagine anyone wanting to speak to him.

"Please, do sit down. Rumor has it that you are newly unemployed. I have a proposal that fits your unique skill set. I think it'll be of interest to you."

Vermeulen bent down to make out who was speaking. He couldn't quite tell. "How do you know I'm newly unemployed?"

"My sources tell me that you just got fired. Besides, you're carrying a cardboard box. That's a dead giveaway."

"I have you know that I quit, I didn't get fired."

"See, I should've expected that. Good for you. Please, come with me for a ride."

Vermeulen climbed into the limo. Since whoever was speaking sat in the front facing the rear, Vermeulen took the opposite seat. The chauffeur closed the door. As his eyes adapted to the dimness inside, he saw a medium sized, somewhat pudgy man. He had a full oval face, a fringe of gray hair rimming the bald pate. He was clean shaven, had small but fiery eyes and a soft mouth. His suit was made from the kind of wool that made wearing it a pleasure no matter the climate.

The man stretched out a hand and said, "François Steyerl. Pleased to meet you."

Vermeulen shook the hand. "You already seem to know a lot about me, but I know nothing about you."

"I'm glad to hear that. I cultivate my privacy carefully."

"What do you want from me?"

"Nothing. I want to offer you a job."

Vermeulen sat up as much as that was possible in the soft leather of the rear seat. "A job?"

"Yes. I endow the 'Just World Initiative.' If you're not familiar with it, it's a global foundation that supports human rights struggles around the world. Based on what I heard about your work over the past decade and a half, I'd say, you have a unique skill set that should serve the foundation rather well."

Vermeulen leaned back in the seat. "I doubt that. I'm a lawyer who hasn't practiced in a decade and a half, and a mostly self-taught forensic accountant, if you want to use a fancy term to describe what I did at the UN. I'm sure you have better lawyers and accountants on your staff."

Steyerl leaned forward and said, "I think you are too modest. And I'm not interested in you as a lawyer or accountant." He hesitated a little. "What has been the most frustrating part of your UN job?"

Vermeulen stared at the man. "What?"

"Let me spell it out for you. You are in a situation where you know how some powerful man—It's usually a man, isn't it?—has defrauded, stolen or otherwise undermined the work the UN is doing. You got all the information you need, you have an open and shut case, but the man gets away. Sure, you end the scheme, you might even get some underling, but the boss is beyond your reach because some powerful country has protected him. How am I doing so far?"

Vermeulen said nothing. That man had his tribulations down to a T.

"I thought so," Steyerl said. "My foundation has a public arm, the one that does good work for human rights. It also has a far lesser known arm. It would be better to say that this arm is actually unknown, clandestine if you prefer. And here I need to count on your discretion, not that you blabbing about our conversation would make any difference. But it would make life easier. May I count on it?"

Vermeulen's skin had gotten tighter with each word

the man said. There was a soft buzzing in his ears. He tried to appear blasé, but wasn't sure he could pull it off.

"Yes," he croaked. "You may."

"Well, this clandestine arm of my foundation ensures that the big man doesn't get away. We're not doing anything nasty or deadly. Let's just say that the big man will reevaluate his life. Of that we make sure. Such means are not always legal by our current definitions, but they are just. Something about your career tells me you'd be the right person for this job. Before you get the wrong idea, believe me, I wouldn't dream of asking you to compromise your ethics. What do you think?"

Vermeulen's throat was as dry as the Arizona desert. He tried to swallow and managed only a painful gasp. The buzzing in his ears had changed a different frequency, as if his mind was tingling with the excitement one feels as the roller coaster car is clicking up to the first mountain. That strange mixture of terror and exhilaration that non-roller coaster riders simply can't fathom.

"May I think about it? And is it okay if I consult with my partner?"

"Ms. Bishonga? Certainly as long as she doesn't write an article about it."

The limo stopped at the curb. As Vermeulen looked out, he realized it stopped in front of his apartment.

"I'll call you tomorrow," Steyerl said. "I hope you say yes."

* * * * *

ABOUT THE AUTHOR

Michael Niemann grew up in a small town in Germany near the Dutch border. Crossing that border often instilled in him a curiosity about the larger world. He parlayed that curiosity into a career teaching International and African Studies, before turning to writing international thrillers. For more information, visit: michaelniemann.com